THE SCARLET BAT

THE SCARLET BAT

FERGUS HUME

A Detective Story

INTRODUCTION

KARL WURF

Fergusson Wright Hume (1859-1932), writing as Fergus Hume, occupies a singular place in the history of detective fiction. Born in England and raised from childhood in New Zealand, he trained as a lawyer before relocating to Melbourne, Australia, where a chance conversation would change the course of his life—and the mystery genre itself.

Aspiring to be a playwright but finding Melbourne's theatre managers indifferent to his work, Hume inquired at a local bookshop about which books sold best. The answer was clear: detective novels by the French writer Émile Gaboriau. Hume purchased Gaboriau's entire output, studied the formula, and set about crafting his own mystery set in the streets of Melbourne he knew so well. The result was *Th Mys tery of a Hansom Cab* (1886), which became the best-selling mystery novel of the Victorian era. Though Hume sold the rights for a mere fifty pounds—a decision that haunted him financially—the book's success was undeniable. It even inspired Arthur Conan Doyle to write *A Stdy in Scar let*, introducing Sherlock Holmes to the world.

Hume returned to England in 1888, settling in Essex, where he would spend the next three decades producing over 130 novels. His prolific output established him as a bridge between Gaboriau's sensational French mysteries and the Golden Age of detective fiction that would flourish in the 1920s and 1930s. He was among the first to incorporate elements like courtroom scenes and coroner's inquests into detective fiction, devices that would become standard conventions of the genre.

Th Scar let Bat, published in 1905 during Hume's most productive period, exemplifies his talent for blending mystery with exotic elements—in this case, a tattooed mark and mysterious symbols that drive the plot forward. The novel demonstrates Hume's gift for creating atmospheric settings and his understanding of how to maintain suspense through careful plotting.

Though none of his subsequent works matched the phenomenon of *Hansom Cab*, Hume maintained a devoted readership who appreciated his straightforward plots and realistic characters. His later years were spent in modest circumstances, but his influence on the detective genre remained significant. When he died in 1932, the literary world had largely moved on, yet his pioneering role in popularizing detective fiction endures.

Readers who enjoy *The Scarlet Bat* will find similar pleasures in Hume's other mysteries. *The Secret Passage* (1905) offers another intricate plot centered on hidden architectural features and murder. *The Green Mummy* (1908) combines Egyptology with detection in a tale of obsession and crime. *The Bishop's Secret* (1900), considered by many to be among his finest works, delivers a compelling ecclesiastical mystery. For those seeking his most celebrated achievement, *The Mystery of a Hansom Cab* remains essential reading—a groundbreaking work that defined an era and launched a thousand imitators.

CHAPTER I

SOWING THE WIND

"I say you're a bad lot!"

"And I reply that you're a liar!"

"Take that!"

"Here's the repayment!"

The man who had spoken first went down like a log. He was a red-headed creature, with a rasping voice and an aggressive manner, evidently one of those who bullied his way through the world, for want of a bold spirit to stand up to him. In this instance he found his match, for the handsome face of the young fellow he insulted was sternly set and considerably flushed. After the war of words came the blow from the bully. His fist passed harmlessly by the head of this antagonist, and a well-delivered return blow caught him fairly on the jaw. Then red-head lay down to consider the lesson he had been taught.

"You confounded scoundrel!" said the other, standing over him. "You may be thankful that I don't wring your neck. You're no good in the world that I can see, and would be better out of it."

"Guess you'd like to send him on the journey into Kingdom Come?" suggested a weather-beaten little man near at hand, who looked like a sailor.

"I just would," said the young man, panting. "What does the ruffian mean by making me a target for his brutal wit? He'd leave the world fast enough if I had my way. Lie still!"

This to red-head, who was rising. But the prostrate man did not obey the injunction, having some fight left in him yet. He scrambled to his feet, and rushed with a lowered head at his enemy like a bull. But the other was ready. He skipped aside, and the red-head met the wood of the counter with a sickening thud. This time he dropped insensible. The sailor man knelt beside the defeated. "I guess you'd better skip, Lancaster," said he. "You've done it this time. An' the police are coming."

It was not the police, but the attendants, who forced their way through the crowd in the bar. Seeing this, Lancaster's friend, by name Dicky Baird, and by profession an idler of the West End, seized his chum's arm and dragged him out of the bar by main force.

"No use waiting for a summons," said Dicky, when the two were in the vestibule. "I think you'd better get home, Frank."

The other stared at a poster which announced that a new musical comedy would be produced that night at the Piccadilly Theatre, with Miss Fanny Tait in the chief part.

"I'm not going till I see her," he said, pointing to this name.

"What, Fairy Fan? Why, all the row was about her."

"Because he abused the woman. She's a good sort, and I like her very much. You know I do, but there's no love."

"Not on your part, perhaps, but Starth loves her, and you knocked him down."

"I wish I'd killed him," said Lancaster, between his teeth.

"Don't talk rashly, Frank," said the other, with uneasiness. "If anything goes wrong with Starth you'll get into trouble."

"Malice aforethought," said Lancaster, carelessly. "Pshaw The man isn't hurt. He'll be up and swearing before the play begins."

It seemed that he was right, for a tall, bulky dark man approached with a smile. "Starth's all right," said he, with a nod. "You've swelled his eye a bit, Frank, but that's all. Berry's going to put him into a hansom. And now we'd better get to our seats."

The others assented, and the trio moved into the theatre. As they passed down the steps leading to the stalls, they caught a glimpse of Captain Berry conducting a swaying figure to the door.

"How did the row begin?" asked Dicky, when they were seated.

"Starth said I didn't know who my father was," said Frank.

"Well, you don't, do you?"

"That's neither here nor there. Starth has nothing to do with my domestic business."

"H'm!" said Baird to himself, thoughtfully.

Frank Lancaster was a dark horse, and although Dicky had known him for some years, he was not aware of his private history. Lancaster kept that to himself, and seemed unnecessarily annoyed by the question of Baird. Dicky could see nothing in Starth's remark which should lead to a free fight, though to be sure Fairy Fan's name had likewise been mentioned. However, Frank seemed indisposed to speak, and like a wise man Baird held his usually too-free tongue.

Miss Tait, commonly known as Fairy Fan, was a popular music-hall star, who danced gracefully and sang sweetly. For a salary largely in excess of her merits, she had deserted the halls for the theatre, and tonight was her first appearance in "The Seaside Girl." Hence the large audience and the

8

subdued excitement. At the present moment she was dancing like a fay and singing like a lark, but the three men nevertheless talked all the time.

"Jolly little thing, ain't she?" said Dicky. "She comes from the Californian Slopes."

"Did she pick up those diamonds there?" asked the dark man, who was a Rhodesian called Darrel, and acquainted with stones of price.

"No. Banjo Berry, who is her uncle, gave them to her. He's a rich man, and lavishes his money on his niece."

"Why does he let her appear on the boards, then?" asked Darrel, heavily.

"Ask Frank, here. He's a friend of Berry's."

"I'm not," growled Lancaster, still ruffled by his late encounter. "I can't bear the creature. His niece is worth a dozen of him."

"Is she his niece?" questioned the Rhodesian millionaire.

"Yes. There's no doubt about that. I respect Miss Berry immensely."

"I thought her name was Tait."

"On the bills. In private she's Miss Fanny Berry. Her uncle is rich, but, in spite of that, she's so vain that she likes to appear on the stage. I like her, and—"

"You're in love with her," contradicted Baird.

"A trifle. Anyone would love such a pretty woman. But I wouldn't ask her to marry me."

"No, Starth will do that."

"She won't have him," said Frank, snappishly. "He's a bad lot."

"A very sore lot at present," put in Baird, smiling.

"It's his own fault," replied Lancaster. "Why can't he leave me alone. It's not the first time he's quarrelled with me."

"Because he knows you are a rival in the affections of Fairy Fan."

"Rubbish, Dicky! Don't get that bee in your bonnet. Starth can marry her for all I care. I merely admire her, and only came into contact with her when Berry wrote asking if I could write her a couple of songs. I came and saw, and—"

"And she conquered," said Darrel. "Who is Berry? I fancy I've met him before. If he's the same man, he hasn't any morals."

"We'll say principles," remarked Baird. "Berry's a fiery-tempered Tom Thumb, who talks American slang through his nose concerning an interesting past of a superlatively shady description. Been a South Sea blackbirding skipper from the looks of him, and I expect he made his money in that way. Ever met him?"

"Los Angeles, now I come to think of it," said Darrel.

Frank looked up uneasily. "Who is he, anyhow?"

"Don't know," responded the millionaire, imperturbably. "He was running an apple orchard when I dropped across him. Clean shot, too."

Baird laughed. "Sounds like a retired pirate of sorts. But he's on the square now. He and Miss Berry have rooms in Bloomsbury, and go to church and have the entry of some decent houses. Frank knows all about them."

"Only that she's a nice woman and a good woman, and that Berry is a ruffian. He won't let Starth marry her."

"I hope not," said Darrel, darkly. "I've known Starth a long time, and he's a bounder. But he's got an uncommonly pretty sister, as beautiful and sweet-tempered as he is the reverse. Hush! Let's stick to the play; we're talking too much."

Frank certainly couldn't be accused of chattering, as he was rather silent. Even the rattling chorus and the jokes of the low comedian could not banish the frown from his brow. And he became aware that a man was looking at him—a fair-faced, effeminate little man, with light eyes and a deprecating manner. Lancaster, in no very good temper, scowled at the man, who immediately turned away his head. As he did so the first act ended amidst loud applause.

"An eighteen months' run if the other act is as silly," pronounced Baird; "but the management won't keep Fan all that time. She's as freakish as a cat, and her uncle is rich enough to allow her to snap her fingers at the Treasury."

"She *is* a cat from the looks of her," said Darrel, grimly. "Come out, boys, I'll put up the drinks."

Dicky assented affably, as the night was warm. But Frank remained behind. "I don't want to run the risk of meeting Starth again. He might come back."

"To fetch his sister," said the big Rhodesian. "Yonder she is in a box with an old lady."

"What a pretty girl," said the frivolous Dicky, and departed.

Lancaster raised his glasses, rather curious to see what Miss Starth was like. He beheld a slender, dark girl, as unlike her brother as possible. Plainly dressed in some gauzy stuff, with a string of seed pearls round her neck, she looked about twenty years of age, but might have been even younger. Apparently she had all the unappeasable curiosity of youth, for her dark eyes roved round the theatre with great eagerness. Finally they rested on Frank, and she flushed when she found he was looking directly at her. First she looked away after the manner of girls, then she stole a stealthy glance at the rude young man, and finally became engrossed in conversation with the elderly lady who was her companion. Frank still looked. He was most polite to the sex, but this face interested him so much that he stared almost rudely. Twice their eyes met, in spite of Miss Starth's ostentatious indifference. She coloured, and he—to his astonishment—likewise blushed. There was something about her which took his heart by storm. To be sure he was susceptible where a woman was concerned, but it seemed absurd to be fascinated by a girl after a few league-long glances. Still, she was distinctly agreeable to him. Fairy Fan he admired after the manner of youth, but she was a pink-and-white doll beside this glorious creature who looked like a queen. Where could his eyes have been to admire the fragile charms of Miss Berry, when true beauty was to be found alone in a stately brunette with coils of shining hair, and eyes like fathomless lakes in the starshine? Fan had been Frank's Rosaline; this vision of loveliness was his Juliet, which means in plain English that he had fallen in love at first sight. But, as he assured himself calmly, such a passion was at once ridiculous and impossible. All the same he continued to "behold vanity," until his divinity grew really angry, and concealed herself behind an envious curtain, which shielded her beauty. At once Lancaster became aware of his bad manners.

"Hang it! I should like to apologise," he thought as his friends returned, and then considered dismally that he had quarrelled past all reconciliation with the brother of his angel, and that there was no chance of a meeting.

Starth hated Frank virulently, because Miss Berry openly approved of the young man's good looks and genuine talents. But even before Fairy Fan appeared to enchant a London public, Starth and Lancaster had never been able to meet without snarling at one another like dogs. Frank was not to blame, being good-natured and much too indolent to fight. But Starth snapped at everyone. That he should have so charming a sister was extraordinary. Even Dicky, the most critical of men, thought so. "Ripping girl, Miss Starth," said he.

"I didn't notice," grunted Lancaster, not wishing to have Baird know too much on account of that gentleman's long, long tongue. He might repeat things to Starth, who could find offence everywhere.

The second act requires no description. It was like the first, but slightly more incoherent. Fairy Fan had it all her own way, as the low comedian had not yet had time to invent his part. When the curtain fell on a pronounced success, with Fan standing in the midst of flowers, Baird bustled out to the bar again with Darrel and his chum. It was to discuss the prospects of the play that they went.

Frank did not notice that the neat man with the light eyes was following them. He was taken up with the weather-beaten Berry, who rejoiced over the triumph of his niece. He was a small man, and had a hard face that might have been hewn out of iron-wood. His lips were tightly closed, his eyes were grey and close-set, and he carried himself in a bouncing, aggressive way, which must have cost him many a fight in the Naked Lands where bounce is not approved of. Berry—Captain by courtesy—looked quite out of place amidst civilised surroundings. A pea-jacket, a tarpaulin hat, a streaming bridge and a rocking, plunging tramp ship would have been more in keeping with his piratical appearance. Why such a Captain Kidd should accompany his niece to London and play the part of a sober citizen puzzled a great many people, Baird amongst the number. But Banjo Berry—such was his odd name—always explained profusely, having no call to do so. Whereby the more astute assumed, and not unreasonably, that he had something to hide.

"Well," said this mariner, gaily, "I guess the play's a go."

"A great success," said Frank, so indifferently that the little man looked at him sharply. Lancaster was wont to be more enthusiastic where Fairy Fan was concerned.

"She sang your chanty well," he remarked, following them to the bar.

"First rate," assented Lancaster. "How's Starth?"

"Sent him home in a cab of sorts," replied Berry, still puzzled. "I guess he'll wake up and apologise tomorrow morning."

"Not to me," said Frank, aggressive at once, in spite of the charming sister. "I don't want to have anything to do with him."

"Ah, pistols and coffee for two is your idea of a meeting," was the Captain's reply. "You'd like to see him buzz into the everlasting darkness, I guess?"

Before Frank could reply, his arm was plucked. In the crowd he did not see who it was for the moment. There was a rush of thirsty souls to the bar, and Berry disappeared in the mob. Still the unknown kept his hand on Lancaster's arm, and drew him towards the door with a gentle pressure. Rather surprised, Frank allowed himself to be so drawn, thinking it was one of his friends. But when the crowd grew thin he found himself face to face with the small, neat man.

"Well?" said Frank, interrogatively.

"I'm glad you didn't answer," said the man with the light eyes. "It is dangerous to answer that man."

"Captain Berry. Why?"

The stranger opened the swing door and stepped into the street. He did not even wait for Frank, but walked along the pavement, dexterously avoiding the people as he walked. Taken by surprise by this odd demeanour, Lancaster followed, and managed to catch up with the man as he was turning into a side street which was deserted. "What do you mean?" asked Lancaster, catching the man by his coat. "Who are you?"

The other stopped under a lamp-post, and laughed in an elfish way. "No matter who I am," he said in a precise voice, "but what I am is another and more important matter."

"Well, what are you?" asked Lancaster, more and more puzzled.

"A man who can read faces and hands and tell the secrets of the future," said the other, gravely.

"Bah!" was Frank's disgusted exclamation. "A charlatan."

"Just so. A charlatan. Yet I am sufficiently interested in you to warn you against coming danger."

"Do you know me?"

"No. I don't know your name or your face, nor anything about you. I happened to be in the bar when you hit that red-headed man, and I saw that the little fellow—"

"Captain Berry?"

"Is that his name? Well, he was trying to foment the quarrel. He is your enemy."

"Nonsense! He has no cause to be my enemy."

"That is the worst kind of enemy to have—one who pretends friendship and strikes in the dark. I read your face, sir, and the face of the red-headed man. If you two meet again—" He hesitated.

"Well?" asked Frank, sharply. "If we meet?"

"One of you will die."

In spite of his scepticism Lancaster felt a chill run through his veins at this speech. "Rubbish!" he said, roughly. "Which one?"

"I sha'n't tell you that," replied the unknown. "You may consider my reply rubbish also. But there is that in your face, sir, which hints at coming trouble. Your fate and the fate of the red-headed man are bound up together. Also, there is a woman."

"How do you know that?" asked Frank, thinking of Fan.

"She is a relative of the red-headed man," said the unknown, "and it is probably—" Here he broke off abruptly. "I sha'n't tell you any more. I may be wrong, I may be right, but the signs are there."

"What signs?"

"Good-night, sir," said the man, and passed swiftly away before Frank could retain him. Lancaster walked to his rooms without returning to the theatre. He laughed at the warning, so vague and absurd did it seem. All the same it haunted him, and he had cause to remember the man afterwards. He never saw the seer again, but, as after events proved, undoubtedly the man was no charlatan.

13

CHAPTER II

REAPING THE WHIRLWIND

Lancaster was by way of being a journalist, and managed to struggle along on an inadequate income. He had no influence, and sweated freely for his money. A few far-seeing editors assured him of a brilliant future, but did not seem anxious to assist him to realise their prophecies. No one knew who Lancaster was, or where he came from, as he never spoke of his past. For five years he had been in town, and, unable to do anything else, had drifted into journalism. But in his heart he cherished the notion of startling London with an up-to-date novel. Pending the joy of waking up to find himself famous, he acted as theatrical critic for the *Daily Budget* , a paper which paid the lowest prices for the best procurable talent, and eked out his income with stray articles. Occasionally he wrote verses, and in this way had made the acquaintance of Fairy Fan, who had read some of his attempts in the papers and thought that he might compose words fit for her rosy mouth to sing.

She took a fancy to him, for he was handsome and well-bred. But even Miss Berry, pretty and astute woman as she was, could not learn anything of Lancaster's past, cleverly as she tried to find out. Her uncle, using coarser methods, tried also, but failed likewise. Only to one man had Frank unbosomed himself, and that was to Eustace Jarman, who had first extended to the lonely young man a helping hand. A memory of Starth's words made Lancaster wonder if Jarman had revealed anything, and he would have sought out his friend to ask him directly had not Jarman dwelt in Essex. However, Frank concluded that Starth had merely made the remarks about his parents in a casual way, and without any real knowledge, so he dismissed that matter easily from his mind.

But he could not so easily dismiss the memory of the quarrel, especially as the charming face of Miss Starth floated persistently before his mental vision. Jarman had introduced Frank to Starth three years before, and the two men had never got on well together. By mutual consent they avoided one another, until Miss Berry brought them together to quarrel over her beauty. Starth thereafter became more and more insulting, until his behaviour resulted in the row of the previous night. Had Frank not seen the beautiful sister he would not have cared much, having small regard for the brother. As it was, he felt depressed the next morning, seeing in that final quarrel an insurmountable barrier to making acquaintance with his divinity.

Being in this frame of mind he was both surprised and pleased to receive a note from Starth asking him to call that afternoon between four and five. It seemed that Starth wished to apologise as he had gone rather far— so he stated in his note—on the previous night. Lancaster was astonished that Starth should behave thus reasonably. The action was unlike him. But as the olive branch was held forth, and as there was a chance of meeting the sister, Lancaster decided to accept. No answer was required, so Starth evidently expected him to come. Frank finished his work for the day, and went to his rooms to dress himself more smartly. If Miss Starth were to be present he wanted to appear at his best, but if she were not—

It was at this point that Lancaster sat down to consider. How did he know that the note might not be a trap? He thought it strange that Starth should come forward in this way, and at a second meeting the man might try to revenge himself for his punishment. A black eye is not forgiven easily by any man, and Starth was the last person to let bygones be bygones. Then, again, if there was to be trouble Miss Starth would not be there, and the careful dressing would be wasted. Lancaster was no coward, but he did not wish to accentuate his bad relations with Starth. He had half a mind to send round stating that he could not come, but the hope that, after all, his divinity might be present, decided him to go. Having made up his mind he completed his toilet, and ended by stowing away a pistol in his hip pocket. It was a loaded Derringer, which Frank sometimes took with him when he went round the slums on dangerous business connected with his journalistic work. On the present occasion it was taken merely to intimidate Starth should he have arranged a trap.

"The man's a coward," thought Frank, as he issued forth into the July sunshine, "so if he threatens in any way I can show him the pistol if necessary. I'd rather use my fists as I did last night, but for all I know he may have a revolver handy. It's as well to be on the safe side."

All the same he rather despised himself for this precaution, and twice was on the point of returning to his room to discard the weapon. Still, Starth was a dangerous man, and might use something lethal only to be met with by a revolver; and if nothing happened no one would ever know that he—Lancaster was thinking of himself—carried a pistol. In spite of his experience of life, Frank was callow in many ways, else he would not have armed himself in so unnecessary a manner.

Starth lived in a South Kensington side street, a blind alley where the houses were small, and each was fronted by a weedy garden. Lancaster found himself after a brisk walk—he never took a cab unless forced to, and disliked a bus ride—facing a blank, dismal house of two storeys with green shutters. It had not been painted for years, and the front was blistered, weather-stained, discoloured, and generally dilapidated. Some attempt had been made to cultivate the patch of ground in front, but, beyond rearing a few marigolds and pansies, the attempt had not been successful. Up a path bordered by oyster shells, Frank advanced to a rustic porch of green lattice-work, entwined with dusty creepers, and rang a jingling little bell whose shrill summons he could hear. While waiting he casually noticed that the right-hand window was slightly open, although the blind was pulled down. Before he could observe further, the door opened so suddenly that it almost seemed as though the person behind had been waiting in the passage.

The person was a small sluttish servant, with gooseberry eyes and a pasty white face. She was attired in her best blue dress, and wore a large picture-hat trimmed with more flowers than adorned the garden. Also she had on gloves, and carried a yellow umbrella. As soon as she saw Frank she burst into voluble speech.

"Yer the gent as wishes to see Mr. Starth, and I am glad to see you, sir, for he said as you was goin' to be 'ere at four, it now bein' half-past, and I'm goin' out, my young man waiting for me. This way, sir, and please be quick, as I am in a hurry. Missus 'ave gone out too, but the tea's all ready and the kettle on the fire."

Almost before she finished this incoherent address, she conducted the astonished Frank up a stuffy staircase, and into a front room. Hastily shoving him into this, she banged the door, and hurried away, presumably to meet her young man. Lancaster, puzzled by this reception, and by the mean look of the room in which he found himself, halted at the door, waiting for his host to speak. Starth was sitting in an armchair by the window, with a book. He threw this down, and advanced to his visitor with outstretched hands.

"I'm glad you've come, Lancaster," he said, eagerly. "I am so ashamed of myself that I hardly know what to say."

"Say nothing more," said Frank, laying aside his hat and cane. "I am only too glad to come to an understanding. I can't comprehend why you quarrel with me."

"Jealousy," said Starth, quickly, and sat down.

"Of me and Miss Berry? Well, you needn't be. I don't love her."

Starth pulled down the blind so as to prevent his discoloured eye showing up too badly. "I thought you were to marry her?" he remarked.

"Certainly not. Such an idea never entered my head. Who said so?"

"Captain Berry."

Frank looked puzzled, then laughed. "I should have thought Berry more ambitious for his niece. I haven't any money."

"That's just it," said Starth, slowly. "If you are poor, how did you come to give her those diamonds?"

"I never did. I heard you gave them to her."

Starth laughed, and glanced round the stuffy room. "Would I live in this dog's kennel if I could afford such stones?" he said. "My dear Lancaster, I'm desperately hard up. Between my sister and myself there is enough to live on, no more."

"I saw your sister last night," said Frank.

"Yes. She lives in Essex, but happened to be in town, so I got her a box. She went back this morning with Mrs. Perth."

"Is that the lady who was with her?"

Starth nodded. "She and my sister live together in a small cottage at Wargrove. But I needn't bore you with my family history. I want you to accept my apology."

"I do, Starth. But why did you mention my parents?"

"It was the only thing I could think of."

"To make me angry, I suppose? H'm! You know nothing about me."

"No. Is there anything interesting to know?"

"I fear not," said Lancaster. "My story is a dull one. Still, I thought that Jarman might have said something."

"He said nothing. I never asked about you," responded the other, quickly. "Fact is, Lancaster, I don't think you and I ever got on well together. My fault, I'm afraid, as I have such a bad temper. I am jealous, too, as I love Miss Berry and want to marry her."

"You can, for all I care," said Lancaster, quietly. "I did admire her greatly, but I never had any intention of marrying her. As to the diamonds, who told you that I gave them to her?"

"No one directly. But Berry hinted—"

"Why should he hint?" said Frank, thoughtfully. "He knows I'm as poor as the proverbial church mouse. Do you think he wants me, or expects me, to marry his niece?"

"Yes, I do," said Starth, promptly; "and that was why I grew jealous."

"Then I can't see his reason. I have no money, no position, and no influence. Miss Berry doesn't love me—"

"The Captain says she does," said Starth, quickly.

"Oh, that's rubbish! She likes me because I write her songs, and we get on well together. As for love—" Frank shrugged his shoulders.

"Have you never been in love, Lancaster?"

Frank grew red and shook his head, looking down meanwhile. Starth's jealous eyes followed his every movement, and he eagerly waited for an

17

answer. But none came. Frank could not bring himself to say that he had fallen in love with a girl he had seen but once, and to say it to her brother. In place of gratifying Starth's curiosity he changed the subject. "What a peculiar servant that was who admitted me," he said. "She was quite angered because I had delayed her appointment with her young man. Had I known, I'd have been punctual."

"It's Tilly," said Starth, carelessly. "A peculiar creature, as you say—a London slavey of the regular type. I believe Mrs. Betts—that's my landlady—gets her cheap from a workhouse. I let her go to see her young man because Mrs. Betts, who keeps her well in hand, is away at the wedding of some cousin or another. I've got all the house to myself till nine o'clock. But, I say, let's have tea."

Frank made no objection, as he was thirsty, and Starth went down to get the hot water. Pending his return Lancaster strolled about the room, and looked at the photographs. There was one of the beautiful girl he had seen on the previous night, and he nearly stole it. Also he was taken with a gorgeous portrait of a tall, thick-lipped negress, which had an Arabic inscription written at the foot. "Who is this, Starth?" asked Frank, when his host returned with the tea-tray and a kettle of hot water.

Starth glanced at the photograph. "A girl called Balkis. I believe she comes from Zanzibar. I met her at the Docks when I was exploring an opium den."

"H'm! She looks as though she had a temper."

"She has. Took a fancy to me, and gave me her picture, with that writing. It's something about Allah and good luck, I believe. I saw her a good many times at that opium shop. She runs it, I believe."

Lancaster sat down while Starth made ready the tea. It struck him, from these remarks, and from a certain strange odour in the room, that Starth smoked opium. Perhaps the drug was accountable for his strange tempers and utter disregard of decency. Frank began to be rather sorry he had quarrelled with the man, since, if he smoked opium, he was to a certain extent not accountable for his actions. Starth, with his swollen face and discoloured eye, looked peculiar and grim, and had a haggard look about him which hinted at excess of some sort.

"Here you are," said Starth, passing along a cup. "Do you take sugar Or perhaps," he added, as he handed over the basin, "you would like a drink of whisky?"

"Tea's good enough for me," said Frank, sipping. "Well, Starth, I'm glad we've come to some sort of understanding. I hate rows."

"So do I, but jealousy always makes my blood boil."

"But, you see, you've no cause to be jealous."

"I can see that now. But Berry kept hinting that it was an arranged thing between you and Fan."

"H'm! I'll have a talk with him. He's no right to make false statements of that kind. I wonder what his game is. I'm certainly not a desirable match for his niece, putting aside the fact that she doesn't care two pins for anyone but herself."

"Are you sure of that, Lancaster?" said Starth, with rather an anxious look. "I'm mad about her, and want to marry her."

"I shouldn't like Banjo Berry for a connection myself," said Lancaster, setting down his cup. "What a strange taste that tea has."

"They never clean the kettles here," said Starth, hastily. "It's smoke or fur inside the kettle, or something. My tea tastes bad also."

Frank refused another cup, and smoked a cigarette while Starth related his feelings for Fairy Fan in detail. Also he mentioned that he hoped to see much of Lancaster, and that he should like to introduce him to his sister. This last remark made Frank's heart leap with joy, but somehow he could not find words to thank his host. Starth seemed to recede a long way, and his voice sounded like that of a phonograph. Lancaster tried to rise, but sank back in his chair drowsily. He felt sure that there was foul play, as he saw faintly the man lean forward to scrutinise him. But his brain was clouded, his speech was thick, and wave after wave of something deeper than sleep poured over him. His last thought was something about opium being in the tea, but he could not put this into words. After that last effort of the mind to overcome the lethargy his head fell back, and he became unconscious.

In after days Frank never could be got to tell his dreams. The mere memory of them would make him shudder. Far away in the land of sleep he wrestled with unknown foes, and passed a time of sheer agony not to be paralleled by any experience of the waking hours. He seemed to have slept for centuries when he came to himself on the sofa, with a furred tongue and an aching head. There was a faint light in the room as the blinds were up, and for a few minutes the young man, still half stupefied with the drug, could not grasp the idea of his whereabouts. Then after an effort or two at thought, his self-consciousness came back with a rush. He rose slowly and staggered into the centre of the room, only to stumble over a body.

It *was* a body, for he fell on top of it. His memory became clearer with the horror of the discovery. He remembered his visit, the empty house, the drugged tea, and, recalling his dread of foul play on the part of Starth, he slipped his hand round to his hip-pocket. The Derringer was gone. When he made that discovery, Frank leaped to his feet with a strangled cry. By this time he had his wits about him; but still remained a vague fear of the thing on the floor.

19

His frock coat had been removed and cast on the carpet beside the sofa. He found it by the feel, and obtained a match out of the ticket-pocket. Striking this he bent over the dead. It *was* Starth. "Great Heavens!" said Frank, under his breath. "Starth—dead—shot!"

Assuredly shot, for there was a small hole under the left eye. The bullet must have passed into the brain, killing the poor wretch instantaneously. As the match flickered out, Frank was left alone in the half-gloom beside this dead thing, trying to think how the poor wretch had come by his death. Then it dawned anew on him that his pistol was gone, that the man had been shot. Who had slain him? What revolver had been used? The first question he could not answer, but the second answered itself. Since his weapon was gone, it assuredly had been used to commit the murder.

But was it murder? What about suicide? Frank tried to argue the case. As he did so, the clock on the mantelpiece struck nine. The sudden tingle of the bell set his blood leaping. He recalled how Starth had expected Mrs. Betts and Tilly back at that hour, and making a dash for his coat, he hastily struggled into it. He must not be found here with the dead man. The row on the previous night, his foolish words, his weapon, his being alone in the house with a man with whom he was well known to be on bad terms—all these things would weave a rope to hang him. Realising his danger with a gasp, Frank lighted another match, and found cane and hat. But he had no more matches, although he desired to search for the Derringer. All he wanted now was to get away, and he hastened down the stairs in a state of agony, the perspiration standing on his brow, and his heart in his mouth.

There was no difficulty in opening the door. He closed it again, and went down the path, through the gate, and on to the road. Here a street-lamp threw a strong light. Under it stood a girl and a young man. "My, sir!" said Tilly, catching sight of his face, "you have been a time with Mr. Starth. I 'ope he ain't angered. He—"

Lancaster waited to hear no more, but walked rapidly down the lane, he knew not whither. All he wanted was to get away from the gallows, from the dead.

CHAPTER III

A FRIEND IN NEED

Popular prejudice regards Essex as a damp, marshy flat, inhabited by mosquitoes, rheumatic yokels, and children of the sea-mist. But Eustace Jarman dwelt on a far-extending plateau, whence from his study window he surveyed Tilbury, Gravesend, the mouth of Thames river, and vast tracts of meadow-lands divided into irregular squares by erratic hedges. His home was three miles from the nearest railway station as the crow flies, and, being cut off from civilisation, by acres of furze-grown common, was as isolated as his misanthropic soul could desire.

Jarman had the reputation of being a solitary man, and those who knew him in literary circles hinted at the destroying influences of the inevitable woman. But Eustace never explained. After a journalistic career in town he disappeared into the Essex wilds, and devoted himself to writing music-hall sketches, short tales, and articles on countries he had visited. As he had been round the world twice or thrice, and knew the manners and customs of various peoples, he was well paid for his contributions. The cost of living at Wargrove was nil, and Jarman was supposed to be saving money. At times he would vanish into the Far East, or seek South America when there was a chance of trouble between tin-pot republics, but he always returned to his Essex plateau, to live a hermit's life. Miss Cork waited on him, and looked after his simple needs, and Miss Cork mentioned frequently that he was the oddest gent she ever set eyes on.

"The Shanty," as he called his place, was an old farmhouse, buried amongst elm and oak trees, and surrounded by an orchard and a flower garden, all more or less in ruins. Jarman would not allow the place to be tidied up, as Miss Cork suggested, loving better the eccentric untrimmed look of his property. The hedges grew sprawling at their own sweet will, long grass flourished up to the very door, and poppies, sun-flowers, and straggling rose-trees showed above this miniature jungle. Eustace possessed three rooms, two of which were occupied by beds for himself and any chance friend, and a third apartment, large and airy, which served as a study, a dining-room, a smoking-room, and a parlour. In this last were collected trophies of Jarman's travels, ranging from Japanese curiosities to South Sea oddities. Books also—but these were everywhere, and over-flowed from the study into the passages, into the hall, up the stairs, and in some degree into the bedrooms. Everywhere there was a scent of tobacco smoke, and Eustace loafed about in flannel bags with an old shooting jacket and a worn cricketing cap on the back of his head.

The house was not very large, and Jarman was over six feet. But he moved with a dexterity remarkable in so huge a man, and was as handy as a woman in looking after his housekeeping. Miss Cork lived at the back, and merely acted as lieutenant in carrying out her master's orders. When she wished to introduce feminine innovations Eustace protested. He loved his savage bachelor life and his hermit-crab shell too much to desire new-fangled customs. Extra civilisation, especially of the womanly kind, meant extra work, and Eustace was a lazy man.

It was a wet July night when Lancaster sought this refuge. All day it had been raining hard, and Jarman was just thinking of putting on his waders for his usual walk, when Miss Cork entered to announce a visitor. On her heels followed Frank, and Eustace stared when he saw him. The stare was excusable, for Lancaster appeared in a silk hat, a frock-coat, and patent-leather boots. He was mired with clay from the roads, torn by the furze of the common, and dripped like an insane river-god. Also, without invitation, he collapsed into the nearest chair, while Jarman's jaw fell still lower at the sight of his white face, his clenched mouth, and his glassy eyes. Miss Cork, half blind, saw few of these things, but she withdrew to the kitchen to soli-loquise on the costume of the visitor, inappropriate alike to the weather and the country. Meanwhile Jarman, behind closed doors, continued to stare.

"What is the matter?" he asked at last.

"I caught the last train from Liverpool Street," explained Frank, in faint tones, "and walked across the Common. I'm dead beat. Give me a whisky and soda."

Jarman supplied this refreshment speedily, and again demanded explan-ations. "But you'd better get into a dry kit before you make 'em," said he, bustling about. "What a crazy rig to negotiate the country in. Been drinkin'?"

"Do I ever drink, you ass?"

"Not your style, I know, but that's the sort that generally goes a mucker in the end. Cut into my bedroom and I'll hand you out a few things. Hang it, man, hold up!"

Lancaster, who had lurched against the big man's shoulder, pulled him-self straight, and tried to smile. Jarman could see that the poor young fel-low was on the verge of hysterics, being overwrought, and quite broken down. Therefore he spoke roughly to brace the slack nerves. With a few choice expletives he chased Frank into the bedroom, made him strip to the skin, and after a thorough towelling, saw him inducted into a pair of flannel trousers and a faded blazer, together with a woollen shirt and a pair of old slippers. Then he demanded if Frank was hungry, and led him back to the parlour.

"No, I'm not hungry," said Frank, dropping into a chair near the fire, for Eustace approved of a fire when the rain fell; "but another whisky—"

"Not a bit of it. You'll get squiffy. You must eat!"

"But I want to tell you—"

"Later! Later! Meantime, bread and meat."

Jarman looted the kitchen, and, having sent Miss Cork to bed, boiled the kettle and returned with a tray. This he placed before his guest, and stood over him while Frank forced ham and bread down a most unwilling throat. Then he gave the young man a pipe, mixed him a second glass of whisky of the weakest description, and demanded explanations.

"I can give them in one word," said Frank, now more composed. "Murder!"

Jarman stared again, and whistled. Then he went to see that the door was closed, and returned to his seat. "Who have you been killing?"

"No one. But I'm in danger of being accused. I am innocent—I swear I am innocent, Eustace?"

"All right, old man," replied Jarman, patting his junior on the back. "I know you wouldn't come to me if you were guilty."

"If I were, would you shelter me?"

"H'm! Depends upon the kind of murder. I don't mind a fair fight sort o' killing. 'Fact, I've shot a man or two myself in the Great Waste Lands."

"But I didn't shoot Starth. I really didn't."

"Starth! What, is he—"

"Dead! Dead! Shot dead. But not by me—not by me."

Eustace chewed his pipe, and stared into the fire, pulling hard. He appeared to be worried.

"Poor girl!" said he at length.

Frank understood on the instant. "Does she love her brother?"

"Do you know her?" asked Eustace, without looking up.

Lancaster shook his head. "I saw her last night at the theatre. Her brother insulted me, and asked me to see him today, as he wanted to apologise—"

"Wait!" Jarman threw up his hand. "The whole truth, if you please."

"I'm telling the truth, if you will only listen."

"Apologising doesn't sound like Starth," objected Eustace.

"I thought so when I got his note, and I am convinced now that his invitation was a trap."

"To have you shot?"

"How do I know?" He was shot himself.

"By whom?"

"I can't say. I was lying in a stupor when it happened."

"Drugged—with opium?" hinted Jarman.

"Yes. Did you know that Starth—"

"All along." Jarman placed the tips of his fingers together. "See here, Frank, I know Miss Starth very well. She lives here with an old lady called Mrs. Perth. Their cottage is only a stone's throw away from my diggings. I met the brother there in the long ago, and—"

"And introduced him to me. I wish you hadn't."

"It's too late now, seeing that the man's dead, to raise objections. I never approved of Walter Starth. A bad lot—a very bad lot. He never liked you. I don't know why. But I didn't think it would come to this."

"Jarman"—Frank started from his seat—"you don't suppose—"

"Sit down, you ass." Jarman pushed Lancaster back into his chair. "I wouldn't take things so quietly if you had killed him. Barring that, I'm glad the man's out of the world. He was no use in it."

"My own words—my own words!"

"When and where?"

"At the Piccadilly Theatre last night. I shouted them in the bar after I knocked him down."

"H'm! Shouldn't talk like that, Frank, it's foolish."

"I know it is. I'm in a fix, that's why I come to you."

"Well," said Eustace, refilling his briar, "the best thing you can do is to tell me everything from the start."

"Where am I to start from. You know about Fairy Fan?"

"Yes; and about Starth's love for her. He looked upon you as a rival, and the knowledge didn't increase his liking for you. Well?"

Frank straightened himself, and forthwith delivered a succinct account of all that had taken place, from the encounter on the previous night to his leaving the house in Sand Lane, South Kensington.

"I took the Underground to Liverpool Street and caught the down train by the skin of my teeth. I didn't even return to my diggings, as I was afraid of being arrested. I'm a marked man now, Eustace. The police will hunt me down. And I am innocent."

"Why didn't you give the alarm when you found Starth dead?"

"Man alive, that would have delivered me into the power of the law."

"I know that. Just asked the question to see what you'd say. H'm! It's a nasty case for you. The circumstantial evidence—"

"I know—I know. Who knows better than I?" Frank rose to pace the room anxiously. "I spoke foolishly about Starth being better out of the world, at the theatre. I took my pistol with me—I was alone in the house with him!—that servant saw me leave, and I daresay noticed my agitation. Jarman, it's awful. I don't see how I'm going to get out of the danger. They'll hang me."

"Steady, old man. They won't hang you. I won't let them."

"Then you'll help me to get out of the country?"

"No. If you cut, you'll surely be caught. By tomorrow every seaport in the kingdom will be watched. You must stay here."

"But I'll be traced."

"I don't think so. Plenty of men go up and down on this line in frock-coats and tall hats. I don't suppose anyone took particular notice of you."

"The train was crowded."

"All the better. There's safety in a crowd. No, Frank, don't leave England. Stop here, and I'll fix you up some sort of disguise. The very daring of the thing may be your salvation. The police will never think that you will remain so near town. I'll make things safe with Miss Cork, and she's the only person who has seen you. When we get time to turn round we can sift matters out."

"What a good chap you are, Jarman!"

"Nothing of the sort. If you were guilty I shouldn't chance the risk of being an accessory after the fact. As it is, I'll see you through the business. It's a nasty affair, there's no denying that. I expect the sister will come over tomorrow to ask for my assistance."

"Oh!" Frank jumped up nervously. "Do you think she'll recognise me?"

"Of course not. She only saw you once, and that at a distance, Besides, I don't suppose she inquired your name. Finally, as I intend to disguise you, she won't guess that anything is wrong. You work the typer?"

"Yes."

"Good! Then you'll stop here as my secretary. I'll dictate, and you'll work the machine. With your moustache cut off, dyed black hair, a stained face, and a pair of goggles for weak eyes, no one will recognise you."

"But no one hereabouts knows me, except Miss Starth, and she only saw me in the glare of the electrics for a few minutes."

"Frank, you're an ass! The *Police Gazette* will have a full description of you. Everyone will be on the look-out. Thank Heaven, you're of the commonplace type. Pink and white, fair hair, blue eyes, well-groomed, military figure, and all the rest of it."

"How will my blue eyes match black hair?"

"We'll say you're Irish, and you can fix up a brogue. Trust me. I've been in several holes myself, and know how to get out of the deepest."

"But, Jarman, who do you think killed the man?"

"I can't say that until I know more. The reason is to be found in Walter Starth's past. He has sown the wind pretty freely, and I can hardly wonder at his reaping this whirlwind."

"Do you think he intended to trap me?" asked Lancaster.

"Yes. He's not the man to apologise. And the house being empty on that evening shows that Starth was up to some trickery. Maybe he intended to kill you. However, he never intended to die himself."

"How do you know? He may have committed suicide."

"Bosh! Starth was the last man in the world to have such an idea. He wasn't cowardly enough. I will say that. Besides, if he wished to commit suicide he would scarcely invite you to see him do it."

"I don't know. He might have left a letter saying I shot him, and then got out of the world to hang me."

Jarman shrugged his huge shoulders. "That's an extreme measure of revenge. If he wanted to get you into trouble, he would certainly like to be present to see how you took your gruel. Another thing, from what you say, your pistol was used."

"I think so. At all events, it was taken from my pocket."

"H'm! He searched you. Anything else missing?"

"The note in which he asked me to call."

"That proves Starth set a trap. I think—no I don't; I can't deliver an opinion until I know more. Go to bed and sleep."

"I can't sleep," said Frank, passionately. "I'm ruined."

But for all that he dropped into a deep slumber almost as soon as his head touched the pillow.

"Worn out, poor wretch!" said Eustace.

CHAPTER IV

TWO HUNDRED POUNDS REWARD

"What do you think of my new secretary, Miss Cork?" asked Jarman next morning, when his housekeeper was laying the table. He put the question purposely to arrange matters for the disguise.

"I didn't see quite rightly, Mr. Jarman, my eyes being weak. Young?"

"And dark and Irish. His eyes are weak to the extent of blue glasses."

"I didn't see them, sir."

"No, poor chap. He broke them crossing the Common, left his baggage in London, and got lost in our country."

"Oh, he'll know it soon, Mr. Jarman. I'm an Essex woman myself— Billericay way—and the country is easy. What's the gentleman's name, Sir?"

"Desmond," said Eustace, lying with an unmoved face. "Desmond O'Neil."

"I'll remember, sir."

"And, oh, Miss Cork, I shouldn't mention about his late arrival and loss of baggage if I were you. The Irish are sensitive."

"As well I know from politics, Mr. Jarman. No, sir, I'll say nothing."

Miss Cork was a tall, lean woman with watery grey eyes and grey hair screwed into a cast-iron knob behind. Her lips were thin, and her nose red by reason of tight-lacing. Miss Cork had a good figure and improved it, in her own opinion, by making her waist smaller. She usually wore a grey dress with cloth slippers, and moved like a shadow. For many years she had been with Eustace, who had produced her from a London police-court where she was being charged with vagrancy. But he never told anyone this, and Miss Cork bore a high character. But she was not popular, as she never gossiped. And a woman who does not gossip in a village is not fit companion for those who want to know their neighbours' affairs. Eustace knew that she would hold her tongue. Nevertheless, he was glad that her limited vision had not been able to take in Frank Lancaster as he had been.

As it was, Mr. Desmond O'Neil appeared late at the breakfast, and Miss Cork, bringing in the bacon and eggs, silently avowed the truth of her mas-

27

ter's description. The new secretary was brown-skinned, with dark hair, and a clean-shaven face, shaded about the eyes with blue spectacles. Miss Cork was rather doubtful about the clean-shaving. From the glimpse she got of him on the previous night she fancied he had worn a moustache, and this she mentioned to Jarman. "It was a smear of clay," explained Eustace. "The poor chap was tumbling in the mud all the time. Were you mired, O'Neil?" he asked, aloud.

"I was that!" responded the Irish gentleman, wondering why his host kicked him under the table.

"The mud do splash high in Essex," said Miss Cork. "I'm a Billericay woman myself, Mr. O'Neil." Then she left the room, and Jarman explained. But Frank continued uneasy.

"I don't like the looks of that woman," he said. "Is she honest?"

"Oh, quite, except what she says about Billericay. She's invented the idea of being a native of those parts, as the villagers here don't like strangers. But she's been with me for three years. I picked her up in London."

"Where?"

"Well, it isn't fair to give her away. She's had a past, although I don't know the rights or wrongs of it. But she'll hold her tongue."

"Suppose a reward is offered, will she?"

"Sure. She owes me too much to play me false," said Jarman, pouring out the coffee. "And where's the reward to come from?"

"The Government—"

"Pooh! Government won't offer much, even if it offers any, which isn't likely. No one else will plank down the money. Miss Starth hasn't much, and there are no relatives. Make your mind easy about the reward. There won't be a cent offered for your apprehension."

"What's Miss Starth's name?" asked Frank, who made a fair breakfast.

"Mildred," responded Jarman, with a flush. "She's the sweetest girl you ever met."

"I saw that from the glimpse I caught of her," said Lancaster, and wondered why Jarman coloured through his tan. He scented a rival, but could not be sure, and, of course, was unable to ask questions. Besides, in spite of his newly-born passion, his position was so dangerous, that he had but one thought, namely, how to escape being hanged on circumstantial evidence.

Frank wished to talk of the matter the moment breakfast was over, but this Eustace would not allow. "You'll have enough of it before you win free," he said. "We must wait until we hear what the newspapers have to say. I daresay there's nothing in the morning lot; but this afternoon we may

28

read something. Then, again, I expect to see Mildred—I mean Miss Starth. She's sure to be wired for."

Frank noticed the slip, and became convinced that Eustace admired the girl more than a little. However, his brain was too filled with his own danger to think of anything else, and he accompanied Jarman on an exploring tour round the village. The idea was that his arrival and appearance and position as secretary should be made as public as possible, so that he might become an accepted fact. After the first few days the villagers would accept him as part of the Shanty household, and cease to discuss him. The subsequent indifference would be another element of safety.

So round the village that afternoon the two went, arm-in-arm. Jarman took his new secretary into several shops, and then to the post-office, which was conducted by a fat woman, who read all the letters and made all the mischief she could. Early as it was, she had a piece of news.

"Oh! Mr. Jarman," said she, puffing, for the day was hot and muggy after the rain, "whatever's come to Miss Starth? I saw her driving like a mad thing to catch the two train. And she only keeps a donkey too—leastways, it's Mrs. Perth who does."

"I suppose she was going to town, Mrs. Baker."

"Then I hope it isn't to a funeral, Mr. Jarman, for her face was as white as a winding sheet. Ah, well, it ain't none of our business."

"No!" said Eustace, emphatically; "it certainly is not."

"That's what I say," replied Mrs. Baker, not seeing the intended rebuke. "As I always says to Baker, if people managed their own affairs without being talked about, people wouldn't be so bothered. And how do you like the country, sir?" This last was to Frank.

"It is extremely pretty," replied Lancaster, cautiously.

"Ah, when you're here long enough, you'll say so, sir. But I suppose you've just come?"

"He came last night, Mrs. Baker, from Ireland?"

"Dear me! I get butter from there. And will you be staying long, sir?"

"I hope so," answered Lancaster, seeing why Jarman had brought him into the company of this inquiring lady. "I am Mr. Jarman's secretary."

"Well, I'm glad you've a companion at last, Mr. Jarman, though a wife would be more to a single gentleman's mind. And I always thought—"

"Good-morning!" interposed Eustace, hastily, and left the shop, tucking a bundle of newspapers and letters under his arm. When they got some distance along the road he laughed.

"What do you think of Mrs. Baker?" he asked.

"She seems to be a kind of gazette. I suppose you took me in so that she could talk of my personal appearance, and my engagement as a secretary, and all the rest of it."

"Precisely. The wider you are known the safer you will be. Mrs. Baker will describe your appearance, and detail how you came from Ireland where she gets her butter. We'll send a few letters through her hands, addressed to Desmond O'Neil, and then she'll drop talking. So even if you are traced by any chance, Frank, there will be no danger of a detective connecting you with the man who is wanted."

Lancaster shuddered. "It's like a nightmare," he said. "Yesterday I was a free man, with a career before me; now I'm an outlaw, with a price set on my head."

"It's unpleasant. But wait—wait. Time works wonders. The real criminal may be discovered. Let us hear what news has come to Rose Cottage."

"Is that where Miss Starth lives?"

"Yes. She and Mrs. Perth share the place. Their united incomes are just enough to keep them in comfort."

"Is Miss Starth engaged?" asked Lancaster, with a side glance.

"No," said the other, with unnecessary fierceness. "Why do you ask?"

"Well, she's so pretty that I thought—"

"Oh, bother your thinking!" broke in Eustace, testily. "Mildred isn't the girl to get engaged in a hurry."

"You seem to know her well, calling her by her name."

"I've known her for some years, and as she is something of a poetess I help her to get her poems into print. She looks on me as a kind of—of father," added Jarman, colouring.

Frank nodded. He guessed the truth, but was too languid to argue it. But he couldn't help asking what Mrs. Baker had been about to observe when Eustace left the shop. "Was she speaking of Miss Starth?"

"I don't know. Mrs. Baker is by way of being a matchmaker, and always couples names. There was a rumour that I was engaged to Mildred."

"It wasn't true?"

"No. I've had enough of women. Seven years ago in 'Frisco—" Jarman checked himself impatiently. "What's the use of raking up old tales. You seem very interested in Miss Starth?"

"Naturally," said Lancaster, sadly, "seeing what I am supposed to have done. If she knew, she would denounce me."

"Not on the evidence you have placed before me," said Jarman. "She's a sensible girl. And the death of her brother will add to her income."

"What an unpleasant speech!" said Frank, in vexed tones.

"We live in a world of facts, my boy. Besides, that beauty is no loss."

By this time they had arrived at the Common. Here Jarman turned down a shady lane, and passed through an arcade of chestnut trees. At the end of this was an open space surrounded by trees, and amidst these a thatched cottage that might have come out of a fairy-tale from the quaint look of it.

The walls were whitewashed, the windows of lattice work, and in front of it flourished a garden filled with old-fashioned flowers, evidently the delight of those who had planted them. A white paling fence separated it from the lane, and over the gate of this leant an elderly lady. Frank recognised Mrs. Perth.

She was a delicate old dame, with an ivory-hued face, smooth white hair, and dressed severely in black from head to foot, even to a black straw hat. She beckoned to Eustace. He knew well enough why she was in mourning, but for obvious reasons asked questions.

"Why are you in black, Mrs. Perth? No bad news, I hope?"

"I don't know if you call it bad or good," she replied, with some asperity. "Walter has been murdered."

Frank, in the background, winced, and dug his cane into the turf. But Eustace took the intelligence with well-feigned surprise. "Murdered! Mrs. Perth! How terrible. Who murdered him?"

"Ah! That's what has to be discovered. Mildred received a letter this morning, telling her that Walter had been found last night shot through the head in his rooms in Sand Lane. Also he was stabbed in the breast—right through the heart."

"Stabbed also," began Frank, incautiously, when Jarman interposed.

"My new secretary, Mrs. Perth—Mr. Desmond O'Neil. He comes from Ireland."

"I am happy to meet you, Mr. O'Neil," said the old lady in a most stately manner. "What was it you said?"

"I was—was—only expressing—my—my surprise," stammered Frank.

"That the man should be stabbed as well as shot," put in Jarman, ever watchful. "I don't wonder at it. Wasn't one mode of death enough?"

"Apparently not. The shot must have killed him, too, as it was under the right eye!"

"The *right* eye," objected Frank, and it was on the tip of his tongue to correct the speech, but he swallowed his words. "How horrible!"

"You may well say that. We don't know all the details yet," said Mrs. Perth, addressing Eustace, "and Mildred has gone up to town to hear what she can. The police are in possession of the house. Let us hope the assassin will be found."

"Let us hope so," muttered Frank, and then aimlessly strolled away to a little distance to overcome a qualmish feeling.

"He's rather a nervous chap," explained Jarman to Mrs. Perth; "bad health and weak eyes."

"He does indeed look pale, Mr. Jarman. I fear I'm not looking well myself this morning."

"No wonder," said Eustace. "The shock—"

31

"Well, it was a shock to us both," interrupted Mrs. Perth, speaking low. "But to tell you the truth, Mr. Jarman, Mildred is more grieved than I am. I never liked Walter. Heaven forgive me for speaking ill of the dead, but—well, Mr. Jarman, you know what a bad man he was."

"We'll bury his reputation with him, poor wretch."

But this Mrs. Perth did not seem inclined to do. "He led Mildred a truly awful life," she continued. "But for my influence she would have parted with her income to him. Moreover, he wished her to marry one of his disreputable friends."

"I never knew that!" cried Eustace, and looked displeased now that he had acquired the knowledge. "Who is it?"

"Mr. Denham. You met him here when Walter brought him down."

"Ugh!" Jarman looked disgusted. "An effeminate little dandy. But I don't think there was any harm in him, Mrs. Perth. He was an ass, pure and simple."

"And disreputable," insisted Mrs. Perth. "He came from the United States, and neither his manners nor his principles are English. I believe he had money, and for that reason Walter desired to bring about the marriage."

Eustace fidgeted. "I oughtn't to ask, of course," said he, "but did this—did Denham propose?"

"Certainly not," said the old lady, promptly, "I saw to that. No, Mr. Jarman, say what you will, Walter is better out of the world than in it. Had he lived he would certainly have ended in gaol. Think what such a disgrace would have meant to Mildred!"

"Oh, I think Starth would always have kept on the safe side," said Jarman. "He had a great notion of looking after his own skin, had Starth. Have you—has his sister any idea as to who killed him?"

"No. Walter's life was distinctly apart from ours. I never allowed him to come to Rose Cottage more often than was necessary, as he worried Mildred, and, indeed, myself. He knew a bad lot of people, and most probably met his death at the hands of one of them. But I must say," added Mrs. Perth, frankly, "that it was kind of this Mr. Berry to inform us of the tragedy."

"Berry?" cried Lancaster, who had again strolled within earshot.

"Yes! Mr. Banjo Berry—a most peculiar name. Do you know him?"

Jarman answered for obvious reasons. "I was speaking about him this morning," said he, hastily. "I suppose the mention of the name in connection with this case recalled it to your mind, O'Neil?"

"Yes," said Frank, taking his cue. "Banjo Berry is not an ordinary name. Did you ever meet him, Mrs. Perth?"

"No. Mr. Starth's friends were not mine," replied the old dame, stiffly; "but this Mr. Berry must have been most intimate with Walter, as he says in his letter to Mildred" (she was again addressing Jarman) "that he intends to offer a reward of two hundred pounds for the detection of the assassin."

Lancaster dropped his stick in sheer amazement and to prevent any betrayal, Eustace took his arm with a significant pressure. "Well, Mrs. Perth, anything I can do shall be done," he said cheerily. "You will let me know when Miss Starth returns?"

"Certainly. We shall both be thankful for your aid."

Mrs. Perth retired into the cottage, and the two friends went on their way, Frank in a state of bewilderment. "What does Berry mean by offering a reward?" he gasped.

"He means to hang you," said Jarman, promptly.

"But he's my friend."

"H'm! He—as you told me—has said that so often that I begin to think he is your enemy."

"Why? I have given him no cause to hate me."

"H'm! Who knows? He was a friend of Starth's."

"That didn't matter," said Lancaster. "Starth himself hinted that Berry wished me to marry his niece. If I was undesirable as her husband before, I am still more undesirable as an outlaw."

Jarman thought, then asked questions. "How did you meet Berry?"

"He called to ask me to write some songs for Fairy Fan, having seen my poetry in the magazines."

"I see. Observe, Frank. Berry sought your acquaintance—you did not seek his. He brought you and Starth together again?"

"Well, he did. I dropped Starth's acquaintance, as you know, because we didn't get on well. He came to know Fairy Fan somehow, and I was constantly meeting him there."

"And this woman made running with you both?"

"Well, she was capricious. Some days she would snub me and flirt with Starth; on other days she would give him the go-by and stick to me."

"Quite so. She divided her favours to arouse jealousy between you."

Frank coloured and looked uneasy. "If you put it that way, she did."

"What was Berry's attitude?"

"I can hardly say, save that whenever he was present Starth and I always had a row."

"H'm! A kind of male Ate," said Jarman, musingly. "Berry was speaking to Starth last night, before Starth insulted you?"

"Yes. But what has that got to do with it."

"Everything! Frank, I tell you this man Berry is at the bottom of the whole mystery. He got you into the trouble, now he means to hang you!"

Lancaster stared. "But his reason?" he asked.

Jarman made an extraordinary reply. "Because of the Scarlet Bat."

CHAPTER V

THE INQUEST

There was considerable excitement over the murder in Sand Lane, especially in theatrical and journalistic circles. The deceased was a well-known figure in Bohemia, as for years he had consorted with actors, with reporters, and with sundry idle men, who, doing nothing themselves, sought the company of those gifted with creative and mimetic powers. Walter Starth, being cursed with enough to live on, had developed into a thorough loafer, and chose Bohemia to dwell in, because its gaslight attractions were congenial to his mind. Occasionally he wrote an article or short story himself, and sometimes walked on in a melodrama as a guest; but he never did any real work, preferring idle talk and constant drinking. He was not a favourite with the Slaves of the Lamp, but his burly figure and red head were excessively familiar. Consequently there was immense curiosity manifested regarding his untimely and terrible death.

Who had killed him? That was the first question which everyone asked. But before the inquest took place it was known that Frank Lancaster was the assassin. How the rumour had started no one knew, but somehow, within twenty-four hours after the discovery of the body, Lancaster's name was on every lip. Now, Frank, moving in the same Bohemia, was as great a favourite as Starth was the reverse, and at the outset everyone declined to believe that he had slain Starth in so brutal a manner. But afterwards the open enmity between the two men was recalled, their attentions to Fairy Fan were mentioned, and an exaggerated version was given of the quarrel in the Piccadilly Theatre. When the inquest was held it was quite believed that Lancaster was the guilty man. His flight proved his guilt.

Frank, concealed under the dyed hair and brown face of Desmond O'Neil, wished Eustace to be present at the inquest, but Jarman did not think it wise to put in an appearance.

"Captain Berry will be there," said he, "and, as I stated before, I am pretty sure that for some unexplained reason he is your enemy. It is probable that he has made himself acquainted with as much of your sayings and doings as he can gather, and he doubtless knows that I am your friend. I'll

34

keep out of it, Frank, lest Captain Berry should be induced to run down here and ask questions. If so, he might spot you in spite of your disguise. Besides, we'll see all that there is to be seen in the papers, and what isn't reported Mildred will explain when she returns."

"Is she stopping in town for the inquest?"

"Yes. Mrs. Perth has gone up also, as the poor girl is much cut up. A brother is a brother, however bad he may be."

Frank reflected for a few moments. "Eustace," said he at last, "do you remember what I told you about Starth taunting me with not knowing my father. That's true, you know."

"Yes. But afterwards he confessed that he said that only to get you dandered."

"How did he know that he would rile me in that way? Why should he hit the bull's-eye with a pot-shot? I fancied at the time that you might have told him something."

"No!" denied Jarman. "I keep my pores open and my mouth shut. It's probable that Starth learnt something about your family history from the egregious Berry."

"But how does Berry come to know anything?"

"That's one of the things we must find out, one of the elements connected with his attitude towards you."

"Do you think he knows what the Scarlet Bat means?"

"Yes. He knows more than you do, and, on the face of it, he purposely made your acquaintance to get you into trouble. Witness the way in which he brought you and Starth together, and secured Fairy Fan's aid to make bad blood between you. He wanted Starth dead and you hanged. At least, I think so; but, of course, I'm groping in the dark."

"But what's hanging to it?" asked Frank, much puzzled.

"I don't know. Money, I should say."

"So far as I know, there's no money worth all this trouble on Berry's part coming my way."

"Observe, my son," said Jarman, paternally, "so far as you know. That is the crux of the whole thing. You are as puzzled as myself over the meaning of the Scarlet Bat. As it's the only mystery about you, save the reason of Berry's enmity, I take leave to jam the two mysteries together. When they make one, we may perhaps be able to get at the truth."

"I don't see how we're to start," said Lancaster, knitting his brows.

"Nor I. Wait till the inquest is over. Then we'll have something to go upon. Berry will be a witness as to your quarrelling with the dead man. Berry will collect evidence to make the case blacker. And when Berry has done his worst, we'll know his cards. See! Then you and I will play our game with a hidden hand. And now, my son, start in with the typing. I have to get this story sent in tomorrow, and you must do something to keep up the fiction of being my secretary."

While Jarman and his friend were engaged in literary pursuits in Essex, the inquest was being held in London on the body of Walter Starth. After the jury had surveyed the corpse, and had particularly examined the bullet hole and the knife wound, either one of which was sufficient to cause death, the police inspector in charge of the case detailed facts. He had been called in by Mrs. Betts, the landlady of the deceased, and found Walter Starth dead in his sitting-room. The body was on the floor, with a wound in the heart and a bullet hole under the left eye. No knife had been found, but a pistol—to be more accurate, a Derringer revolver—was discovered in the fireless grate. There was no sign of a struggle. Everything was in its place. The man, apparently taken by surprise, must have died instantly. It was impossible to say whether he was knifed first or shot afterwards—but that was part of the doctor's evidence. A card had been found torn in two and lying on the floor. It bore the name of Frank Lancaster, and an address. On the silver plate of the Derringer were the initials "F. L.," so the inspector, presuming that Lancaster, owner of the pistol, was the assassin, had called at that address given on the card to arrest him.

At this point the coroner said that witness was assuming too much.

Inspector Herny submitted that the revolver used was the property of Lancaster, that the torn card bore his name, and that the servant Matilda Samuels stated that a man answering to the description of Lancaster had called to see the deceased. Also Lancaster and Starth had quarrelled at the Piccadilly Theatre on the night before the committal of the crime, and Lancaster had been heard to threaten the deceased. Finally, Captain Berry, whom the inspector had come into contact with at Lancaster's chambers— where he was paying a visit—stated that the two men were bitter rivals for the hand of his niece, Miss Berry, known on the stage as Fairy Fan.

"Why was not Lancaster arrested?" asked the coroner.

"He fled, sir," replied Herny. "After the committal of the crime, he did not return to his rooms. The last seen of him was when he passed Matilda Samuels a few minutes after nine o'clock."

The doctor who had examined the body deposed that either wound was sufficient to cause death. From the condition of the body he thought that the man was killed between six and eight o'clock. It was the doctor's opinion that Starth had been shot first and stabbed afterwards. He could give no absolute reason, save that if the suspected person using a knife had thus secured his end, he would hardly fire a shot into a dead body, especially into the head. "The noise would have attracted the neighbours," said the doctor, "and as the man was dead, there would be no sense in acting so foolishly. But in a vindictive spirit the assassin might certainly have mutilated the body with the knife. I am convinced that he killed Starth with the revolver."

The coroner interposed. Twice the witness had referred to the assassin as "he." How did he know that the criminal was a man?

The doctor answered that he did *not* know, but the presumption favoured a male criminal. It was improbable that a woman would be such a straight shot (the doctor had been in South America and talked so), and, moreover, the knife had been driven so deeply into the heart that he doubted whether a woman would have strength to make such a wound. Besides, after firing the shot and securing her purpose, a woman would never have had the nerve to stop in the room for over an hour.

"There is no evidence that any woman stopped in the room for an hour."

The witness explained that he was thinking of Inspector Herny's remark of Lancaster having been seen by the servant leaving at nine. If Lancaster were guilty, he must have stopped in the room with his victim's body for over an hour. The murder took place between six and eight, and Lancaster did not leave till after nine.

"Most irregular, these remarks," said the coroner, discontentedly. "You have no right to assume so much. Which wound killed the man?"

"Either wound would cause death," said the doctor, sticking to his opinion, "but it is my belief the shot was the cause. The mutilation was an afterthought."

When this witness stepped down, Mrs. Betts the landlady was called. She knew nothing at all. On that day she had gone to a wedding—one of her cousins—and had been absent from midday till half-past nine. She returned to find Tilly (the servant) in hysterics, and her lodger dead. She then called in the police. Mrs. Betts never knew that her lodger expected anyone. He had said nothing to her. She had never given Tilly permission to go out during her absence, and had severely reprimanded her for leaving the house. It was Tilly's duty to have remained in until Mrs. Betts returned. The landlady declared that she never heard of any quarrel, that she never saw Lancaster, and that she knew of no one likely to have killed her lodger. Mr. Starth was a quiet gentleman in the house, whatever he may have been outside. He rarely had a visitor. Captain Berry was one of the few who called. Sometimes Mr. Starth would go away for a week, and always returned looking ill.

All this and much more of little account was extracted from the garrulous landlady, but she could throw no light on the darkness of the crime. She was succeeded as a witness by Tilly, whose evidence was delivered amidst floods of tears. The poor little wretch had been severely frightened when she entered the house after leaving her young man.

"I went to take Mr. Starth's lamp," she said, sobbing, "as he allays liked oil an' not gas. He was lying a deaden, so I 'owled and dropped, till missus shook me up. There wasn't anyone in the house. But that gentleman what called come out just as I wos talking to Alf. He looked white an' strange like. I spoke of the long time he'd bin, but he said nothin', and jus' cut."

"Were the two men on good terms?" asked the coroner.

"Well, sir," said Tilly, hesitating, "I can't 'ardly say for certing. I wos left in the 'ouse when missus went to the weddin', and Mr. Starth, he called me up, arskin' if I wos in the humour to see Alf, which is my young man, a bricklayer. I sed, 'Right oh!' and he tells me I could cut when a gentleman called to see him. 'There might be a row,' ses he, 'cos this gent 'ates me awful, an' I don't want you to 'ear bad language,' ses he. So I gets ready for Alf, and when the gent comes after four, and very late he wos, I shoves him into the room and cuts."

"Did you hear the greeting given by Starth to Lancaster?"

"No! I jus' shoves him in, and cuts."

"It was Lancaster who called?"

"Yuss. Mr. Starth ses as the gent he expected wos Lancaster by name, an' a fair, yeller-'aired cove. He seemed to 'ate 'im, tho' he ses as it wos Lancaster who 'ated 'im," finished Tilly, confusedly.

"Do you think Mr. Starth got you out of the house so as to quarrel freely with his visitor?"

"Yuss. He said as there would be a row."

"Could anyone have got into the lower part of the house during your absence?"

Tilly stole a look at hard-faced Mrs. Betts. "Why, bless y'no, sir. I wos perticler about lockin' an' barrin' the winders. But Mr. Starth could 'ave let anyone in. I left him with Mr. Lancaster, that's all I knows. W'en I come back after leaving Alf, I sawr 'im dead, w'en I brought the lamp. I nearly dropped with 'orror, an' after puttin' the lamp down I ran to woller on the kitchen floor with fear till missus come an' shook me up. I wos too feared to holler fur the perlice."

When Tilly was dismissed with a streaming face to the companionship of Alf, who lurked at the back of the court, Captain Berry was called. The little skipper looked harder than ever, and delivered his evidence in a dry fashion, with unwinking eyes and without saying more than was needful. His language smacked of the Great Waste Lands.

"Yes, sir, I guess I knew the corpse, and Lancaster. They fair hated one another, and there was always a shine between them when they met. My niece sent 'em fair crazy. They both wanted to marry her, but she shied when they asked her. She didn't want to run in double harness with either. Not much. I tried to make them two boys friends, but they wouldn't cotton

38

to one another nohow. Starth *did* liquidate considerable, and at the Piccadilly Theatre made trouble. Oh! he came right along, callin' Lancaster
high-and-mighty names. I wanted to put the stopper on Starth's jaw, but
Lancaster sailed in and levelled him straight. A pretty hitter is Lancaster;
but I don't call it square of a man to wish another out of the world."

"Did Lancaster say that?" asked the coroner.

Berry spat and nodded. "Several times, you bet. He said he'd like to
wring Starth's neck, that he'd be better out of the world than in it, and that
he'd like to kick him out of the world. Oh, there was an holy show. I took
Starth home, but he never let on that he was goin' to make it up with Lancaster next day. They made no appointment as I heard on. Oh! I guess Lancaster had a row with Starth in his own shanty, and let out at him with the
Derringer. A clean shot, sir." Berry spat again. "The knife? Don't know
anythin' of th' knife. But I heard as Lancaster was in 'Frisco once, so he
might have imported a bowie. Yes, sir, that wound was made by a bowie."

Berry said much more to the same effect, and appeared to be quite sure
that Lancaster was guilty. He was followed by Baird, who had been imported into the case by the skipper on a word to Inspector Herny. Baird admitted reluctantly that Lancaster had threatened to kick Starth out of the
world, and that the two men were on the worst of terms.

Afterwards followed the cause of the trouble. Fairy Fan, exquisitely
dressed, and quite overcome with emotion, deposed that the two men both
asked her to marry them. She refused both, as she wished to stay with her
dear uncle. Starth and Lancaster hated one another, but she never thought it
would come to this. Starth usually started the quarrel, but it was always
Lancaster who threatened. He frequently expressed a wish that Starth was
dead. Lancaster told her that when slumming for his newspaper he sometimes carried a revolver. The weapon produced in court was his. She had
seen it once. It had belonged to his father, Lancaster said. The elder Lancaster's name was Frank also, hence the initials on the silver plate. The
death of Starth and the wickedness of Lancaster had inflicted two several
shocks on her, so that she had been out of the bill at the Piccadilly Theatre.
She never thought Lancaster was so bloodthirsty. He always seemed to be
such a quiet young man. Starth's language was certainly most insulting.

Mildred Starth was then called. She deposed that she was a sister of the
deceased. She lived in Essex, and saw very little of her brother. They got
on pretty well, but she was fond of a quiet life, and her brother was never
happy unless he was leading a fast one. On the night previous to the
murder she was in town. Her brother was in the box at the Piccadilly
Theatre; that was the last she saw of him. He seemed excited and a little
overcome with drink. She had heard him express hatred of Lancaster, but
he was careful in her presence not to explain the reason. She had never

heard him threaten Lancaster, but twice she had heard him express fears lest Lancaster should kill him. He described Lancaster as a ruffian from San Francisco. Witness had never seen the accused man.

This formed the gist of evidence collected by the police, and it was quite enough to permit the coroner making a speech strongly condemning Lancaster. He said that no doubt Lancaster had intimated his intention of calling on Starth, as there was no reason to believe that Starth, who was manifestly afraid of his opponent, had invited him to come. Lancaster had undoubtedly brought the revolver with him, and it would seem that he had called on deceased with the intention of committing the murder. Perhaps Starth—as seemed probable—had torn Lancaster's card in two (the pieces having been found), and the insult had fired Lancaster's rage. Hence the murder. It seems that no one heard the shot; at all events no one could be found who could give such evidence. The jury must therefore take the doctor's opinion that Starth had been shot between six and eight. It was impossible to say why Lancaster had remained behind with his victim's body until nine. But he apparently did, as he was seen leaving the house by the servant, Matilda Samuels. The jury had inspected the body, they had heard the evidence and the cause of death, and on the facts before them would give their verdict.

This was easily given. Without the least hesitation the jury brought in a verdict of wilful murder against Frank Lancaster. After that the crowd went out, and the neighbourhood buzzed with excitement. The one question asked was whether the police knew the whereabouts of the guilty man.

The police did not, and to a reporter Inspector Herny confessed that he had absolutely no clue. Lancaster had vanished like a water bubble.

40

CHAPTER VI

A SCRAP OF PAPER

When the big dailies arrived at the Shanty containing accounts of the inquest, Lancaster was perfectly convinced that Jarman was right. Captain Berry was his enemy sure enough, though for the life of him Frank could not conjecture the cause of such hostility. Also it seemed as though Fairy Fan was likewise against him, since—according to Frank—she lied freely during her five minutes' evidence.

"Starth might have asked her to marry him," he explained to his friend, when they were strictly alone, "but I certainly never did."

"Had you any idea of doing so?"

Lancaster hesitated, not being willing to reveal his deepest and most sacred feelings even unto this staunch friend. "I don't know to what lengths my infatuation might have carried me."

"Oh then you did love her?" said Jarman, alertly.

"That depends on what you call love. I certainly had a fancy for her. I thought her pretty and fascinating, and she was always on her best behaviour with me. I think she liked me more than a little."

Eustace laid one big finger on the *Daily Telegraph* significantly. "It looks like it," said he.

"Berry's put her against me," replied Frank in disturbed tones. "I'll swear that she would never lie like that, unless she was put up to it in some way. She *did* like me, although she was always too selfish to love anyone but herself. Jewels and laces, carriage and pair, admiration and cutting a dash—that was what Fairy Fan desired. I could not offer her these things, so she was careful not to compromise herself with me in any way. I never got so far as asking her to marry me, though I don't know but what I mightn't have been such an ass had I not changed my mind."

"And what caused you to change your mind, my son?"

Frank looked oddly at the big man, and then fixed his eyes studiously on his pipe, while making an evasive reply. "I saw someone I liked better," he explained, "and then my admiration for Fairy Fan seemed to vanish like a cloud of smoke. After I saw that other face I thought no more of Fan, and was able to tell Starth with a clear mind that I didn't care about her. I'd have danced at his wedding with pleasure."

"H'm! And who is the—no, I have no right to ask that. But to continue with the lady's evidence. We know the the first. And the second?"

"I never expressed any wish to her that Starth should die. I told her, certainly, that I sometimes carried a revolver when slumming. But I never mentioned that it belonged to my father, nor did I show it to her. Lastly, I never said to Fan that my father's name was the same as my own."

"Was it?"

"Well, yes. Francis, same as mine."

"And did the revolver belong to him?"

"It did. I got it from my aunt. There was a silver plate on it with my father's initials, and my own, of course."

"She might have seen the revolver produced in court," said Jarman, thoughtfully; "but why should she state that it was your father's?"

"Chance shot!" suggested Frank.

"No. She knew the initials on it were your father's and not yours. H'm! She's in this conspiracy along with Berry."

Lancaster rose to pace the room in an exasperated manner. "Why should there be a conspiracy?" he demanded.

"You've asked me that before," said Jarman, calmly, "and I have replied that I think money is at the bottom of it. Evidently Berry forced his acquaintance on you; and Fairy Fan made the running to create jealousy and bring about this catastrophe. Money, my boy!"

Frank sat down in despair. "I don't see it," he said, pushing his hands into his pockets. "Supposing there is money (though for the life of me I can't think where it's to come from), why is it needful for me to be hanged before Berry and Fairy Fan get it?"

"That's what puzzles me," said Eustace, nodding. "If they wanted you out of the way, they could have polished you off at Sand Lane as easily as they did Starth."

"Do you think they killed him?"

"I do, or else they employed someone else to do it. But you were lured there to be inculpated in the crime, and, begad! They've managed finely to put the rope round your throat. The money—well, I can't make it out, considering the means they've taken to get you into trouble, but there's money in the matter some way. And a mighty big sum too, seeing they've gone as far as murder."

"But it's all so vague; and all supposition on your part."

"I admit it. All the same I can theorise in no other way, unless—"

"Well, what is it?"

42

"I was going to say that perhaps it's blackmail. They may find out where you are and come forward, offering to save your neck from being wrung if you pay them well."

"That inculpates themselves. Besides, if I am entitled to money of which I knew nothing, it was easy enough for Fan to marry me. Then all would have been square for Berry and her without having had to slay Starth and outlaw me."

"Sure enough," groaned Jarman, who was getting more and more puzzled. "What it all means I can't say. You have been outlawed in due form, and the police are after you. All you have to do is to remain quiet and not give yourself away, as you nearly did to Mrs. Perth the other day."

"I hadn't my feelings under control," said Frank. "Her talk of that stab in the breast startled me. I can't understand why I didn't see it at the time."

"Did you feel the man's heart?"

"No. The sight of the bullet wound under the left eye was enough for me. All I wanted to do was to get away and hide."

"Well, then, as you had only a match, and didn't feel the poor man's heart, it's easy to see how you missed the knife wound." Jarman took up the paper again. "The doctor says that Starth was shot first and mutilated afterwards."

"But why should the poor wretch have been mutilated at all?"

"I can't say. It looks like a piece of savagery to me. Though, to be sure, I think mutilation's a wrong word to be used for a clean stab. If his ears had been cut off now, or—"

"Don't!" said Frank, with a shudder. "It's horrible! The man was shot dead, and then stabbed to make sure. That's how I read it."

"Well, the person who sent him into the other world must have been anxious to make certain." This time it was Eustace who paced the room. "I only heard of one corpse being treated like that before."

"Where was that?" asked Lancaster.

"In San Francisco some years ago!"

"Who was it, and why was he slain twice—for that's what it amounts to?"

Jarman did not answer immediately. It was close on eight o'clock, and he stood looking out of his study window into the luminous night. He and the secretary had been haymaking throughout the afternoon, and the shaven expanse of a particularly rough lawn was dotted with haycocks pictur-esquely disposed. Beyond was the untrimmed hedge which Jarman could never allow to be cut, and under this grew straggling white rose-bushes, the flowers of which showed starlike in the glimmering light. Over the hedge through a vista of leafy elms could be seen the far-extending country, and the lights of Tilbury in a long line like flying illuminated railway carriages.

A clear, starry sky and a yellow harvest moon completed the beauty of the scene, and the nightingales were singing wildly in the copse at the bottom of the meadow. Jarman heaved a sigh of delight.

"It's a peaceful scene," said he, with a look of pure pleasure. "Why do I go into gaslight and noisy crowds when I can dwell always in this Arcadia?"

"Well, you don't," said Frank, not seeing where this speech would lead to. "You haven't been in a London theatre or drawing-room for ages."

"True enough. I keep out of those things. But I was saying that San Francisco was noisy."

"Were you? I didn't hear you," said Frank. Then, as Jarman again made no reply, he spoke up rather pettishly. His position didn't soothe his nerves in any way, poor fellow. "You can trust me, Eustace."

"How do you know I was becoming confidential?"

"Because you talked sentiment about the scene before you."

Eustace returned to his seat and laughed rather sadly. "You're an observer, my son," said he. "Yes. You have told me about your past—we must have a repetition of that story some day, for reasons you will easily understand—now I'll tell you my romance."

"About a woman?"

"Yes. Did you ever know a romance that didn't include a woman? And this one of mine included a corpse, too."

"Shot and stabbed?"

"Both—in the streets of 'Frisco six or seven years ago. The man's name was Anchor."

"Are you talking of the corpse?" asked Lancaster, settling himself.

"Of what else. He was a lucky miner, and, having made no end of money, he built a new raw palace near 'Frisco, where he settled with his wife."

"Ah!" said Frank, intelligently, "she's the woman."

"Quite so, and I loved her for all I was worth, till I found her out."

"Eustace," remarked Lancaster, finding these details scrappy, "if you will start in an' sail plainly, I won't interrupt."

Jarman took a pull at his pipe. "I'll give the gist of it in a few words," said he, slowly. "I was doing some journalistic work in 'Frisco, and ran across Anchor. He was a big, burly, rough chap, but a whacking good sort. We chummed up, and he invited me to see him. I was introduced to Mrs. Anchor, and fell in love with her."

"What was she like?"

"You promised not to interrupt. Never mind what she was like. My taste then is not my taste now."

"Mildred!" thought Frank, but said nothing.

"I think she liked me more than a little. But after I visited at her house for a time, I found that Anchor was turning nasty."

"Jealous, I suppose?"

Eustace nodded. "But upon my soul he had no cause to be. I was as straight as a die. It's not my fashion to loot other men's wives. I think Mrs. Anchor did her best to make him jealous. After a time I became sure, and then found out—it matters not how—that she wished to get rid of her husband. I was to be the man to remove him."

"Confound! Did she want you to murder the man?"

"Well, that was her idea. But all this I didn't find out for a long time. Anchor grew nasty, and I rarely went to his house. But Mrs. Anchor used to come and see me in the city sometimes."

"Was that quite straight?"

"No, it wasn't, in one way. But, you see, she came to tell me that she was afraid that her husband would kill her. I wasn't up to her game then. A third man came in. His name was Sakers—a nasty, dry, bad-tempered chap. He and Mrs. Anchor became thick as thieves. Then she gave me the go-by."

"Oh! I suppose she hoped Sakers would kill her husband?"

"Yes. It seemed that Anchor was ruined. His wife spent all his money, and the raw new palace was sold. The pair came to live at 'Frisco, and Sakers loafed on the Front with Mrs. Anchor."

"Were you still in love with her?"

"I was. I tell you, Frank, I really did love that woman. She was the most fascinating woman I ever met, and I've flirted with them in all countries. Well, after a time, she chucked Sakers and came to me. I gathered that she knew of some money which could be got if her husband was out of the way."

"How?"

"Well, I didn't inquire. She proposed so plainly that I should shoot Anchor—seeing that even her pranks couldn't make him jealous enough to get up a duel—that I grew angry. That was an eye-opener. But even then if she'd dropped the business I might have gone on loving her, but she up and slanged me properly. Then I saw what a bad mind she had, and showed her the door. What her scheme was I don't know. After that, a week later, Anchor came to see me."

"To make trouble?"

"No, poor chap. He came to make it up. Said that he had been mistaken in me, and that he didn't believe all the lies that were told about my being in love with Mrs. Anchor. Then he cried, and said that she had bolted with Sakers."

"Why wasn't he man enough to follow, and shoot?"

"He was off that night to Chicago, where the two had gone. But he came to see me to explain. It seemed that there was some money—about a million—that he had something to do with. He promised to see me again before he left for Chicago, and to give me some papers about the matter. It was by the midnight train he was going, and he was to call back at eight. I went to the door of my house with him—it was in a quiet side street, and we stood chatting at the door."

"But why didn't he bring the papers with him?" asked Frank.

"He didn't know if I'd take them, and, moreover, was afraid of being robbed and killed by—well, I can't say who by, but Sakers was mixed up in the business."

"I see. Mrs. Anchor had told Sakers what she told you, and he, less scrupulous, intended to kill Anchor to get these papers."

"That's about the size of it. But the whole thing was so vague that I couldn't get at the pith of it. Anchor would tell me nothing until he came back with the papers at eight. All he said when we shook hands at the door was 'Tamaroo—'"

"Well, go on. Tamaroo what?"

"He didn't get any further," said Jarman, "for at that moment he was shot."

"Shot! In the open street?"

"It was a quiet side street, and, being about meal-time, there was no one about. Also it was almost dark. The man who shot Anchor must have been concealed in a corner close at hand. I turned, and saw him cutting along the street. I followed, calling for the police. But he bunked into a crowded street, and I lost him. I went up to a policeman and made him come back with me. I had been away for fifteen minutes on the chase. Anchor was still lying before my door, but in addition to the shot wound there was a knife in his heart. In this instance Frank, the knife was left in the wound. It was a brand-new bowie, and nothing could be made of it in the way of evidence."

"What happened then?"

"Well, at first I was thought to be guilty, but I soon cleared my character. Anchor was buried, and I never saw nor heard of Mrs. Anchor, nor Sakers again."

"What about the papers?"

"I never heard anything of them either. But it appeared that when Anchor was seeing me a negro came to his lodgings to wait for him. As he didn't turn up the negro skipped. I fancied he might have been an emissary of Mrs. Anchor's to steal those papers. But none were found."

"And who killed Anchor?"

"Well, I fancy Sakers fired the shot. But who knifed him I can't say."

Frank rose, and walking to the window stretched himself. "It's a gruesome story," said he; "and what did Tamaroo mean?"

"I can't tell you. That was the one word the poor fellow said before he was stretched a corpse. Well, Frank, after that I got sick of the West and came home. A strange romance?"

"Very. But I can't make top nor tail of the business. It is strange that Anchor should have been both shot and stabbed as Starth was."

"For that reason I tell the story. Keep it to yourself, Frank. I do not care about wearing my heart on my sleeve."

"I'll say nothing," assented Lancaster, "and you know quite enough to round on me if I do. I say"—he peered through the window into the moonlight—"who is the lady?"

Jarman rose, and looked over Frank's shoulder. There was a white figure crossing the lawn. "It's Mildred—Miss Starth."

Frank made for the door. "I'll go to my bedroom," he said. "I am not able to meet her yet, as I might give myself away. Besides, she may wish to talk to you about the case."

"H'm! Yes, it's just as well. Clear out. I'll let you know all that is needful."

So Frank disappeared, and Jarman opened the front door to his visitor. Mildred looked very weary. She wore a white dress with black bows, and saw him looking sideways at it when she entered the study.

"I haven't had time to get proper mourning," she said, sinking into a chair. "Mrs. Perth is furbishing up an old dress for tomorrow."

"I wasn't thinking of that," said Jarman, mendaciously. "Have some wine, Miss Starth? You look so tired."

"I'm worn out. That awful inquest, and poor Walter's death." She hid her face in her hands. "It's all so sudden, so terrible! I have been in bed ever since I returned."

"So Mrs. Perth told me. I know the verdict."

"Do you think it is a true one?" asked Mildred, suddenly.

Jarman was taken aback. "How should I know?"

"The jury say that Mr. Lancaster killed Walter. But as I was leaving the room someone—I don't know who—slipped a paper into my hand. I have brought it to you, as I can't understand."

She handed Jarman half a sheet of notepaper. On it was written in an unformed, childish hand three words— "Frank. Innocent. Tamaroo!"

"Tamaroo!" Jarman leaped up. "Tamaroo! What does it mean?"

CHAPTER VII

CUPID'S BARGAIN

While Jarman was receiving Miss Starth at the door, Miss Cork had brought in the lamp and pulled down the blinds. In the yellow light Mildred could see that his face was pearly white. As Eustace was not usually emotional, she guessed that the paper she had given him must be interesting enough to surprise him out of his ordinary self.

"What is it?" she asked nervously. "Oh! What is it?" Her nerves were slack, poor girl, from the anxieties of the last week.

Jarman did not answer directly. That he should have stumbled on the word "Tamaroo" in this unexpected manner, immediately after telling his story to Frank, surprised him not a little. The coincidence was extraordinary, and, he suspected, providential. He could not see what connection there could be between the murder of Anchor in San Francisco and that of Walter Starth in Sand Lane, but the mysterious word "Tamaroo" seemed to link the two. Perhaps it might prove the clue to the mystery of the last crime. Jarman sat down to hurriedly arrange his thoughts, but he was unable to answer Mildred for a time. After her exclamation she remained quiet, clasping and unclasping her hands, shaken to the core of her soul by the disturbed looks of this ordinarily phlegmatic man.

"I don't know what it means," confessed Jarman finally, and looked again at the paper. "This is written by an uneducated person, and by one who knows Lancaster well enough to address him by his Christian name. Who slipped it into your hand?"

"I don't know," said Mildred again. "I was passing out with the crowd after the verdict had been given, and I felt this being pushed into my hand. My fingers closed on it mechanically. For the moment I never thought to look round for the person. When I examined it outside it was, of course, too late."

"H'm! That's a pity. If we could only find who wrote it there might be some chance of clearing up the mystery."

"Then you think there *is* a mystery, Mr. Jarman?"

"About your brother's death? Certainly I do. I know Lancaster very well. Indeed, it was I who introduced him to your brother, and I am absolutely certain that he is not the man to commit so brutal a crime."

"But his threats on the previous night?" objected Mildred.

"Mere foolish speaking. And, far from proving his guilt, they, to my mind, hint at his innocence. Had he intended to kill your brother he would have been more circumspect in his language."

"But if Mr. Lancaster is innocent, why did he run away?"

Jarman shrugged his shoulders. "You can't expect a man to have all his wits about him at such a moment. He was"—here Jarman was about to explain the drugging, but on second thoughts he did not think it wise to appear to know too much—"he was in the house alone with your brother, whom he had threatened," he continued, "and when the murder took place saw that there was every chance of his being accused. To avoid being arrested on circumstantial evidence, he fled."

"Have you any idea where he is?" asked Miss Starth, quickly.

"No," replied Jarman, deliberately. "I have not seen Frank Lancaster for some months. He was always in town, and, as you know, I rarely go up. You believe him to be guilty?"

"Everything seems to point to his guilt."

"I admit that. But I am convinced from what I know of him that he is perfectly innocent."

"If so," said Mildred, shrewdly, "he must at least know who killed my brother, seeing that he left the house *after* the death."

"I don't profess to explain," said Eustace, who was unwilling to lie more than was necessary to shield Lancaster. "Did your brother ask Lancaster to call on him?"

"No!" replied Mildred, decisively. "Walter was rather afraid of Mr. Lancaster. They were bad friends for some reason, and Mr. Lancaster threatened to give Walter a thrashing."

"Did he threaten to kill him?"

Mildred hesitated. "Well, Walter said that Mr. Lancaster would shoot him if he got the chance, as he always carried a revolver."

"Lancaster only carried a revolver when he went slumming."

"He wasn't slumming when he visited at Sand Lane."

"No! I can't explain that. All I can say is that, from what I know of Lancaster, he might have thrashed your brother, but he certainly would not murder him."

"But Mr. Darrel tells me that Mr. Lancaster was very bitter against my brother."

"When did he tell you that?" said Jarman, who knew Darrel, and, regarding him as a possible rival, did not approve of him overmuch.

"Today, when I got up. Mr. Darrel is staying at the Rectory for a few days. You know, he is a friend of the rector's."

"Yes, I know," replied Eustace, thinking he must put Frank on his guard, since Darrel might recognise him. "Why did Darrel come down?"

"On a visit to the rector. But he also said that he came to see if he could help me in any way."

"I can do all the help that is necessary," said Jarman, jealously.

"I told him so, and, then, Captain Berry is anxious to assist."

"H'm!" said Eustace, pulling his big moustache. "Mrs. Perth told me that he had offered a reward. Very good of him."

"Captain Berry was a great friend of Walter's. He wrote me the sad news almost immediately."

"Almost too immediately," replied Jarman. "What time did you get his letter?"

"By the eleven post."

"Then it must have been posted in London before midnight, and the fact of the murder was not known to the general public till next morning. How came Captain Berry to have such early information?"

"I don't know," said Miss Starth, blankly. "Do you think—"

"I think nothing," interposed the big man, quickly. "I have never met Berry, and I know nothing about him. But Mrs. Perth doesn't seem to entertain a good opinion of him."

Mildred, in spite of her grief and sadness, could not help smiling. "You know that Mrs. Perth never approved of Walter's friends. She was my governess, you remember, and still thinks it's her duty to look after me."

"And after that Denham man."

"Oh! he is only a boy—" said Mildred, with contempt, "and a very silly boy. Walter brought him down twice, but I don't suppose he'll come here again."

"Where did Starth meet him?"

"At Captain Berry's. Mr. Denham came from San Francisco with Captain Berry. They are great friends."

"And thereby hangs a tale," muttered Jarman, who was intensely suspicious of the skipper and his associates. "Well, and what are you going to do now, Miss Starth?"

"I can do nothing," she said, with a helpless gesture. "I have seen our lawyer about Walter's affairs, and Walter's income comes to me. I don't know what to do about his death except wait."

"For the capture of Lancaster?"

Miss Starth moved uneasily. "I am not revengeful," she said, "and my brother was not such a good man as he should have been. But if Mr. Lancaster is guilty he ought to be punished."

"Yes. *If* he is guilty. But presuming his innocence—"

"He will have an opportunity of proving that when he is tried."

"Ah!" said Jarman, pulling again at his moustache, "then you anticipate that he will be captured?"

"Captain Berry says he will never rest until he is captured. We had a long talk about the matter."

"Has Berry any clue?"

"No. Neither has Inspector Herny. Since that servant saw Mr. Lancaster leave the house, nothing more has been heard of him. I don't want him to be captured. His being hanged wont bring poor Walter to life, and that paper makes me doubt if he is guilty."

"Did you show this to Berry?" asked Jarman, who still held the paper.

"No. I showed it to no one, not even to Mrs. Perth. I wished to consult you about it."

"I am glad you said nothing, Miss Starth," said Jarman. "May I keep this paper? I may be able to find out something, you know."

"Certainly. I shall be glad if you will help me."

"I wish to help you in every way. You know that."

Jarman's voice shook a little, and the woman in Mildred took the alarm. She rose to go, whereupon Jarman insisted on seeing her to Rose Cottage. "But there is no need," protested Mildred, "the moon is shining, and I am quite safe. Don't trouble."

"It's a pleasure," insisted Eustace, putting on his cap, and being thus obstinate Mildred let him have his own way. She was even secretly pleased, as she liked Eustace extremely.

They stepped out into the moonlight, and took their careful way between the haycocks. The night was very still. Occasionally there would float towards them an outburst of song from the copse-hidden nightingales, diversified by the hoot of an owl, or the whirr of a distant train steaming towards London. Mildred had simply thrown a lace shawl over her head to run across to the Shanty, and her face looked wonderfully pure and white in the ivory radiance of the moon. Eustace felt his pulses throb with suppressed excitement, and the blood tingled pleasantly in his veins. He was in love with Mildred, he was jealous of Darrel, and these passions lifted him somewhat out of his usual self. The romance of San Francisco appeared the veriest prose beside this lyrical night. Yet he felt that he could not break in upon the grief of the girl with his tale of love, and so walked sedately by her side, holding himself well in hand.

As they passed into the lane, and under the chequered shadows of the elms, Mildred felt the influence of her companion. She was not in love with Jarman, or with anyone, but she liked and admired him immensely, and, granted that the fairy prince did not come along, was not unprepared to listen should he speak. Still, the feeling of sorrow for the death of her brother lay heavily upon her, and she sighed as the cool night wind ruffled her dark hair. After a time, to break the silence, she asked Jarman about the new secretary.

"Mrs. Perth told me that he was very handsome," she said.

"Oh, he's good-lookin' enough," replied Eustace, "but his spectacles rather spoil him. Weak eyes, you know."

"I was not aware that you intended to engage a secretary."

"I have so much work to do."

"You might have engaged me," said Miss Starth, reproachfully. "I can type quite as quickly as you can dictate, and you know I am always glad to assist you."

"I know that," said Jarman, suppressing a strong inclination to take her in his arms. "We have done some work together."

"*You* have. I don't know what I should have done without you to correct my verses and help me to get them printed. I was only sixteen when I showed you my first poem."

"Yes. And very shy you were over it. Natural in a schoolgirl."

"I am not a schoolgirl now, Mr. Jarman."

Who knew that better than Eustace? "I wish you were," he muttered.

"Why? You should be glad to see me grow up, Mr.——"

"Why so formal, Miss Starth—Mildred. Call me Eustace."

"I should like to—Eustace," said the girl, frankly—too frankly, alas, for any feeling of love to lurk in the words. "You know how fond I am of you," and she squeezed his arm playfully.

"Mildred!" He could stand it no longer, although he felt that this was not the time to speak of love. But the influence of the hour, of her words, and the feeling of jealousy inculcated by Darrel's arrival made him confess his secret. "Mildred?"

"Yes." She detected the change in his voice, and grew nervous.

"I—I—love you!"

"Mr. Jarman—I mean Eustace!"

"I didn't mean to speak," went on the man, rapidly. "I know you have heavy troubles to face. But I wish to help you. If you would accept me as your husband, if you would lean upon me through life, I would do all that I could to save you from being worried."

Under the shadow of the trees, a stone's-throw from the white gate of Rose Cottage, Mildred stood still, her hands clasped before her. A shaft of light piercing the leafage shed its radiance on her beautiful face, and Eustace put a constraint on himself. Under his breath he quoted the Arabic proverb: "Blessed be Allah who made beautiful woman."

"Eustace, I never thought of this!"

"And you are angry?"

"No—no. I'm not exactly angry. But—"

"You love me, then—you love me!" She could feel his breath on her cheek, and shrank away from the passion expressed in his deep voice.

"I am not angry, but I don't love you. Wait!" She flung up her hand as she heard his sigh. "I like you—oh, yes, I like you more than anyone I ever met."

"More than Darrel?"

"Mr. Darrel; I don't care a bit for him. I wish you wouldn't talk so." She stamped her foot. "You know how troubled I am about poor Walter's death, and we were getting on so nicely."

"You and Walter?"

"No, poor fellow. You and I. We were such companions, and I always told you everything—and now talking like this!" Miss Starth's eyes filled with tears. "It's a shame."

"I can't help loving you."

"Well, I love you—in a way. No, don't come any nearer. I—I—looked on you as a—a—father," sobbed Mildred.

"Oh, Heavens! There's no more to be said after that. Let me remain in that relationship."

"No. That is"—Mildred dried her tears, and became alarmed because she thought she was inflicting pain—"that is—you know, I don't mind—well, if you can't guess."

"Does that mean you will marry me?" asked Jarman, catching his breath.

Mildred rolled her handkerchief up into a ball, and became more of a woman and less of a schoolgirl. "I will marry you on one condition."

"What is that?" he asked, eagerly.

"That you find out and punish the person who killed Walter."

Jarman's heart leaped. "Do you mean Lancaster?" he asked, alarmed.

"No—if what that paper says is true. I mean the real person. You say that Mr. Lancaster is innocent, and I know you too well to doubt your word. Find the real person, and—" she bent forward as though to seal the bargain with a kiss. But before her face could touch his own she drew back, and flittered towards the gate.

"Mildred!" he cried. "Mildred!"

"Good-night!" floated back faintly, and he heard the closing of the door. Alone with the night and with his great happiness, he tried to realise his good fortune. "She doesn't love me yet," he thought, as he walked back to the Shanty on tip-toe excitement, "but she will—she will. Heaven bless her How could I have loved Mrs. Anchor? This is the real thing, and Mildred— oh! What a boy I am yet." He wiped his face. "Of course I'll find out who killed her brother, both to win her and to save Frank. Dear Frank—poor fellow!" Jarman felt immensely sorry for Lancaster being, as it were, out in the cold. "I must tell him."

And tell him he did, blurting out the news almost before he filled his pipe. "I say, Frank, I'm going to start in and find out who killed Starth!" he declared.

"Miss Starth has asked you to do so?" said Frank, trying to suppress his jealousy.

"Yes. And she is going to reward me, if I am successful, with her hand."

Lancaster stared. "I—I—hope you'll be happy," he gulped. "She'll get a good husband."

"And I an angel for a wife."

"An archangel—a Madonna—a saint," said Frank, incoherently. But his heart ached.

CHAPTER VIII

A PLEASANT SURPRISE

The Rectory was like a bee-hive. Mr. Arrow was the happy father of ten healthy children, and his wife was pretty well worn out looking after them. One of the boys was at Sandhurst, a couple were at school, but the majority of the children remained to make the old house lively. Why Darrel, who loved his comforts, should come to such a noisy establishment, Arrow could not conjecture, although he was glad to welcome him. Darrel himself declared that he came to see his old tutor, and Arrow accepted the flattering compliment. But when he found that his guest paid three visits to Rose Cottage in as many days, the rector began to mistrust the excuse. However, he said nothing to Darrel, as the Rhodesian was rich, and might be trusted to do something towards launching the young Arrows into the bleak world.

Darrel was a big man, as huge as Jarman, but black and sulky in his looks. His manners were soft, and he resembled a large tom-cat more than anything else, particularly when speaking, as he positively purred. With the children he was a favourite, as he always presented them with gifts; but it was understood that on condition of this largess, they were to leave him alone. Consequently, he had all his time to himself, and spent it dodging about Rose Cottage, or filling the little parlour with his gigantic person.

Mrs. Perth rather liked him, as he was always deferential to her, and she was not averse to his courtship of Mildred, for that was what his continual, and not always welcome, presence amounted to. But the girl herself thought Darrel possessed a violent temper, and always declared that she would not marry him if he were as rich as Vanderbilt. However, as the Rhodesian came ostentatiously to condole with her on account of her trouble, she could not very well express herself as she wished. Moreover, in a measure, she was now engaged to Jarman, but she told no one of the agreement she had made with him, not even Mrs. Perth. It was now over a fortnight since the death of Starth, and as he was buried, Mildred was recovering her spirits. She had never cared particularly for her brother, who was something of a bully, and had seen so little of him that his death made scarcely any difference in her life. Consequently, beyond that she was in mourning, she showed little sign of the catastrophe. And Walter had only himself to thank for the calmness with which she accepted his decease.

One afternoon Mrs. Perth was out, and Darrel sat with Mildred drinking tea in the parlour. It was a small room filled with chintz-covered furniture, and looked extremely cool. The window was open, and Darrel, who felt the heat, sat near it cup in hand. He was dressed in spotless flannels, and looked better-looking and less black than usual. Mildred, in her sombre dress, was fanning herself vigorously.

"I wish I could feel as cool as you do," she said, enviously.

"It's more looks than anything else," replied Darrel in his heavy way. "I'm warm enough—quite. How I'll stand town I don't know."

"When are you returning?" asked Miss Starth, indifferently.

"Tomorrow—if you don't want me to stay."

"I have no control over your movements, Mr. Darrel."

But the coldness of the tone had no effect. "I mean, that there may be something I can do for you. Now that your brother is dead—"

"Mr. Jarman is looking after things for me, thank you," said Mildred, stiffly. "The only thing you can do is to find out who killed Walter."

Darrel raised his bushy eyebrows. "There's no difficulty about that, Miss Starth. The verdict of the jury—"

"Was wrong. I can't believe that this Mr. Lancaster committed so horrible and apparently purposeless a crime."

"Have you any reason to believe him innocent?"

Mildred, for obvious reasons, did not answer this question directly. "I can't see his motive," she said, looking down pensively.

"The evidence of that lady at the inquest—"

"I know nothing about any lady," retorted the girl, flushing. Then, to change the conversation and mark her sense of Darrel's bad manners, she asked a question. "Did you know Mr. Lancaster?"

Darrel nodded. "I thought I told you," he said. "He was sitting next to me on that night I saw you in the theatre."

"The night before the tragedy," said Mildred, shuddering. "What is he like to look at?"

"Fair chap, blue eyes, and—"

"Wait!" Miss Starth recollected the man who had stared at her. "Do you mean to say that he was the gentleman who sat next to you?"

"Yes. I said so. Fair hair, and—"

"I know," she broke in hurriedly. "He was looking at me; our eyes met, and he—oh he didn't look like a man who would commit murder."

"I shouldn't have thought it of him myself," said Darrel; "but if he didn't, who did? That's the point."

"I wish you to find that out if you will."

"Certainly. I'll do my best, on conditions."

"Conditions!" Mildred stared, and looked annoyed.

"Yes," said the Rhodesian, stolidly; "promise to be my wife, and I'll hunt down Lancaster."

Mildred gasped. This was the same bargain as she had made with Eustace, so the situation was duplicated. But she more than liked Jarman, and cared very little for Darrel. Moreover, now that she knew the suspected man was the one who had stared at her, and to whose face she had taken a fancy, she was inclined to agree with Eustace that he was innocent. So refined a man could not possibly have committed so brutal a crime. And, finally, she was displeased that Darrel should again broach a subject about which she had asked him to be silent.

"I told you before, and I tell you again, Mr. Darrel, that I cannot become your wife," she said, with some heat.

"Why not?" asked the man, stolidly.

Mildred grew exasperated. "Because I don't love you."

"Love may come after marriage."

"I prefer it to come before," she declared. "I won't marry you."

"Yes, you will," said Darrel, closing his obstinate mouth; "your brother was in favour of the match."

"At one time, but not lately."

"I know, and I can't understand why he changed."

"Whether he changed or not doesn't matter," said Miss Starth, sharply; "the thing is out of the question."

"No, it isn't. I've made up my mind to marry you, and marry you I shall."

She rose and turned on him indignantly. "Do you threaten me?"

Darrel rose also, but did not reply directly. "I never made up my mind yet to get a thing that I didn't succeed," he said. "I wanted to be rich, and I am rich. I want you to be my wife, and I intend to make you my wife."

"No! No! No!" She stamped her foot three times.

"Oh, yes," said Darrel, calmly. "Think it over. I go to town tomorrow, but will come back in a month. I'll expect my answer then."

"Take it now," she cried, indignant at his impertinence. "No!"

"That's not the answer I require," he said, collecting his cane and hat. "You must say yes."

"I won't!"

Darrel took not the slightest notice, but held out his hand. Mildred declined to take it, and repeated her refusal. The big man turned to the door. "I'll come in a month for my answer," said he, and went out.

Mildred was very angry at his persistence, but she had quite as strong a will as Darrel, and determined that nothing would induce her to become his wife. But she dreaded his return, as she knew he was not easily shaken off. For the moment she was minded to tell Eustace, but a reflection that such a confidence might lead to a quarrel, made her change her mind. "But I'll never marry that Darrel," she declared. "Never—never—never! I wonder, indeed, if I'll marry Eustace. I like him, but I don't love him. And one should love when—" here she blushed and sat down. Her thoughts wandered to the pleasant face of the young man in the theatre, and she recalled his persistent gaze. He had evidently been attracted by her, and she — "No," said Mildred to herself, "I'll never believe that he murdered Walter!" after which remark she began regretting that she had made a bargain with Eustace. Decidedly her conduct was flighty, but late events had unsettled her mind. She was not usually so vacillating, but at the present moment she was too bewildered and upset to know her own mind, save that she would never marry Darrel. "And perhaps not Eustace," she concluded.

Meantime, Eustace was in the seventh heaven. For the last few days he had gone about singing, and Lancaster was rather exasperated. It seemed unfair that Jarman should have all the happiness, and he should have nothing but trouble. Then he blamed himself for being selfish. Jarman had been, and was, a good friend to him, and Jarman had known Mildred for many years. He, Frank, had not even spoken to her, so it was ridiculous and ungrateful of him to be jealous of his best friend on such slight grounds. He did all he knew to preserve a cheerful face, but at times grew gloomy. Eustace put his fit of the dismals down to a too vivid realisation of his danger. He would not allow Frank to speak more than was necessary about the murder, as he did not wish him to brood over it. But he was not idle, and one morning announced that he was going to to town.

"I'll be away for the day," he said, "so you can make yourself comfortable, Frank. Look out that Darrel doesn't see you."

"Darrel has gone back to town," said Lancaster, "so one of the young Arrows told me. He returns in a month."

"Mildred will be glad he has gone. He was always hanging round her."

"Why didn't you put a stop to that?"

"I have not the right as yet. You see, I am not formally engaged to Mildred, and will not be, until I have discovered the assassin."

"Why not denounce me, and bring about the engagement at once?" said Frank, with some bitterness.

Jarman stared. "Because in the first place you are innocent, and in the second I should not like to build up my life's happiness on your ruin. I thought you knew me better than that, my friend."

"Forgive me. I am a beast," said Lancaster, penitently. "But the fact is, I —I—"—he gulped down the truth—"I am not myself."

"Don't wonder at it, considering the fix you are in. Cheer up. I may learn something today likely to give me a clue to the truth."

"From whom?"

"From your friend, Fairy Fan."

Lancaster jumped up from the breakfast-table. "What?"

"You look surprised, but it is so. I am going to see her today—by appointment!" and he displayed a perfumed note.

Frank glanced over it, and discovered that Miss Berry would be pleased to see Mr. Leonard Grant at her rooms in Bloomsbury at one o'clock on that day.

"Why did you write to her?" asked Frank, handing this back.

"The use of my *nom de plume* should tell you that," replied Jarman. "I want to have a quiet chat with that lady, so I wrote as Leonard Grant—under which name I produce my sketches—and asked her if I could do one for her. As I have a certain reputation, she seems inclined to entertain the idea."

"Why didn't you write under your own name?"

"What an ass you are, Frank! Firstly, the *nom de plume* is required to intimate who will write the sketch, since Eustace Jarman is unknown as a dramatist. Secondly, did I write in my own name I might give myself into the hand of Berry. He must have learnt from Starth that I am your friend, and thus might seek to know too much."

"You could baffle his inquiries."

"Oh, yes. But if he chose to come down and see me, I could not baffle his spotting you. It's best to be on the safe side, and even in that disguise the man is clever enough to recognise you."

"That doesn't say much for my disguise," said Frank, grimly.

"Pooh! The make-up is good enough to baffle a casual observer, but Captain Berry is exceptionally clever. He might not recognise you, certainly; on the other hand, he might. No, Frank, as Leonard Grant I'll see Miss Berry and learn all I can."

"She won't discuss the matter with you."

"Perhaps not, but I'll try and get her on the subject. I may even meet with Berry, and then we'll see if I can't pump him. So you make yourself comfortable here, Frank, while I go to town. I think you might take the newspaper to Mrs. Perth, and meet Mildred."

"I don't know her," said Frank, flushing.

"Mrs. Perth will introduce you," said Jarman, "and I am sure you will get on well with her."

"Too well," thought Frank. But he said nothing, not even if he would go over to Rose Cottage.

Jarman bustled about, and finally set off across the heath, which was the nearest way to the railway station. His plan of action was to seek Berry and his niece as a complete stranger, and to learn, if he could, what they were about to do. He had a clever pair to deal with, but Jarman was smart himself, and not for nothing had rubbed shoulders with the astute citizens of the great republic. Moreover, apart from his wish to please Mildred and to save Frank, there was a certain element of exhilaration about this chase after an unknown criminal that appealed to his love of adventure.

"I've got detective fever," he thought, as he swung into a third-class smoking, "and the disease won't be cured till I run the true assassin to earth."

On arriving at Liverpool Street, shortly after twelve, he walked to the tube railway at the Mansion House Station, and thereby gained Oxford Street. From Tottenham Court Road he strolled to Bloomsbury Crescent, where Miss Berry dwelt with her uncle, and reached the door of the house a few minutes before one o'clock. A neatly-dressed maidservant admitted him into a cool drawing-room. While the maid informed her mistress of Jarman's arrival, or rather that Mr. Leonard Grant was at hand, Eustace looked curiously round the room. From its contents he hoped to learn something of the character of Fairy Fan.

But there was no need to read her character in this way. Almost before he commenced his examination she appeared at the door, and came forward with a smile. Suddenly she stopped, and the colour ebbed from her face. Jarman gasped and stared, as well he might.

"Mrs. Anchor!" he said, under his breath. "Mrs. Anchor I might have guessed."

CHAPTER IX

THE OLD ROMANCE

Mrs. Anchor, *alias* Miss Fanny Berry, was a pretty little creature even when the searching morning sunlight was full on her face. She had no absolute need of paint and powder to make her attractive. In a tea gown of delicate blue, with a head of fluffy golden hair, and a piquant face, she looked—as the saying is—as pretty as a picture.

Jarman eyed her sternly, and wondered how he could ever have loved a woman possessed of such obviously meretricious charms. Her mouth was hard, and there was an unpleasant glitter in her blue eyes which did not bode well for Eustace. After her failure in San Francisco the lady was intensely suspicious of Jarman, deeming him too scrupulous. Eustace saw the inquiring light in her eyes, and, having his own game to play, he pretended to forget the past, and to be overjoyed at the meeting. Now that he knew who Fairy Fan was, he felt quite certain that Captain Berry would answer readily to the name of Sakers, and hoped to see him before the termination of the interview. Meanwhile, to abate the suspicions of the little lady, he made himself agreeable. And Eustace could be extremely pleasant when it suited his book.

"Mrs. Anchor," he said, advancing with outstretched hands, "this *is* a surprise."

"An agreeable one, I hope?" replied the lady with an artificial laugh, but searching his face keenly.

"Very agreeable. I have often thought of you, Mrs. Anchor."

Womanlike her thoughts reverted to his love, and she strove to see if she yet had him in her toils. But Eustace did not flush, and the calm expression of his face baffled the reading of his thoughts. A puzzled look which meant, "I-wonder-why-you-called!" crept into her expressive eyes, but beyond this she governed her feelings excellently. But Eustace had interpreted the look, and to rearrange their friendship hastened to explain.

"I have never seen you at the theatre," he said, easily, taking a chair, "so it never struck me that Fairy Fan, who was delighting the British public, was the same as Mrs. Anchor of San Francisco."

61

"Nor is she," replied the little woman, seating herself on the sofa. "After the sad death of my husband, I took my maiden name again."

"Miss Berry?" inquired Eustace.

"Fanny Berry," she replied, nodding. "I am over here with my uncle." She glanced uneasily at the door, thinking he might come in. "His name is Banjo Berry. He is a merchant captain, but in 'Frisco you knew him as Edward Sakers."

"Oh I thought—"

"I know you did," she interrupted petulantly, "and so did everyone else. But he is my relative, and nothing more. Owing to some trouble connected with the casting away of a fruit schooner on a South Sea reef, he was obliged to call himself Sakers. As I told you, my husband's behaviour became so impossible that I had to leave."

"You never told me that," said Jarman, serenely; "but at our last interview you hinted that I might fight Anchor with revolvers."

"I don't deny it. The man treated me shamefully. I was a good wife to him." Miss Berry—as it is best to call her—squeezed out a tear. "But he—he—well, what's the use of going over the old ground. You know how jealous he was."

"And I know how he loved you," said Eustace, pointedly.

"What about yourself?" she responded flippantly.

"I never lost the right of calling myself your husband's friend."

"No," she taunted, "you hadn't the pluck to do that. You pretended to love me, yet when I would have given you myself and a fortune you drew back."

"The price was too high. And you got someone else to put him out of the way."

Fairy Fan rose indignantly. "I never did!" she declared vehemently. "I was in Chicago at the time. When Anchor's conduct became unbearable I went with my uncle to that city. It was there that we heard of his death."

"Shot and stabbed, wasn't he?"

"Yes. But not by me—not by my uncle, although he was angry at the way in which I had been treated. I left Anchor and intended to get a divorce —but circumstances made me his widow."

"Did it make you a rich woman also?" asked Eustace, remembering the last interview he had with her.

"No," she said quietly. "You never gave me time to tell you about the money. Anchor speculated, and lost his fortune. However, he knew, through some Indian, of a treasure—a Spanish treasure which was buried in a certain place. I wanted him to tell me the secret, but he would not. When he died he took the secret along with him. I am as poor now as I was then, and I shouldn't be acting at the Piccadilly Theatre if I wasn't."

"Why was the death of your husband necessary to your learning the secret?" demanded Jarman, quickly.

Fairy Fan arranged herself on the sofa and took out a case, which she opened, "It wasn't," she said, blandly, selecting a cigarette. "But I feared I wouldn't get a divorce, and so I wished him out of the way. You were too scrupulous, although all you had to do was to pick a quarrel with him. You were a better shot than he was."

"I don't commit murder even for love, Mrs. Anchor."

"Berry, if you please. Love!" she repeated, lighting the cigarette. "You don't know the meaning of the word. Had you really and truly loved me you would have rid me of the man who struck me."

"Did he strike you?"

"I was beaten black and blue. I told you so," she retorted. "Would any woman put up with that treatment? I hated the man!" She clenched her small fist, and her face grew angry. "I would have killed him myself had I been able."

"Perhaps, as you didn't, you got someone else to—"

"How dare you say that, Eustace!" Jarman winced as she called him by the old name. "I tell you I knew nothing of the matter. If you have come here to denounce me for the murder of my husband, you have wasted your time. There is no evidence which can connect me with that crime, or my uncle either. We are quite at our ease—quite!"

"I never thought of doing such a thing," said Jarman, drily. "My coming here is a pure accident. I live in Essex, and rarely come to town. I had not the slightest idea of your identity. It was simply and solely to write you a sketch and make money that I came."

"Why did you write under a false name?"

"Bah! You understand well enough. I am known as Leonard Grant in this line, as I'm not proud of the occupation of writing these drivelling things. You—so far as I knew—were a stranger to me. I wrote you under the name I was best known by, to do the sketch. Fan—"

"Don't call me Fan!" she said petulantly.

"Well, I treated you so badly that I don't deserve much at your hands, my dear," he said, with feigned penitence, "but for the sake of old times let me call you by the old name."

"My uncle will not like it. He will be here soon, and should he hear you call me by so intimate a name he will be angry. He is very, very particular."

Jarman privately thought that an ex-skipper, who had cast away a schooner and had to change his name for that reason, had no need to be so scrupulous. But he did not believe in the relationship, and suspected that Fairy Fan was telling glib lies. However, it suited him to accept the story she set forth, and he swallowed the scrupulous Captain Banjo Berry along with the other fiction.

"I'll call you Miss Berry when he comes, but till then——" He looked imploringly.

She gave him a coquettish smile. "Very well, till then, Eustace!"

Jarman knew perfectly well that she was calculating to make use of him, and wished her to think so. Should she accept him as a colleague in the swindle which she and her so-called uncle were perpetrating, he might more easily penetrate the secret of Starth's murder.

"Then tell me, Fan, was it ever discovered who killed Anchor?"

"How you harp on that, Eustace! Yes. An old partner of his, whom he cheated in connection with a mining claim, shot him."

"And who thrust the knife into his heart?"

"A Chinaman. He found the body, or rather, he found Anchor dying, and intended to rob him. When Anchor opened his eyes and tried to sing out for the police Lo Keong knifed him. The Chinaman has been hanged, but the man who fired the shot got away. And now don't let's talk any more about the matter; it gives me the horrors. I'm doing very well here, and I hope to make a lot of money. Then I shall retire."

"And marry again?"

Fairy Fan shot a second provocative glance. "Perhaps," she said.

"H'm!" Jarman resolved to startle her. "So Walter Starth was not to your taste?"

He woefully failed to bring about the desired result. Fan was too old a hand to be startled. "You've been reading the papers?" she said.

Jarman nodded. "I saw that both Starth and the man who is supposed to have killed him loved you."

"They did, and I refused both of them. Nice boys, but a couple of paupers. If I marry again, I marry money. But why do you use the word 'supposed.' Frank Lancaster murdered Starth, sure enough."

"So the jury say, but——"

"And so I say. I know exactly how it happened. Starth thought that I was going to marry Lancaster, and they had a row. Then Frank, who always carried a revolver, shot him."

"And knifed him afterwards like your friend, Lo Keong, did Anchor."

"That *was* strange," admitted Fan, thoughtfully. "I don't think such a nice boy as Frank would act so brutally; and it's odd that my husband should have been treated in the same way."

"A coincidence, I suppose," said Eustace, indifferently, knowing that Fan was watching him closely. "What's become of Lancaster?"

"I don't know. I wish I did. He should hang."

"I thought you liked him, as a nice boy."

"So I did," she replied, "but I liked Starth better."

"Oh!" Jarman found it difficult to believe this. She eyed him suspiciously, and he would have explained himself further, but that Banjo Berry, followed by a young man, entered the room.

"Uncle," said Fan, rising and anticipating Eustace, "who do you think Leonard Grant, who wants to do the sketch, is?"

"Well, this is very curious," said Berry, shaking Eustace by the hand in the warmest and most friendly way. "Jarman, of 'Frisco."

"That's me," responded Eustace. "How are you, Sakers?"

Berry winked. "Don't need that name now," said he. "There's no chance of my getting run in for piling up that old schooner at Samoa. I'm Banjo Berry now. M'own name, and it's a hummer in the South Seas."

"I've been explaining all that to him," said Fan, impatiently. "I say, Mr. Jarman"—Eustace observed the punctiliousness—"do you know this boy, Natty Denham?"

The boy, so-called, was a callow young gentleman of twenty-five, dark-haired and brown-complexioned. He had a pleasant smile but rather a vacant expression, and in Jarman's mind was sized up, not exactly as a fool, but as a youth of rather weak will. He thrust forward a slim hand, and gave Eustace a nerveless handshake.

"How do you do?" he said, talking very fast. "I never met you in 'Frisco, but I saw you often. I'm Chicago m'self, and came to this old country along with the Captain and Miss Berry."

"You never met in 'Frisco?" asked Fan, addressing Jarman.

"No. I heard you talk of Mr. Denham, though."

It seemed to Eustace that both Fan and her uncle were rather relieved by this admission, and he wondered what connection this fool could have with the game the two were playing. He fancied that Denham was the pigeon, and Berry & Co. the hawks. It also struck him that if he could get Natty to himself he might find out something, always supposing that the young fellow knew anything. Later on, after a desultory and friendly conversation, Natty gave him an opening.

"I say," said he, "you live down in Essex?"

"Yes. At Wargrove."

Natty nodded to Fan and the Captain. "I knew," he said. "Can't understand how it slipped my memory."

"What slipped your memory, Bub?" asked Berry, sharply.

"Why, that he"—he nodded towards Eustace—"was in Essex. When Starth took me down to see that pretty sister of his, he said something about Jarman. I remember now."

"Why didn't you tell me, Natty," said Fan, in so cooing a voice that Eustace guessed she was thoroughly angry.

65

"I forgot. Can't remember anything," rattled on the youth. "I say"—suddenly turning to Eustace—"awful about poor Starth. Eh?"

"Oh, give it a rest," cried Berry, savagely. "You've done nothing but jaw of that since it happened. Jarman, wasn't it you who introduced him to Lancaster? Quite so. H'm! Guess Lancaster's an almighty friend of yours. Eh?"

"Well, he was," drawled Jarman, seeing that his reply was awaited with much interest, "but now—" Eustace shrugged his shoulders. "I don't much care to consort with criminals."

"Right, sir. You don't happen to know where he's skipped to?"

"Certainly not. He legged it sharp to escape the police."

"He won't escape me," said Berry, grimly. "I'm goin' to get that young man lynched, you bet. I loved Starth just like a son."

Jarman laughed. "Yet Starth wasn't a lovable man," he said.

"Oh, there was no end of good in him when you got at it," replied the little skipper, solemnly. "Besides, we had a scheme on to make money."

"What sort of a scheme?"

"Never mind," said Berry. "He's dead now, and the scheme's up a tree."

"I suppose Miss Starth's cut up?" said Denham to Eustace.

"Naturally. Her only brother."

"I guess she needs a heap of consolation," went on the young man artlessly. "It's just in my mind to go down and see her."

Jarman was not at all pleased at this proposition and was inclined to reply in the negative. But a bright thought struck him—a very daring thought of the nature of bluff. Denham was a fool, and not at all observant. It might be that if he came down and saw Mr. Desmond O'Neil he might be able to dispel any suspicions which might afterwards take shape in the minds of Fan and her uncle. With this idea he gave Natty an invitation.

"Come and stop with me," he said cordially. "There is no one with me but my secretary, an Irish chap called O'Neil. You'd get on well with him."

Natty seemed inclined to accept, but looked at Berry for instruction.

The skipper nodded. "Go by all means, and have a good time."

"You never ask me," said Fan, reproachfully, to her old lover.

"I'm afraid a bachelor establishment is not quite a paradise to ladies," said Eustace, laughing; "but if you will spend the day I'll be very pleased. When will you come down?" he asked Denham.

Berry answered. "He can come on Saturday," said he, "as I'm going to-morrow to see an old friend for a couple of days. I'll be back in the morning—Saturday morning, that is. I don't want Fan to be left."

"Is it Balkis you're going to see?" asked Denham.

Jarman nearly uttered an exclamation of surprise, for Balkis was the name of the negress in the portrait which Lancaster had seen in Starth's rooms. Berry didn't seem pleased at Natty's speech, and Fan frowned. But they both laughed indulgently.

"It isn't Balkis," said Berry, "but a marine officer I'm seeing in connection with Lancaster. He's left the country, and I think I know the ship he's skipped by."

"That's clever of you," said Jarman, rising to take his leave. "If you catch him, Captain, you'll do more than the police."

"Huh!" scoffed Berry. "Your police are fools. Most people in this old country are. I can squash the lot of them. Lancaster too, you bet!"

Eustace laughed when on his way home. He was pretty certain that, having already made a false start about Lancaster, Berry would *not* squash him. Jarman hoped to gather a great deal from Natty's prattle.

CHAPTER X

A QUEER MARK

Frank was not at all pleased when he heard that Denham was coming down to the Shanty. The experiment was too risky, as there was every chance that the young man would recognise him, in which case he would at once put the revengeful Berry on the scent. But Jarman did not look at the matter in this light, and explained himself after sundry questions.

"Have you met Denham often?" he asked.

"Yes. He was always dodging round the Berry establishment."

"I thought he lived with them."

"No, he had diggings some way off. Berry, so he told me, is a kind of guardian to him."

"Does a man require a guardian at the age of twenty-three?"

"Denham's twenty-five. He's almost the same age as I am, although I look older," said Lancaster; "and I should think, seeing what a fool he is, that he will require a guardian all his life."

"Then you think he's more fool than knave?" asked Eustace, ruminating.

Frank nodded emphatically. "I don't think he's a rascal at all, whatever the Captain may be. Denham's just a silly, good-natured ass, who would give his head away. He has a weak will, and is quite under the thumb of Berry."

"Did you fraternise with Denham?"

"No. His cackle got on my nerves. But he knows me well enough to spot me should I betray myself."

"Then you must not betray yourself," said Eustace, decidedly. "So far as looks go, he won't know you. I would defy even a detective to penetrate your disguise."

"Denham may twig me by my voice."

"I don't think from what I saw of him that he is so observant. Besides, I shall give you something to roughen your voice. You can say you have a cold."

Frank stared at his friend. "You seem to be up to all the tricks."

Jarman nodded. "I thought of being a detective myself once, and I practised for a time. I have all the materials for disguise here. I told you so when I made you up as Desmond O'Neil. I can get into the skin of a character with ease, and that's what you have to do. You are not Frank Lancaster, remember, but Desmond O'Neil from County Kerry."

"But, I say, Eustace, why do you want Denham down here?"

"Well, I wish him to report to the Berry lot that there is no concealment about me. They may suspect that I know something of your whereabouts, and I don't want either one to drop down upon me. Denham is a fool, and what he sees he will report to them in his artless fashion. Consequently, Berry and Fan will trust me. I want to get in with them and learn what they are up to."

"Do you think Denham can tell you?"

"No," said Eustace, promptly, "I don't. Whatever the game is, that boy is in the dark. He has much too loose a tongue for Berry to trust him with his secrets."

"But what's Berry bothering about him for?"

"That's what I want to find out. Denham may know something. For instance, he mentioned the name of Balkis, as I told you."

"What's the use of that?" asked Frank, gloomily.

"This much. Starth had her portrait, and Berry is in touch with her. I want to learn why Berry calls at an opium shop at the docks. He's going there, I'm sure, to see Balkis."

The two were standing by the window chatting in this way. As Eustace repeated the name of Balkis there sounded a low moan, which made the speakers turn. Miss Cork, with the tablecloth over her arm, stood at the open door, her thin face as white as the linen she bore. Apparently she had entered silently, as was her wont, to lay the table for luncheon, and had overheard the name. Like a statue she stood, her vacant eyes fixed on Jarman.

"What's the matter?" he asked.

Miss Cork's lips moved. "Balkis!" she said in a whisper.

"What about Balkis. Do you know the name?"

"Balkis!" said Miss Cork again. Then she threw down the cloth and ran back to the kitchen. Eustace followed and found her moaning in a chair. Rather brutally he shook her.

"What's all this?" he asked.

Miss Cork went on moaning. "I had a child—" she began; then shut up, and not another word could he get out of her.

After many fruitless inquiries Eustace returned to the sitting-room to explain. "I told you I didn't trust her," said Frank, whose fears took shape at once. "She is a silent, secretive woman. I am sure she will get me into trouble. Why should she know that name?"

"I can't say. And now she talks of some child—her own, she says. But you needn't be afraid, Frank, she's as true as steel."

"I don't trust her," said Frank, doggedly. "Where did you pick her up?"

Jarman, driven into a corner, replied reluctantly: "In a London court."

"A police-court?" inquired Lancaster; then, when he received a nod, went on: "Then she's dangerous. What do you know of her past?"

"Nothing. She never speaks of it. The poor wretch was taken up for vagrancy, and afterwards was handed over to the missionary. I knew the chap, and he told me what a capital cook the woman was, and how she needed a good home to put her right. She came to me as Miss Cork, and I have had no reason to regret having played the part of a good Samaritan. But it's strange that the name of Balkis should upset her."

"Won't she explain?"

"No. She is a very obstinate woman when the fit takes her."

But the fit apparently did not seal Miss Cork's mouth on this occasion. A soft knock at the door told of her return, and she presented herself quietly. Picking up the cloth she proceeded to lay the table, and without looking at the men proceeded to exculpate herself.

"I ask your pardon," she said, in her whispering voice. "I ask your pardon, Mr. Jarman, and yours, sir, but the name Balkis—" Here she stopped, and laid her hand on her heart. "I had a child of that name."

"Ah!" said Jarman, sympathetically, while Frank still looked suspicious. "And the name brings sad memories to you?"

Miss Cork nodded. "I'm a married woman," she said softly, "but my husband left me to starve—with the child, and—and—"

"And the child died?"

"No?" she burst out fiercely. "The child was stolen!"

"By whom?"

Miss Cork stopped, and her fingers worked convulsively, as though they were clutching at a throat. "I wish I knew—I wish I knew!" she said, savagely, and the expression of her lean face surprised Jarman, who had always considered her an apathetic woman. Perhaps his looks warned her that she was betraying too much of her unknown past, for she pulled herself up with a faint titter.

"I'm a Billericay woman myself," she began, when Jarman cut her short.

"That's nonsense!" he said sternly. "You know you are not."

"I've said all I have to say," said Miss Cork, quite irrelevantly, "and if you aren't pleased, Mr. Jarman, I'll go."

"I don't want you to go, and I ask you nothing," he replied.

"My child was called Balkis," went on Miss Cork, "and she was stolen five years ago. I've been looking for her ever since. She will be seventeen years old by now, and I lost her five years ago—yes, five years ago," she kept on repeating. "I've been looking for her ever since."

"A strange name Balkis?" said Jarman, watching her.

"My husband was in the East. It came from the East, that name. I'm a Billericay woman myself, and—" She giggled, then shook her head and withdrew swiftly.

The two men looked at one another.

"She's quite mad, and harmless," said Eustace.

"Quite mad, and dangerous," replied Frank. "I don't trust her."

Confirmed in this opinion by the strange demeanour of Miss Cork, he watched her closely. She muttered to herself frequently, and kept counting on her fingers. Sometimes she would utter the name of Balkis and laugh. Her laughter was not pleasant. It did not seem to Frank that she retained any pleasant memories of the name—yet if it was that of her child she should have done so. Jarman did not trouble about Miss Cork's eccentricities. The meals were well cooked and well served, and there was no fault to be found with the woman's housekeeping. She was odd in her manner, and appeared to be labouring under suppressed excitement. Twice Frank caught her listening, but not in sufficiently open a way to admit of rebuke. As his position was a delicate one he became alarmed; but trusting in Jarman's influence over the woman, and his claim to her gratitude, he tried to dismiss his fears.

Denham duly arrived, and speedily made himself at home. Thanks to some herbal decoction given to him by Eustace, Lancaster welcomed the visitor in a hoarse voice—a regular nestling's note. Natty did not recognise in Mr. O'Neil, the dark secretary, the fair-haired Frank Lancaster, whom he had seen frequently in Bloomsbury. He was completely deceived, and Frank felt more at his ease, being now certain that his disguise was all that could be desired. And, luckily, Natty did not give him much of his frivolous company, as he was mostly with Jarman or hanging round Rose Cottage.

By this time Frank, introduced by Mrs. Perth, had made the acquaintance of his divinity. She likewise never suspected any disguise, and was quite at her ease with the new secretary. Frank's heart beat hard when she offered him her hand, and he could hardly see her face for a mist before his eyes. Now that he heard her voice, and saw her gracious manner, he fell more in love with her than ever. It was a strange feeling, and one that he had not experienced in his wooing of Fairy Fan. But, from the misery he suffered, there was no doubt that it was genuine passion.

Mildred was very amiable with him, and they were together a great deal. Mrs. Perth had taken a fancy to Frank, whose manners she pronounced perfect, and talked much to him. She even discussed the death of Walter Starth, and the probability of Lancaster being the assassin. But by this time Frank had schooled himself into hearing the case talked of without moving so much as an eyelid. In a couple of weeks he became quite an accepted fact in the life of Rose Cottage, and, indeed, of the village. Even Mrs. Baker had ceased to ask him questions. Several letters addressed to Desmond O'Neil, with the Dublin postmark, had arrived, so Mrs. Baker was quite satisfied that he came from the country whence she procured her butter. From being a nine days' wonder in that quiet Essex hamlet Frank became a comparative nonentity, which was exactly the state of things Jarman wished to bring about. Thus, when Denham arrived on his three days' visit, there was nothing likely to connect the secretary with the bedraggled man who had arrived so late at night. And Miss Cork, in spite of her odd ways and Lancaster's suspicions, kept her own counsel most faithfully.

One afternoon Frank, now quite at his ease in his disguise, strolled over to the cottage to ask for afternoon tea. He brought a book of poems in his pocket, for Mildred was fond of hearing him read. Frank could read admirably, which is a rare accomplishment, and often he would declaim poems to Mrs. Perth and Mildred. But on this occasion there was no chance of enjoying Browning, for Jenny Arrow from the Rectory was present. She was a kittenish damsel of eighteen, with a freckled face, a turn-up nose, and a gay, vivacious manner. Also she had a vein of romance, and cherished an unrequited affection for the dark secretary. She confided this to Mildred.

"Doesn't he look a romance, dear?" said Jenny, when gazing from the drawing-room window she saw Frank approach. "Don't you love him, Milly?"

Mildred laughed, "I have had quite enough of love," she said. "That Denham boy worries my life out. Then there's your brother Billy."

"Oh, Billy's an ass!" said Jenny, contemptuously. "He falls in love with everyone he sees. I suppose you will marry Mr. Darrel?"

"Certainly not," said Mildred, quickly. "What put such an idea into your head, Jenny?"

The young lady nodded sagaciously. "Oh, I know," said she; "it's not to see poor pa that Mr. Darrel comes down here. Ma saw that. Ma says he's in love with you, and, being rich, you're sure to marry him."

"I would never marry for money, Jenny," said Mildred, thinking of Eustace. "Mr. Darrel will never make me his wife."

"Oh, but he's so very rich."

"Then marry him yourself."

"I would rather marry Mr. O'Neil."

Mildred laughed again, but all the same, for some reason inexplicable to herself, felt annoyed. "Here *is* Mr. O'Neil; you'd better propose."

"Mildred, if you reveal my love—oh! how I shall hate you."

But Mildred, watching the approaching figure of the man she knew merely as O'Neil, did not reply. She was wondering why she was so attracted towards him. He was not particularly good-looking, nor had he shown any marked preference for her society. Indeed, she had laughed with Mrs. Perth over the attentions which O'Neil paid the old lady. But there was something about the secretary which made Mildred's pulses beat as they never beat in the presence of Jarman. Perhaps, although she never knew, it was a case of telepathy, for Frank was always moved beyond his usual self when in her presence. But he never revealed it by his manner. Mildred, however, was not sufficiently a psychologist to analyse her feeling, so did not search too closely into the reason of her sensations. Still, she could not help wondering why she felt annoyed by Jenny's silly remark.

"I think you had better take that Denham boy," said Mildred to Jenny. "He bothers me greatly, and he's the kind of donkey who would fall in love with anyone."

"I don't regard myself as anyone," said Jenny, with dignity. "Besides, he's not half so nice as Mr. O'Neil."

Mildred acknowledged this with a sigh, and welcomed O'Neil with a blush, which he marked and wondered at. "Where is Mr. Jarman?" she asked.

"He has gone bathing with Billy and Denham," said Frank, standing outside and looking in at the window. "I have done my work, and came to be rewarded."

"With what—cakes and ale?" asked Jenny, languishing.

"Their modern equivalent in the shape of afternoon tea."

"Let's have it outside on the lawn. Oh, Mildred, do!"

Miss Starth assented. "Mrs. Perth is lying down," she said, "and as the room is rather hot, we may as well have a picnic on the lawn."

Forthwith she ordered the tea, which was brought out by the one servant of the establishment. But Jenny had to lay the cloth, and Frank was told to place the tables under the noble elm. In a few minutes they were all seated, Mildred and Frank in chairs, and Jenny lying gracefully on the lawn. Every now and then she looked up adoringly at the secretary, who took no notice. But Mildred did, and so strong became that absurd feeling of irritation that she could willingly have slapped Jenny.

After a desultory conversation, Jenny asked when Denham was returning to town. "Billy will be sorry when he goes. He's awfully fond of Mr. Denham. The adventures that man's had in America are extraordinary."

"He comes from America, doesn't he?" asked Mildred, idly.

Jenny nodded. "And Billy says he's been a sailor, he thinks."

"He doesn't look much like a sailor," said Frank, contemptuously. "He has been wrapped up in cotton-wool all his life."

"Oh, no, he hasn't indeed," said Miss Arrow, eagerly. "He has lived in Mexico, and among the Indians—not the Red Indians, you know, but amongst those Cortez found."

"The Aztecs," said Mildred. "My dear girl, there are none left."

"Oh, yes, there are, Mr. Denham says so. Billy calls him Natty, because that's his name, and he and Billy are going to explore for hidden treasure. There's lots of it in Mexico."

"Denham's been reading romances," said Frank, disbelievingly.

"No," insisted Jenny, "he's had all sorts of adventures. Why, when he was just a baby, he was carried off by these Indians."

"How do you know?"

"He says so, and they tattooed him on the left arm, Billy says."

Frank sat up suddenly. "On the left arm?" he asked. "With what?"

"With a Scarlet Bat—the oddest thing, Billy says— Oh! What's the matter?" Frank, profoundly moved, had fallen back in his chair.

CHAPTER XI

FRANK'S STORY

Seeing Frank's disturbed face, Mildred also became alarmed, but he managed to pacify both her and Jenny in a few words. It was impossible to tell the truth, therefore he was obliged to romance. "I think the heat is too much for me," he said, smiling, "and your mention of tattooing, Miss Arrow, recalled a disagreeable story."

"Tell it to us," said Jenny, eagerly. "I love ghastly tales."

"I wouldn't shock you by repeating this one," said Lancaster, finding it difficult to improvise. "It's about a leper."

Mildred uttered an exclamation of disgust. "Ugh! how dreadful. I don't want to hear it."

"I do," cried Miss Arrow, with the avidity of a ghoul. "You must tell it to me on some other occasion, Mr. O'Neil."

"I will, if you will tell me more of Mr. Denham's tattooing."

Jenny shook her head. "I don't know any more. You must ask Billy. He has this Scarlet Bat on his left arm, that's all I know."

"Did he ever tell Billy how it came to be there?"

"I told you. The Indians marked him. I can't say the reason."

Frank was silent. He was particularly anxious to know why Denham was marked in this peculiar way, and resolved to find out before the young man returned to town. As it was, the tattooing was another link in the chain which, to his mind, connected Berry with the crime. However, he kept his ideas to himself, and would have taken his departure to think them out at leisure but that he had a purpose to achieve connected with the photograph of Balkis. He knew that Walter's effects had passed into the hands of Mildred, and wished to obtain the portrait, for reasons which he afterwards explained to Jarman. Mildred herself gave him a chance of introducing the subject without awakening suspicion.

"You have been working too hard," she said, in reference to Lancaster's late emotion, "and it is so very hot."

"Perhaps I have," he assented, glad of the excuse; "but Jarman is anxious to get a new story finished quickly. It's an Eastern tale."

75

"Tell it to us," said the bold Jenny, sitting up and hugging her knees.

"Jenny, how can you!" corrected Mildred. "Mr. O'Neil must keep all those sort of things quiet."

"I can tell you this much, Miss Arrow, that Jarman wants a few words of Arabic, and we can't find them."

"I never knew him to be at a loss before," said Mildred.

"Well, he is this time, so you can crow over him, Miss Starth. He is anxious to get some Arabic letters. You haven't such a thing, I suppose," he added, half jokingly.

"Good gracious! Where could I— Wait," she said, rising, "there's a portrait which belonged to poor Walter. There are some Arabic letters on it. Mrs. Perth told me they were Arabic. But she may be wrong."

"As a governess she ought not to be," put in Jenny. "Get it, Mildred."

While Miss Starth hastened into the house, Jenny stared up into Frank's face in quite an embarrassing way. "Are you going to stay long at the Shanty?" she asked.

"That depends upon Mr. Jarman."

"Oh, then you'll stay as long as you like. He's very fond of you."

"He is a very good friend to me," said Frank, quietly.

Jenny nodded. "He is to everyone, I think. Mildred's fond of him. He has helped her a lot with her poetry. I like him better than Mr. Darrel. Do you know Mr. Darrel?"

"I have heard of him," replied Frank, cautiously.

"I don't like him at all," said Jenny, shaking her head vigorously. "He's a great friend to pa and ma, and very rich. But he doesn't come down to see them," she tittered. "No, Mildred's the attraction."

"Does Miss Starth like him?" asked Frank, quickly.

"She says she doesn't; but, of course, he's so rich. But I would rather she married Mr. Jarman, wouldn't you?"

Frank was spared the pain of replying to this embarrassing query by the return of Mildred with the portrait, which she placed in his hands. "It's the picture of a negress," she said, "and the letters at the foot—"

"They are Arabic sure enough. Who is the woman!"

"I don't know. It is a fancy portrait, I suppose."

"Probably. Can I take this away with me for a few days to copy the letters, Miss Starth? I'll return it safe."

"Oh, take it by all means. Look, Jenny, there's beauty."

Jenny sat up, and looked at the face earnestly. "It's something like Mr. Darrel," she said at length.

"Nonsense!" said Mildred, looking in her turn at the picture. "But, really, I don't know. What do you think, Mr. O'Neil?"

There was a resemblance to Darrel. The same sulky expression, and thick lips, and arrogant air. "Perhaps she's a relative of his," giggled Jenny. "He was born in the West Indies, you know."

"This portrait was taken at some place in Rotherhithe," said Mildred, pointing out the photographer's name. "But it is like Mr. Darrel."

"Quite as ugly," said Jenny; "though it's mean of me saying that," she added, "for Mr. Darrel gave me a lovely brooch last time he was down. He's coming again in a month. Do you know, Mildred?"

"Yes, I know," replied Miss Starth, in no very pleased tone.

Frank slipped the portrait into his pocket, as Billy Arrow came on to the lawn followed by Jarman and Natty. Billy was nearly twenty-one, and a Sandhurst cadet, but a great deal of the schoolboy remained in him. "We've had a rippin' time," said the young gentleman, throwing himself on the lawn.

"Would you like some tea?" asked Mildred.

"Rather. Tea would be saucy. Let me get it," and Billy swept into the house like a whirlwind.

Frank saw that Jarman looked rather disturbed, and wondered what could be the reason. He guessed that he had learnt something relative to the Berrys from Natty, and was anxious to know what it was. But he could not question Eustace at the moment, therefore curbed his curiosity until a more seasonable time. Meantime Natty was paying compliments to Mildred.

"You do look well, Miss Starth," he babbled in his inconsequent way —"and what a slapping day! We had an A1 dip. You should have come along, Mr. O'Neil."

Frank suppressed a smile, thinking how soon his disguise would have vanished had he accepted this offer. "I have been more pleasantly engaged," he said; "here comes Billy and the tea."

Billy was a first-rate hand at getting what he wanted. He brought a tray laden with strawberry jam, a large bowl of Devonshire cream, some hot cakes, and a fresh pot of tea. "You'll starve us out of house and home, Billy," said Mildred, when these were arranged before her. "What will Mrs. Perth say?"

"She'd say eat well, and not too quickly," said Billy, selecting a cake, while Jarman looked on amused.

"You're still a boy, Billy."

"So am I," said Natty, taking a slice of bread and cream, "in spite of being nearly twenty-five. I'm not that till the twenty-fifth of September, you know."

Frank looked up quickly, and glanced sideways at Jarman. That was the date of his own birthday, and then he, like Natty, would be twenty-five. This coincidence, taken in conjunction with the tattooing, puzzled him not a little. Jarman also looked perplexed, and asked a question. "Where were you born, Denham?" he demanded.

"At Zacatecas in Mexico," prattled Natty. "No end of a place. But I went to school in New Orleans. Yes, sir—to a slap-up school. My dad said I'd have to have the best education possible, so that I could look after the money when it came."

"Are you coming into a fortune?" asked Frank.

"Rather—to no end of a fortune. But it's a long yarn. I'll tell it to you some night, Jarman. It's good for your books."

"I shall be delighted to hear it."

"I get the money after my twenty-fifth birthday," said Natty, "and then I'll buy you all presents. Billy shall have a horse."

"And what will you give me?" asked Jenny.

"A husband," replied Natty. "And you, Miss Starth?"

"I'll have a husband also," said Mildred, frivolously, and then was sorry when she said it, recalling Natty's attentions. Jarman also was annoyed, and addressed himself to the young man.

"You must first catch your hare," he said gravely. "And I suppose your guardian, Captain Berry, will have to be consulted."

"No, I guess not. His control ceases when I get the dollars."

"On your twenty-fifth birthday?"

"*after* my twenty-fifth birthday. I can't say how long!"

Jarman said no more, being afraid to press his inquiries. Natty was a babbling fool; still, it was not wise to arouse his suspicions. He might mention them to Captain Berry and Fan, when there would probably be trouble. And Jarman wished that estimable couple to look upon him as one wholly unconcerned in their shady doings. By assuring them of his lack of interest he hoped to throw them off their guard.

The conversation became more or less frivolous, as was natural amongst such young people. Jarman was the eldest present, and he felt his forty years painfully. He even began to ask himself if it were fair that he should make Mildred his wife. She was young, he was elderly, and he remembered the proverb of May and December. He was not exactly December yet, but he was getting rapidly into the sear and yellow leaf. The reflection made him sad. When he went home with Frank—Natty remaining behind to play a game of tennis with Billy—he talked very little. Frank likewise was silent for a time, but ultimately he spoke first.

"I was rather startled today?" he said, as they neared the Shanty.

"Eh, what was that? Nothing wrong?"

"No. But Jenny Arrow told me that Denham, according to Billy, had a Scarlet Bat tattooed on his left arm."

"I know," said Jarman, quietly. "I saw it today when he was bathing. I intended to surprise you with the news. Strange that you should have made the discovery on the same day as I did. The long arm of coincidence again, I suppose."

Frank paid little attention to this, being taken up with his own thoughts. "You know I have a Scarlet Bat tattooed on my right arm?"

Jarman nodded. "I remember, and I suggested that as it was the sole mystery in your life, it might have to do with Berry's desiring to have you hanged. Now that we know Denham is marked in a similar way, it puts the matter beyond a doubt."

"I can't see how," said Frank, frowning.

"Wait till we get inside," said Jarman, "then we can talk at our ease."

Not another word was spoken until they entered Jarman's den, and sat down in the coolness. The blinds were down and there was a pleasant darkness. Jarman closed the door, then took a seat opposite to that into which Lancaster had thrown himself.

"Tell me again of your past," he said. "I want to refresh my memory."

"There's so little to tell that I wonder you don't know every word by heart," said the other, drearily.

"You only told me once, and my memory is a bad one. Go on."

While Jarman lighted his pipe, Frank told how he had been sent home from San Francisco by his father when he was two years of age, and placed under the care of a Quaker aunt called Miss Dorothy Drake. "She lived in Devonshire, at a place called Kingsbridge," went on Lancaster, "and there I was brought up till it was time for me to go to college. I studied at the Elizabethan Grammar School in that town. My father was always coming home, but never appeared. Then, when I was ten, he stopped writing altogether. But my aunt had the money for my education sent to her regularly. I went to Oxford, as you know, and then came, five years ago, to make my mark in London. And a pretty mark I have made!" said Frank, bitterly.

"You never spoke of this past to anyone?"

"No. My aunt particularly told me not to do so. I can't see, myself, why I should have kept silence though," he added, frowning. "There's nothing wrong about my past that I can see."

"No. It would seem as though your father was anxious you should live as quietly as possible, so as not to attract the attentions of adventurers of the Berry type."

"I don't understand."

"Well, that tattooing on your right arm! You never knew what it meant?"

"No. I asked my aunt and she could not tell me. It was on my arm—the Scarlet Bat I mean—when I came from America. Denham, I understand, says that his tattooing was done by Indians."

"H'm! He might believe that," said Jarman, sceptically, "and I daresay he's as ignorant of what the symbol means as you are. But Berry knows."

"What makes you think that?"

"Because he is hounding you down, and you are marked in a similar way to that boy whom he has in his clutches."

"Do you think Denham is in his clutches?"

"I am sure of it. The boy believes in him thoroughly, and is quite under Berry's thumb—poor wretch. He knows nothing about the significance of the Scarlet Bat, or Berry would not trust his babbling tongue within reach of my ears. But you told me that there was a chance of your learning something about yourself?"

"Yes. Aunt Dorothy said that when I was twenty-five, she had been told by my father to give me a sealed envelope. What it contained she did not know. In fact, Jarman, my aunt knew nothing, save that my father was a great traveller, that he married in America, and that when my mother died he sent me home. She thinks he is dead, because she has not received a letter from him for so long. I don't agree with her, as all this time the money has been forwarded for my education and keep."

"Are you still receiving money?"

"Yes. Twenty pounds a month. But I don't touch it. Aunt Dorothy is poor, so I give it to her and work for my own bread and butter."

"H'm! You're a good fellow. Who pays you the money?"

"White & Saon, lawyers in the City."

"Can't they tell you anything?"

"Maybe they might be able to do so, but they refuse. All they say is that the money comes from their San Francisco agents, and that they are empowered to pay it to me."

"Have they any papers?"

"No. I asked them. They said they had none. I must wait for that sealed envelope."

"On your twenty-fifth birthday," mused Jarman. "Observe, my son, Denham states that he is to come into money *after* his birthday. He is the same age as you are."

"And his birthday is on the same day, which makes it stranger. There is money knocking round, as you guessed. But I can't see how it is to come my way."

"You may learn when you open that envelope."

"I'll know soon then. Next month I'm twenty-five. Poor Aunt Dorothy. I wonder what she thinks of my scandal."

"Didn't you write her?"

"No. How could I. I feared lest the police might see her and make inquiries? She is a truthful old lady, and, although she would not betray me, she would give herself away by being confused. No, Eustace, it's best that my aunt should know nothing of my whereabouts."

"Well, she will know soon, as I intend to call on her next week."

"What for?" asked Frank, surprised.

"To get that envelope, and to learn all I can from her about your father's life in America. There's money I tell you, Frank, and it comes either to you or Denham."

"How do you make that out?"

"Because you are both marked with the Scarlet Bat. And Berry," said Eustace, with emphasis, "is doing his best to get that money."

CHAPTER XII

THE UNEXPECTED HAPPENS

Denham took his leave with profuse thanks to Jarman for a pleasant visit. He departed without the least suspicion that Frank was other than he was represented to be. Eustace drew a breath of relief when he dismissed him at the railway station.

"That's all right," he thought, as he took his way homeward. "Denham will represent me as a kind friend, and will do away with any suspicion in the Berry mind as to my having a card up my sleeve. Now I can make another move."

The next move was to see Miss Dorothy Drake and learn all particulars about the sealed envelope. Also Frank wished to know what had become of his effects, which had been left behind in his London rooms. As his nearest relative, it was probable that Miss Drake would lay claim to them until such time as he should reappear. Eustace therefore decided to go a few days after Denham's visit, and called on Mildred to explain his absence. For obvious reasons he did not explain himself too fully. Not until Frank was proved innocent did Jarman wish her to know that he was identical with Mr. O'Neil.

"I shall only be away a week, Mildred," said Eustace, taking her hand; "you won't forget me in that time?"

"I am not likely to forget you at all," replied the girl, wearily.

"Mildred, you are not looking well."

"The weather is so trying," she said hesitatingly, "and Walter's death has damped my spirits."

"I wish you would not dwell on that, my dear. He was not worth it."

"Still, he was my brother when all is said and done. If he had only died a natural death, I would not mind so much. But it is terrible to think of his tragic end. Are you making any attempt to discover the truth?"

"Yes. My journey is connected with the attempt."

"Where are you going?"

"No," said Jarman, smiling, "don't ask me that. Not until I am successful shall I reveal my methods. And at present I am groping in the dark."

"Have you no clue?"

Eustace hesitated. "I can hardly say that I have. There are certain suspicions in my mind, which may or may not prove correct. But when I return I may be able to tell you something."

"Do your suspicions still point to the innocence of Mr. Lancaster?"

"Yes," said Jarman, firmly. "I am more convinced every day that he is the victim of a conspiracy. But his innocence will be hard to prove. Mildred"—he again took her hand—"when I'm away I want you to be kind to O'Neil. He has no relatives, poor fellow, and is in sad trouble. Don't let him feel lonely."

Mildred nodded, but could not trust herself to speak. Had she consulted her own inclinations she would have seen nothing of the secretary during the absence of his employer. Daily she grew more and more interested in the so-called O'Neil. She learnt to watch for his coming, to hang on his words. He had said nothing to her likely to be construed into admiration, and was always cold and guarded in his utterance. But this very coldness increased her liking for him. She assured herself that it was merely "liking," but in her heart she knew that love had awakened. The thought of this, coupled with the remembrance of her half-engagement to Eustace, made her nervous and confused. She could not meet her lover's eye, and he returned to his home wondering at the inexplicable change. However, he finally put it down to grief for the loss of her unworthy brother, and to prevent her from brooding he asked Frank to see her as frequently as he could during his absence.

"Certainly," said Frank, with an effort to be cheerful; "if you do not think she will find me out."

"How can she She has never set eyes on you at close quarters, as you were."

"No," muttered Lancaster, guiltily, recalling the night in the theatre and the genesis of his futile passion. "I suppose not." Then, to change the subject, he asked Eustace to be sure to let him know all that transpired between himself and Miss Drake. "And give her my love."

"And tell her you are innocent?"

"Oh, she won't need to be told that," said Frank. "Aunt Dorothy will never believe that I did such a wicked thing. Heaven bless her! By the way, you don't think there is any chance of Berry coming down?"

"Not the slightest. Any suspicions he may have entertained about my knowing your whereabouts will be dissipated by the babble of Natty. I took the greatest care to load him up with a story likely to satisfy even the suspicions of Captain Banjo. I shouldn't be surprised," added Jarman, reflectively, "if Berry approached me with an offer to join forces."

"What good would that do him?"

"Well, I know about the murder of Anchor, and, moreover, as I was your friend I might—in his opinion—know something likely to help him in acquiring this fortune."

"Then you really think there is a fortune?"

"After the talk of Natty about his birthday, I am perfectly sure that there is a great deal of money knocking about. It ought to come to you; but Berry's machinations, unless thwarted, will put it into the pocket of Denham."

"If so, he won't benefit."

"Oh, yes, he will," rejoined Eustace, grimly. "When Denham is in possession of the fortune, he will die as Starth did. He will follow poor Anchor to the other world in the same way. Then Fan and Berry will retire to live happy ever afterwards."

"It's all theory," grumbled Frank.

"Quite so. But that's my reading of the mystery. However, your aunt may throw some light on the subject. She will probably tell me more of your father's life than she told you."

But Lancaster was not to be convinced. "I don't think she knows anything," he said. "Better see those lawyers, White & Saon."

"I'll look them up when I return to town."

Jarman, having settled his plans, went off, and Frank found himself in sole possession of the house. Miss Cork waited on him assiduously, and he noticed that she was not so eccentric as usual. As yet he had not tried the experiment of letting her see the photograph of Balkis, which was his true reason for obtaining it from Mildred. Frank did not believe Miss Cork's story of the lost child, and was certain that her emotion at the mention of the name was due to some other and less respectable cause. It might be that she knew Balkis herself, and as Balkis knew Berry—according to Natty's slip of the tongue—Miss Cork might be able to throw some light on the mystery of the black woman's connection with Starth. Frank determined to place the photograph where Miss Cork could see it, and then when she was moved to terror or surprise by the sight of the face, to insist on an explanation. What she said might not lead to the detection of the true assassin, but it might reveal something about Berry likely to show why he was conspiring against the life and liberty of an innocent man. But this again was all theory, as was Jarman's belief that the tattoo mark of the Scarlet Bat was at the bottom of Berry's rascalities. Still, if Frank wished to win clear of his difficulties, it behoved him to try in all directions, on the chance of finding a clue to the mystery.

Frank therefore displayed the photograph of the big negress in a prominent position, for the startling of Miss Cork, and then took his way to Rose Cottage. He knew, that, seeing he loved Mildred, he ought not to go, in spite of the unsuspicious Jarman's direct wish. But Lancaster, loyal as he wished to act towards his friend, could not help drinking in the sweet poison. By this time he was convinced that Mildred liked him more than a little, and he gave himself a kind of delicious pain in watching this fruit which he could never hope to pluck. He thought that when she knew his real name her liking would vanish, to be replaced with loathing for the assassin of her brother, as she must surely think Lancaster to be. Then she could marry Jarman, and be happy. Frank argued in this way. All the same, he knew that he was giving way to weakness in trusting himself in her sweet presence. This feeling was so strong on him, when he approached the cottage, that he was minded to retreat, and make some excuse for not calling again. What made him change his mind was the sight of Darrel in the garden. But that Frank was in love and knew that Darrel was a suitor for Mildred's hand, a timely thought of his danger would have made him retreat. As it was, he went boldly forward, trusting in the perfection of his disguise. It had not been pierced by Denham, so it was unlikely he would be unmasked by so slow-thinking a man as Darrel. And it made the young man furiously jealous to think that Darrel should persecute Mildred with his attentions. He tried to think that in coming between he was actuated by friendship for Jarman, but, in his own passionate heart, he knew well that it was a personal resentment. Mrs. Perth had brought her everlasting knitting into the garden, and was seated in a cane chair under the elm. Near her was Mildred, looking in Frank's helpless eyes more beautiful than ever. And to make him the more jealous, Mildred was winding a ball of red wool for Mrs. Perth from a skein held by Darrel. The Rhodesian was, as usual, big and sullen, and appeared much too gigantic for the little garden. It was a modern picture of Hercules and Omphale; and Frank, realising his own helplessness, raged inwardly, as he was smilingly welcomed by Mrs. Perth. Mildred, after a nod, cast down her eyes with a flush on her face, and attended assiduously to her work. Hercules scowled.

"I'm so glad to see you," said Mrs. Perth in her precise voice. "Do you know Mr. Darrel?"

Naturally, Frank said that he had not the pleasure and was introduced at once. Darrel lifted his heavy eyes with a grunt, and paid no further attention to the secretary. But he was quite as jealous as Frank; and Mildred, the cause of this feeling in both breasts, became aware that the weather was thundery. However, she chatted brightly, and divided her attentions equally, being helped by Mrs. Perth. That good lady never suspected what was going on under her nose.

"Your cold is better," said Mrs. Perth, when Frank was seated.

As a matter of fact it was, as Eustace had left off giving Frank the means to hoarsen his voice after the departure of Denham. "It is better," said Frank, almost in his usual tones. "Jarman has been doctoring me. I'll soon be well."

Darrel pricked up his ears and looked at the dark young man. "Have I ever met you before?" he asked.

Frank kept his countenance, although he felt that he was in an awkward position. "I think not," he said coldly.

While Darrel's lazy eyes strayed over him slowly, Mrs. Perth put in a brisk word. "Mr. O'Neil comes from Ireland," she said. "Have you ever been in Ireland, Mr. Darrel?"

"No," he responded, still eyeing Lancaster, who sustained his scrutiny unmoved. "I should never have taken Mr. O'Neil for an Irishman."

"That means you have no brogue," said Mildred to Frank, smiling. "But he had one when he came, Mr. Darrel."

"You have been here a long time to get rid of it, then?" said Darrel.

"Just a few weeks," replied Frank, calmly.

Mrs. Perth, with the best intentions, brought Lancaster under the guns of the enemy. "You came just when we were in deep grief over that horrid murder," she said, clicking her needles.

"Yes. I remember you saying something about that," said Frank.

"I have been in Scotland," said Darrel, suddenly, and taking side-looks at Lancaster's unmoved face, "so I don't know what has happened. Have they caught the man who did it?"

"Mr. Lancaster?" said the old lady. "No, they have not."

"And I hope they never will," said Mildred, flushing. "From what Mr. Jarman says, I believe Mr. Lancaster is innocent."

"Oh!" said Darrel, turning away his eyes from Frank, "so Jarman takes up the cudgels on behalf of this murderer. I remember he was a friend of Lancaster's."

"And is," said Frank, incautiously.

"You should know," said Darrel, quietly, and with a keen glance, "being his secretary."

"I have heard Jarman speak of this matter," replied Frank. He knew that Darrel's suspicions were aroused, and tried to keep the colour from his cheeks. He looked directly at Darrel, and the eyes of the two men met. It was Darrel who first withdrew his gaze.

"No," he said at length, "you're not a bit like Lancaster, although you have the same tone of voice."

"Has he indeed?" said Mildred, with interest.

"Lancaster was fair-haired and white-skinned," went on Darrel.

"Whereas I am a dark Celt," said Frank, drawing a long breath, as he deemed the danger was at an end.

"Well, don't talk any more about the matter," put in Mrs. Perth, sharply. "You'll upset Mildred, and the affair is too horrible to discuss."

Upon this hint Darrel turned the conversation into other channels, and devoted himself to Mrs. Perth. Frank thus had an opportunity of chatting with Mildred. They talked on the most indifferent subjects, but all the time each one knew what the other wanted to say. Such sudden love seems incredible to those who have never loved; but anyone who has fallen a victim to the great passion knows how suddenly the devouring flame blazes into a conflagration. The two had seen little of one another, all things considering, and they had never become confidential. Yet they loved one another, and it needed only an unguarded moment of emotion for the truth to be openly acknowledged between them.

Darrel, with his side-glances, saw their embarrassment, their flushed cheeks, their efforts to appear easy, and took note of all. But with great self-control he continued his conversation with Mrs. Perth. For quite an hour he talked, and then rose to take his leave, at the same moment as Frank announced his intention of departing.

"I am stopping at the Rectory," said Darrel, when they passed through the gate. "You come my way, I think?"

"For some little distance," replied Frank, always on his guard, but suspecting no evil on the part of his companion.

For a time they strolled on in silence, down the lane, and out on to the dusty white road. Then Darrel commenced to converse on indifferent matters, and told stories about Africa. Also he stated his experiences in America. "I was at Los Angeles," he said.

Frank remembered how at the theatre he had said that he met Berry at Los Angeles, but made no comment on the remark. Darrel still continued to talk, till they halted in a quiet side road, whence Frank branched off to the Shanty. There Darrel stopped. "Miss Starth is in love with you," he said abruptly, his jealous eyes on the young man's face.

"What do you mean?" demanded the secretary, indignantly.

"And you are in love with her," went on the Rhodesian.

"I don't know what right you have to say these things."

"This much right," said Darrel, calmly. "I love Miss Starth, and I intend to make her my wife. If you clear out and leave her alone, I'll say nothing; if you don't, I'll have you arrested. You understand me, Lancaster."

Frank's heart almost stood still. "I am not—"

"Bah!" said Darrel, cutting him short, and pointing to his left hand. "When you disguise yourself, you should remove your ring. I fancied it was your voice when you spoke, and I saw that habit you have of slipping that ring up and down your finger. Also the ring itself, I remember it quite well."

Frank cursed his folly. The ring was a noticeable one, set with two black pearls. More of a lady's ring than a man's it was, but he wore it because it had belonged to his mother. There was no chance of keeping up his assumed character in the face of such evidence. "But I assure you, Darrel, I am innocent," he protested.

"I don't care two cents if you are innocent or guilty," said Darrel, coolly. "Starth was never a friend of mine, and objected to my marrying his sister. I've set my heart on making her my wife, because I love her with all my soul. She loves you."

"No, she doesn't!"

"She loves you," persisted Darrel. "Do you think I can't tell. I'm too deeply in love with her myself to make any mistake. I'm not going to have you queering my pitch. If you leave her alone and clear out, I'll hold my tongue."

"And if I don't?"

"I'll write to the London police. Inspector Herny will be glad to get you into his clutches. Now you know," and without further words Darrel turned on his heel and lumbered down the road like a heavy, clumsy steer.

For a few moments Frank stood alone in the shadow, feeling as though the brightness had died out of his life. He felt that he did not much care if he were arrested, so wearing was the *rôle* he was playing, but the thought that Mildred would be told, that she would look upon him with loathing, made him shudder. He tried to stifle his thoughts, and hurried into the house to think what was best to be done. At that moment he sorely missed the wise head and staunch friendship of Jarman.

The door of the Shanty was wide open. Wondering at this, for Miss Cork was of that suspicious nature which always kept windows barred and doors closed, Frank stepped into the drawing-room. He glanced towards the mantelpiece where he had placed the photograph of Balkis. It was gone. A sudden suspicion seized him. He went to the kitchen. It was empty. Miss Cork had, vanished, and had taken the portrait with her!

CHAPTER XIII

A QUAKER LADY

Kingsbridge is the quaintest of towns and was of great importance before the era of steam. Then fruit schooners ran as far as the Azores, and smuggling was a fine art; but now the glory and excitement has departed, and Kingsbridge is a quiet, clean, country town set in the heart of the Devonshire hills. At the top of the steep High Street dwelt Miss Dorothy Drake, and from her window she could behold the silver waters of the estuary and a panorama of undulating lands. The window was Miss Drake's favourite seat, and there she sat knitting for many a long hour, watching the landscape changing under the wonderful colours of the sky.

She was a quiet, homely little person, usually clothed in a grey stuff gown, and wearing the white, close-fitting cap of the sect she belonged to. Her serious face was the hue of old ivory, and she had mild blue eyes, the pensive expression of which, added to the calm look, soothed all to whom she spoke. When anyone was in trouble, he or she—it was usually a she—came for advice and comfort to Miss Drake, and both were freely given. She kept only one servant, a stout wench called Kezia, who adored her mistress, and who made it the study of her life that Miss Drake should be comfortable. The old lady had a little money of her own, and with this and the twenty pounds a month which came from America she lived in what she regarded as a luxurious way. But Miss Drake's luxury would have been the penury of other and more modern people.

The room in which she sat was as quaint as herself, and almost as small. The furniture was old, and polished brightly by Kezia. The curtains and hangings were faded, but the room was brightened by numerous antimacassars worked by its owner. There was a china cupboard containing hoarded cups and saucers, strange seashells on the mantelpiece, and portraits in oil of Miss Drake's ancestors on the walls. She did not claim descent from the famous Sir Francis, but admitted that she derived her blood from a distant branch of the family. At all events, the love of travel and seafaring was in the Drake blood, for two of Miss Drake's brothers had been merchant captains, and her only sister had travelled in quest of a situation to America.

They were all dead now, and Miss Drake remained awaiting her summons in the small room in the small house at the top of Kingsbridge High Street. Miss Drake missed her nephew. She was much attached to him, and had done her best to bring him up since the time when he was entrusted to her charge at the tender age of two years. But Frank's ambitions had led him to London, and Miss Drake, knowing that it behoved him to fight the battle of life, had let him depart with a sigh. Sometimes he came to see her, and these occasions were always festivals. When the news of Frank's trouble came, Miss Drake sturdily refused to believe it, and prayed earnestly that Frank's innocence would be made evident in God's good time. She firmly believed that it would.

All the same, in spite of her undoubted faith, Miss Drake was much agitated over the matter. As the weeks went by and nothing was heard of Frank, she fretted over his disappearance until the good Kezia grew quite alarmed. But after a time, so long as no mention was made of the matter, she became calmer, and waited patiently for the result of her prayers. When Eustace called she was at once alarmed, divining that the arrival of this stranger had something to do with the trouble of her poor lost boy. She saw her visitor at once, and gave him tea out of wonderful egg-shell china. Eustace liked the old lady at sight, and strove to set her at her ease. In this he succeeded, for by the time they arrived at the most serious portion of their conversation Miss Drake was quite alert. She had been greatly cheered by Jarman's insistence on Frank's innocence.

"Though I never believed he was guilty," she said, in her quiet voice. "Friend Jarman, thou hast been a brother to him. Thy reward will come."

"I don't ask for any reward, Miss Drake. I am not the man to see a fellow like Frank—such a good fellow, too—go under without doing my best to help him. Well, I have told you that he is with me in disguise, and you know all the circumstances of the crime."

"So much, Friend Jarman, as the police could tell me."

"The police? Oh! has Inspector Herny been here?"

Miss Drake nodded, and looked at her knitting with her head on one side like a bright-eyed robin. "This Mr. Herny took possession of Frank's goods in the name of law and order. He found a letter addressed to me, and learnt that I was aunt to my poor boy. He came to learn if Frank had fled to me."

"I thought he would," said Jarman, drawing a long breath.

"I was not able to tell him anything," resumed Miss Drake, "but I insisted that Frank was innocent. Beyond a few papers, all Frank's goods have been sent here. I have paid up the rent of his rooms, and they are now let to another tenant. So when Frank comes to me, Friend Jarman, he will find that his worldly affairs are as settled as I, in my poor weak way, could arrange them."

"You have done splendidly, Miss Drake. And now that we know how we stand, I will come to the object of my visit. I want you to help me to prove Frank's innocence."

Miss Drake's hands trembled, and she stopped knitting. "Gladly would I do so, but thou art mistaken. I can do nothing."

"That depends upon what you know of Frank's father."

"I know very little, Friend Jarman. My sister Ruth met him in San Francisco, and married him. I never saw him myself. Why do you ask?"

"Well, it's this way, Miss Drake. I believe that Frank is the victim of a conspiracy, which involves a lot of money. You know that he had a Scarlet Bat tattooed on his right arm?"

"Truly I know that. Many a time have I seen it when he was a child. But I do not know what it means?"

"Did you never inquire?"

"From whom could I inquire, Friend Jarman? Frank knew nothing, and his father would not tell me. I never asked, as I did not think it was worth while. But had I inquired, Friend Lancaster would not have replied. According to Ruth, he was a silent and secretive man."

"Is Mrs. Lancaster alive now?"

"Alas! no. She died when giving birth to the boy. Friend Lancaster kept the baby with him for two years. Then, as he was going on some expedition, he sent the child to me, with a stipend of twenty pounds a month. I brought up the lad as I best knew how. He had a good education at the school here, and then departed to college. Afterwards, he dwelt in London as you know. That is his story. All I know."

"But the twenty pounds is paid regularly?"

Miss Drake nodded. "Through White & Saon, of Kirk Lane, London. I wished Frank to take it to himself, but he always refused. I use a part of it, but much I put aside. So," said the old lady, looking over her spectacles, "if he should be tried, or if he is in need of money now, Friend Jarman, I have a hundred or so waiting for him."

"It will come in handy," said Jarman, idly. He was disappointed at the scanty information afforded by the old lady. "Have you any letters from Mr. Lancaster?" he asked.

Miss Drake rose, and produced from a cabinet a bundle of envelopes with the American postmark. These she placed in Jarman's hands, and, having obtained permission, he examined them carefully. While he did so the old lady examined him stealthily and anxiously. Twice she frowned, as if trying to solve some problem.

91

"There's nothing here likely to throw any light on the subject," said Eustace, tying up the bundle again in the faded blue ribbon.

"What didst thou expect to find, Friend Jarman?"

Eustace pinched his nether lip in perplexity. "I thought to find some mention of Banjo Berry," he said, frowning, "for it seems to me that he is at the bottom of all this business. For some reason he wants Frank hanged."

"An evil man—an evil man!" said Miss Drake, shaking her head.

"Oh, he's one of the worst," continued Eustace; "but in these letters"— he laid his hand on the bundle—"there is no mention of him. These only ask after the boy and announce the remittance of money. But I notice," said Eustace, looking at his hostess sharply, "that there are no late letters."

Miss Drake nodded. "Quite so, Friend Jarman. For many years there have been none. Friend Lancaster stopped writing to me when his son was aged ten. That is nearly fifteen years ago."

"So I understand," said Eustace, pondering. "Frank is twenty-five in September. His birthday is in a few weeks."

The old lady took off her spectacles and rubbed them with a vexed air. She appeared about to say something, but closing her mouth firmly she went on knitting. Jarman was annoyed as he saw that she was not quite open with him. However, he made no direct comment, but resumed the conversation as though he had noticed nothing. "Do you think old Mr. Lancaster is dead?" he asked.

"I cannot say, I think he is," said Miss Drake, with a worried look, "but Frank thinks otherwise, Friend Jarman. He would have gone to San Francisco to learn, but that I asked him to wait till his twenty-fifth birthday."

Jarman recalled Natty's remark that he was entitled to money after his birthday in September. Frank was the same age and was born on the same day, so it would seem from Miss Drake's remark that to his birthday also there was something attached. "Is Frank entitled to any money?" he asked. "Is there a will, or—"

"There is no money as far as I know, Friend Jarman," said Miss Drake, rising; she paused, then went on. "But my heart misgives me."

"Why should it?"

"There is some mystery about the boy," continued Miss Drake, still agitated. "That mark on his arm is strange—and then the sealed letter."

It was for the mention of the sealed letter that Jarman had been waiting. Now that Miss Drake had mentioned it of her own free will, he no longer disguised the object of his visit. "It was to get that letter that I came down."

"Why?" asked Miss Drake, suspiciously.

"Because I think it may solve the mystery of Berry's enmity. Miss Drake," he went on, earnestly, "this man Berry has in his clutches a fellow called Denham, who seems to be an ass as far as I can judge. Denham is of the same age as your nephew and was born on the same day. He also has a Scarlet Bat tattooed; but he is marked on the left arm. I believe that there is a sum of money—a fortune—perhaps the one to which Denham alludes. Berry is trying to get Frank out of the way, so that Denham may obtain the money, in which case he will have the handling of it. Of course this is all supposition, but I can account for the extraordinary circumstances in no other way."

Miss Drake heard him quietly, her bright eyes fixed on his earnest face. "I believe thou art a good man, Friend Eustace," she said, "and, for the sake of my poor boy, I will trust thee. Sixteen years ago, just before Friend Lancaster stopped writing, he sent me an envelope which he asked me to give Frank on his twenty-fifth birthday. I intended to do so with my own hands, but as this trouble prevents me from doing so, I will give the letter to thee—" She stopped and folded her hands as though in prayer. "I trust I am doing right," she murmured to herself, "but the man seems good and kindly."

"I swear you can trust me, Miss Drake. I have Frank's interests at heart. I shall take the letter back, and ask Frank to open it."

"But it was not to be opened until his twenty-fifth birthday."

"Under the circumstances I think it should be opened at once," pleaded Jarman, earnestly; "there is no good to be gained by waiting. And, remember, Frank is in great danger. Should Berry succeed in tracing him, he will denounce him at once to the police. If Frank is tried, I don't see what defence he can put forward."

"But he is innocent, poor lamb."

"I am sure of that. But the circumstantial evidence is too strong."

Miss Drake thought for a few moments. "Friend Jarman," she said at length, "by his unhappy position Frank is tied hand and foot, and thou must act for him. If thou dost think that the letter is vital to the proving of his innocence, why not open it now?"

Eustace shook his head. "I can't say if the letter will prove his innocence," he said doubtfully, "but it may be a clue to the mystery. I prefer that Frank should open the letter."

"I will get it for thee," said Miss Drake, rising. "One moment," said Jarman as she walked to the door. "Have you ever heard the name of Tamaroo?"

"No. A strange name. But I know it not."

"It's not mentioned in the letters either," said Eustace to himself as the old lady left the room, "yet it has something to do with the Scarlet Bat, and *tht* I am certain has to do with the mystery. A peculiar affair." He thrust his hands into his pockets and looked out of the window. "I can't see what it all means."

Miss Drake returned and placed in his hands a common-looking envelope which, from the fold, had evidently come inside another letter. It was addressed to "My son Francis!" and was sealed with red wax. Jarman drew near the window and looked at the seal. Then he muttered an ejaculation —"The Scarlet Bat again!"

"Yes," said Miss Drake, divining his astonishment, "the seal is the same as the mark on the poor lad's arm."

"I am more convinced than ever that this has to do with the solution of the mystery," said Jarman, placing the letter in his pocket-book. "Wherever we look we meet with the Scarlet Bat. I shall take this to Frank, and on my way to Wargrove I will call on White & Saon. They may know something. By the way, have you a photograph of Mr. Lancaster?"

"Yes. Ruth sent me a photograph taken with her husband when they were married," and Miss Drake, taking a picture in a silver frame from a distant corner of the room, showed it to Jarman.

Mrs. Lancaster was a sweet-looking, mild woman, not unlike Miss Drake, her sister. But Lancaster was a picturesque, resolute man, with a firm mouth and a pair of rather fierce eyes. Frank resembled both his parents, but favoured his mother most. Jarman examined the photograph carefully, then rose to go. "I shall tell you what this contains when Frank opens it," he said, "and if possible I shall get Frank to come down and see you."

CHAPTER XIV

A PUBLIC CLUE

Jarman did not let the grass grow under his feet. With the sealed letter in his pocket-book he returned that same evening to London. He put up at a small hotel for a few hours, and, leaving his bag there, went to see White & Saon towards midday. Had he consulted his own inclinations he would have gone immediately to Wargrove, as he had a great curiosity to see Frank open the sealed envelope. But he thought it best to follow on the warpath as long as possible, on the chance of something new turning up. It didn't do to waste time with so active an enemy as Berry.

Near the Mansion House he met Dickey Baird, who was always prowling about the City in connection with mysterious stocks and shares. His friends declared that Dickey lost more money than he made—but Dickey always talked with the air of a Rothschild. He knew Jarman very well, and saluted him gaily. Eustace was not averse to talking with Baird, thinking Dickey the ubiquitous might have something to say of the Captain and his niece. After the exchange of a few words, Jarman introduced the subject of the murder as speedily as he dared without attracting attention.

"I say, Dickey, have you heard anything of Lancaster?"

"No, poor chap. He's cleared out. I daresay he's in America. In fact, I know a fellow who thought he saw him in Liverpool."

"No doubt," replied Eustace, thinking it was best to encourage this idea and put Berry on a wrong trail. "The most sensible thing he could do was to cut."

"But I say, Jarman, you don't believe that he's guilty?"

"Don't you?" asked Eustace, alertly.

"No. Or if I do," added Dickey, rather inconsequently, "it was an accident. I'll never believe that a good chap like Lancaster killed another in so brutal a way."

"What do you mean by an accident?"

"Well, you see, Frank rather admired Starth's sister—"

"Ha!" said Eustace with a start. "I remember, she was in a box."

"Rather looking the beauty of the world. Ripping girl, just the sort of Diana of the Chase I'd like to marry."

"Go on—go on!"

"Well, Frank thought she was a ripper, and wished to know her. Of course, Starth's rowdy manners prevented a proper introduction. Frank never intended to quarrel with Starth on that night. He was all for making it up and getting to know the beauty. But Starth was so insulting that Frank had to stand up for himself. He lost his temper did Frank, and made a lot of silly speeches which were used afterwards in evidence against him. Hang it!" added Dickey, in an injured tone, "that beastly Berry hauled me into the thing, and I had to tell the rot that Frank had been talking. I said he was a silly ass at the time. But he never meant any of it. It was all sheer rage at that pig Starth, and you know he was a pig, Jarman. I wonder you made a friend of him."

"He wasn't much of a friend."

"You introduced Frank to him, anyhow."

"Only in a casual way. Go on. Let's hear your theory."

"Well, the last thing Lancaster said to me on that night was that he was sorry he had such a row, and that he wished he could make it up. I guess he went to see Starth next day for that purpose. There was another row, and Frank shot him. He would carry that revolver of his, though I was always telling him what a fool he was. So if he did shoot Jarman he shot in a rage, same as when he called the names. I hope he'll save his neck."

"Do you think there's any chance he won't?"

"Not so far as the police are concerned. But the skipper swears he'll hunt him down. You know he offered a reward of two hundred?"

"Yes. Has anyone got it?"

Dickey shook his head. "No. And Berry's offering five hundred now. I can't think why he's so keen on catching Frank. He pretended to be a friend of his and wasn't fond of Starth from all I saw, although they were as thick as thieves."

"Do you think Berry really means business?" asked Eustace after a time. "All this offering a reward might be an advertisement for Fan."

"It might. But if jaw goes for anything he's bent on collaring Frank. He swears he'll hunt him down, if it costs him a thousand. I say," he added, looking wise, "I believe Berry and Starth were in business as partners over something and the business has gone bang. That's what made Berry mad."

"What sort of business?"

"I can't say. But when Starth was drunk he used to jaw about a million pounds he hoped to make some day. Berry shut him up once pretty sharp when he burbled like that, so I think Berry was in it."

"If it's anything shady, you may be sure Berry has something to do with it," said Eustace. "Goodbye, Dickey, I must be off."

When on his way to Kirk Lane Jarman mused over the information. He was sure now that the invitation of Starth had been a trap into which the man himself had somehow fallen. The amount at stake was a million, which was large enough a sum in Berry's eyes to justify even the murder of one man and the hanging of another. No wonder Berry offered a reward for the apprehension of Frank, if in the capture lay his chance of securing so large a fortune. But what puzzled Eustace, and what had puzzled him all along, was why it should be necessary to hang Frank. Had Lancaster been entitled to the money it would have been sufficient to have killed him, and while lying drugged on the sofa he could easily have been despatched. Indeed, the drug itself might have been administered in a sufficient quantity to polish him off. "It's an infernal mystery," said Jarman, flogging his brains to arrive at some conclusion. "I can't see the pivot on which the thing turns. Perhaps these lawyers may supply a clue."

Messrs. White & Saon were most respectable solicitors. They occupied a dingy, dark office at the top of Kirk Lane at the end furthest from Cheapside. The senior partner was engaged, but Jarman was told that he could see Saon. He had with him a letter of introduction from Miss Dorothy Drake, and sent this in with the clerk. After some delay he was conducted into a kind of dust-hole with a grimy skylight, packed with books and boxes and law papers. In the centre of this sat a spick-and-span gentleman of over fifty, with a heavy face and a smiling, easy-going mouth. He held the open letter of Miss Drake, and welcomed Jarman politely. "We are very glad to see any friend of our esteemed client," said Mr. Saon. "And what can I do for you Mr.— Mr.—" He consulted the letter. "Mr. Jarman?"

"I want to know something about Mr. Lancaster?" said Eustace.

The smiling face grew serious. "I don't quite understand," said Mr. Saon, stiffly. "We have no knowledge of the whereabouts of that unfortunate young gentleman. Had he placed himself in our hands we should have done our best at his trial, As it is, we are in darkness."

"I see you are unwilling to speak openly," said Jarman.

Mr. Saon placed the tips of his fat fingers together. "Why," said he, "it's a delicate position—a very delicate position. You come to us armed with a letter from an esteemed client who asks us to tell you all you may ask. But the client in question, Mr. Jarman, happens to be a lady, and ladies—if you will pardon me—rarely have any idea of business."

"I have, however," replied Jarman, drily—although he could not blame the lawyer for his caution—"and when I tell you that I am the most intimate friend Mr. Lancaster has, perhaps you will not object to tell me something about his father."

Mr. Saon sprang from his seat in sheer surprise. "His father!" he repeated. "Dear me? Mr. Jarman, I understood you to inquire about the son—our unfortunate client."

"Oh!"—Eustace passed over the point of the remark—"then you admit that Frank Lancaster is your client?"

"You allude to the son, I presume?"

"Of course. I said Frank."

"The father's name is also Frank," replied Saon. "If you don't mind, we will talk of father and son, as more explicit. May I ask why you make these inquiries?"

"I wish to prove the innocence of the son."

"Oh! Then you believe him to be innocent?"

"Certainly I do. What do you say?"

Mr. Saon coughed delicately. "I say nothing. The facts are not before me. I sincerely hope that the son is innocent. But if he had been well advised he would have placed his case in our hands."

"And then would have been hanged for his pains!" said Eustace, roughly, for he saw that this dignified gentleman was bent solely on making money; and whether Frank had been proved innocent or guilty, would have been equally pleased, provided the bill of costs was discharged. "As a matter of fact, I advised the son to lie low!"

"Ah! Then I understand that you have seen him since his misfortune?"

"I have. I was the first person he came to."

Saon's face showed great interest. "Are you aware that there is a reward offered for his apprehension by a friend of the deceased?"

Eustace nodded grimly. "I know the amount of the reward and the friend also. Do you wish me to earn it?"

"No, no; certainly not! You shock me—you inexpressibly shock me, Mr. Jarman. But if you really know the whereabouts of our unfortunate client, tell him to come to us, and—"

"I'll do nothing of the sort," interrupted Jarman, "the evidence is too strong against him."

"But if he is innocent?"

"Innocent men have been hanged before now, Mr. Saon. No, sir, you let me manage the matter in my own way. When I have in my hands sufficient evidence to save Lancaster—the son, of course—from being hanged out of hand, you will step in."

"Well"—Saon scratched his chin—"I am not prepared to say but what that may not be the wiser course. And you wish to get some information from us to bring about this state of things?"

"I do. You receive a sum of money monthly from 'Frisco."

"From San Francisco," corrected the heavy man. "We do."

"Does Mr. Lancaster the father send it?"

"That I can't tell you. Our agents there are very respectable, as you may guess, and for many years they have sent us this sum monthly. We pay it to Miss Drake—our esteemed client—at the request of that unfortunate young gentleman. But it is understood that the money really goes to him."

"Is Mr. Lancaster the father alive?"

"We cannot say."

"Have you ever asked your respectable San Francisco firm?"

"No, certainly not. There is no need to. We receive the money and we pay it over. That is all that concerns us."

"Do you know anything about the father?"

"Nothing, absolutely nothing. Twenty-three years ago he sent home the son to Miss Drake—our esteemed client—and arranged with our San Francisco agents to pay a monthly sum of twenty pounds for the child's keep. The child is now the unfortunate young man in question, but the money is still paid. I know nothing more."

"Would you mind making inquiries of your agents?"

Saon shook his stupid head. "I don't think it would do, Mr. Jarman; no, I really don't think it would do. So long as the money arrives, we have no right to pry into private business."

"But to save Frank Lancaster?"

"Not even for that. We have our own high position to think of." Jarman could have thrown a book at the head of this dignified ass, who would have let a man die to preserve what he called his position. But it was no use getting angry, lest the man should refuse to say more, therefore Jarman swallowed his temper and continued his questions.

"Do you think the father is still alive?"

Saon did not reply for a moment. Then he looked up. "I said just now that I did not know," he said in a more reasonable tone; "but the fact is I do. Do you think that such information would really be of service to the son?"

"I am sure of it."

"Then I can tell you that Mr. Lancaster, senior, is dead."

"Dead! And when did he die?"

"That I can't say. It was a negro who told us."

"A negro!" Jarman looked astonished, and wondered what was coming.

"You may well look surprised, Mr. Jarman. But a negro came to see us —a grey-haired negro, possessed of great muscular strength although he was but small. He inquired about Mr. Lancaster the son, as he had information to impart to him about the death of Mr. Lancaster the father. He refused to tell us anything beyond what I have said."

"Why didn't you send him to the son?" asked Jarman, testily.

"Because we did not know where the son was to be found."

"Oh! The negro came after the murder of Starth?"

"Yes; a week later. We told him that our unfortunate client had been accused of the crime and had escaped justice. The negro then departed, although we offered to do all we could towards proving the will."

Jarman pricked up his ears. "Is there a will?"

"I suspect there is, Mr. Jarman, and I suspect that the negro is the bearer of it. Had Mr. Lancaster the father made his will in San Francisco he would have executed it in the office of our esteemed agents. As it is, we have not heard from them. But, strange to say," added Saon, "the twenty pounds has been paid this month as usual. I really don't know what to make of it."

"Nor I. I suppose there must be a will?"

"I think so, since the late Mr. Lancaster is dead and was a man of means. If you can find this negro—"

"What is his name?" interrupted Eustace.

"We cannot tell you that. He refused to inform us. In fact," added Mr. Saon, drawing himself up, "for an African he was impertinent."

"Why didn't you kick him?" said Eustace, rising. "H'm! Is this all you can tell me?"

"All. And if you will let us know where Mr. Lancaster the son is to be found, we shall have much pleasure in proving the will."

"The will has to be found first, and the negro," said Eustace, coolly; "and also Frank Lancaster has to get his neck out of the noose before he can let himself be arrested."

"Quite so. I admire your caution, Mr. Jarman. Still, if Mr. Lancaster the son will only place himself in our hands—"

Jarman's patience with this old ass was exhausted. "He would be hanged within the month. Good-day." And he hurried away, leaving Saon a frozen statue of indignation.

But he was not so indignant as Eustace returning to his hotel. "Silly fools!" he said, wrathfully, to himself. "They'd juggle with a man's life just to get their costs. Frank sha'n't show up, to be slaughtered by them, if I can help it. That negro! H'm! And Balkis is a negress. I wonder if the man was a spy of Berry's trying to find out the whereabouts of Frank? I must think this over. Upon my word!" lamented Eustace, hailing a hansom, "the more I go into this case the more mysterious it seems. Well, there's one comfort, the sealed letter may give us a clue to the mystery. I'll go down by the six train, and may know all about it before retiring to rest."

At his hotel he alighted and went in. Then he suddenly recollected that he had not sent a wire to Frank. To be on the safe side, although he was sending it to O'Neil, he went to the telegraph-office himself. On his way hither he, knowing the neighbourhood well, took a short cut through some by-streets. As he was turning a corner he heard a fresh young voice singing some song, the burden of which was "Tamaroo! Tamaroo!" Hardly believing his ears, Eustace dashed round the corner to hear who was repeating the last word which poor murdered Anchor had uttered. He came nearly on top of a ragged urchin, a true guttersnipe, who was dancing gaily in the gutter to the music of his own minstrelsy:

> *"Oh, he gits a 'eavy screw,*
>   *Tamaroo! Tamaroo!*
> *An' 'is father is a Jew,*
>   *Tamaroo! Tamaroo!"*

"Where did you hear that song?" interrupted Eustace, seizing the boy.

"Garn away with y'. It's m'own words an' music. 'Ow Tamaroo!'"

"Where did you hear the word?"

"That's my business. Tie it up, cocky," said the brat.

"See here, my lad, you tell me where you got the word Tamaroo and I'll give you a shilling."

"Wot! A whole bob? Right y'are, gov'ner. 'Twas 'Melia told it me. 'Melia kin read an' she got it orf a wall a hour ago. It 'ull be all over Londing soon. 'Ow Tamaroo! Tamaroo!' Ain't it a prime word?"

"Show me where Amelia got it?" Eustace saw that the melody of the word had caught the boy's ear, but he could not understand what he meant.

The boy conducted him down one street and up another, till he brought him up against a huge hoarding before some houses in the course of erection. There appeared the huge placard of a Scarlet Bat with outspread wings, as on Frank's arm. Beneath, was printed in gigantic red letters the mysterious word "Tamaroo!"

CHAPTER XV

A STRANGE DISAPPEARANCE

Jarman returned fuming to Wargrove. He was a clear-headed man, who liked to foresee what was coming, so that he might arrange his plans. But at the present moment he could not see an inch before his nose, and rather lost his temper in consequence. The unexpected appearance of the Scarlet Bat, and of the mysterious word "Tamaroo" on London hoardings perplexed him extremely. At first he thought that this might be a new move on the part of the astute Berry, but on consideration dismissed this idea.

"Berry is not anxious for publicity," argued Eustace, when in the train, "as it would attract attention to his underhand schemes to get this money. Again, I don't believe Denham knows anything, not even the meaning of the tattooing on his left arm. He would want to be told why the Bat appeared on posters, if it was Berry's work, and the Captain might not be disposed to furnish an explanation. No, there is some other person taking a hand in this game, and with that person I must come into contact. If the person is an enemy of Berry's we may work together to thwart him. On the other hand, the person who has plastered London with these posters may want the fortune himself, in which case he will be equally an enemy to Frank. He may want him hanged also. But it may be a woman," conjectured. Jarman. "That Balkis seems to be mixed up in the matter, not to mention the negro who called on the lawyers. H'm! I wonder what the barbaric element is doing in this galley?"

He turned and twisted and argued the matter in every way, but by the time he arrived at Wargrove he was as much in the dark as ever. His only chance of making any discovery likely to elucidate the mystery lay in the contents of the sealed letter. Anxious to see Frank and to tell him all his adventures, Jarman walked rapidly to the Shanty. When he reached it, he was surprised to find that it was shut up. Windows and doors were barred, and, not having a key, Eustace could not obtain entrance into his own home. There was no sign of Miss Cork or of his friend.

"What does this mean?" Jarman asked himself. "Can Frank have been arrested? But in that case Miss Cork would still be here."

The situation was puzzling, so Jarman set to work to learn details and make discoveries. He sought out an old gardener who lived in a cottage adjacent to his own house. This ancient, Bowles by name, was a bent, wheezy old creature, very garrulous. Jarman could not have hit upon a better man for information, as Jacob Bowles had the key of the Shanty.

"That dark gentleman, he guv it to me," said Bowles, surrendering the key to its owner. "T'other day he guv it to me—you might call it the day afore yesterday—yes, you might, Muster Jarman. The dark gent, he guv it me sayin' as you'd be back, Muster Jarman, and would be wishful to get into your house like."

"Did he leave any message?" asked Eustace, still perplexed. Bowles scratched his head. "I can't say rightly as he did, Muster Jarman."

"Do you know what has become of Miss Cork?"

"No, Muster Jarman, I can't rightly say as I do. But my missus, she did say as Mrs. Baker saw Miss Cork gitting to the station three days back. Aye, Muster Jarman, you might say three days."

Eustace remembered that this was the day of his departure, and questioned the female Bowles. But she simply repeated the information given by her husband, adding that Miss Cork had been seen by the ubiquitous Mrs. Baker walking rapidly towards Mardon railway station. "Across the Common, as you might say," said Mrs. Bowles, cautiously.

Considerably perplexed Eustace returned to his deserted house. It was plausible to think that Frank might have taken fright and have fled. But the disappearance of Miss Cork was remarkable. So far as Jarman knew, she had always expressed herself pleased with the situation, and certainly never stated that she was going. He hurried into the house, hoping to find some message from Frank. In this he was not disappointed, for on the writing-table lay a letter addressed to Jarman. The big man wrinkled his brows, and opening it read it at once in the waning light:

DEAR EUSTACE,

I have to go. Darrel, who is stopping at the Rectory, recognised me, and for reasons which need not here be set forth it is probable he may denounce me. I think it best to go away, but will let you know as soon as I can what I am doing. I left a photograph of Balkis lying about, and after seeing it Miss Cork ran away. I believe she knows something about the negress and is in league with the gang we know of.

Having digested this letter, Jarman sat down to think over the matter. He had always been afraid lest Darrel should recognise Frank, and wondered that his friend had not the sense to keep out of the way of so dangerous an acquaintance. But he could not conjecture any reason for Darrel's denunciation of the unhappy man. However, as Darrel was staying at the Rectory, Jarman decided to go over on the morrow and hear what he had to say. But as regards Miss Cork?

"H'm!" thought Jarman, while getting a scratch meal together. "I wonder if there is any truth in Frank's belief? She certainly seemed startled when she heard the name of Balkis, and pitched that yarn about her child being called so. I don't believe she has a child of that name—or, indeed, a child at all. However, she seems to have taken fright on seeing the photograph. I wonder where Frank got it? Ah! I remember. Starth had a photograph, and probably it was passed on to Mildred. Frank could get it from her. But why should Miss Cork run away, and where has she gone?"

He could not answer this question without further information, and only Frank could give details. But Frank was gone also, and Jarman wondered whither the poor persecuted young fellow had fled. He did not dare to make inquiries, lest he should attract the attention of the police. The only thing to be done was to remain passive until such time as Frank chose to write from his new place of concealment. Then he might see him and learn details about the inexplicable flight of his housekeeper. Meantime, it would be just as well to see Mildred and learn if his surmise about the photograph was true. After a hurried meal, Jarman walked to Rose Cottage.

The maid who answered the door was a fat, red-faced creature and was the only domestic employed by the two ladies. She stated that Miss Starth was lying down with a bad headache—had retired early to bed, in fact—but that Mrs. Perth was still in the parlour. Jarman would have walked in, but Mrs. Perth herself appeared, and seemed indisposed to admit him. Jarman put down this unwillingness to her prim manners, as nine o'clock at night was certainly not the time to pay a visit to two single ladies. But on seeing her face in the moonlight, he noticed that she looked disturbed. However, she appeared friendly enough—why should she not be?—although declining to let him in. When the maid retired he had a few minutes' conversation with her on the doorstep.

"No," said Mrs. Perth in her decisive tones, "I have not seen Mr. O'Neil lately. He called once after your departure, Mr. Jarman, but since then has not favoured us with a visit."

"Do you know that he has gone away?" asked Eustace.

"Gone away?" replied Mrs. Perth. "What do you mean?"

"What I say," said Jarman, rather chafed. "He has gone away, and I thought that you might know where he is?"

Mrs. Perth drew herself up in a prim manner.

"Why should I know, Mr. Jarman?" she said stiffly. "Your friend's movements have no interest for me. It seems to me that you should know best where he is. I presume he gave you notice, being your secretary?"

"He left a letter saying he was going. I never expected him to leave so suddenly."

"There appears to be a mystery about him."

"Oh, not at all," rejoined the big man, quickly, "but he is an odd fellow, and doubtless left in a freakish way. I only came to ask, as I thought he might have called before going."

"He called only the once, when Mr. Darrel was here. He and Mr. Darrel went away together."

"Have you seen Mr. Darrel since?"

"Oh dear me, yes. He is stopping with Mr. Arrow."

"Does he know that my friend has left?"

"I really do not know," replied Mrs. Perth, with a fatigued air. "He made no remark."

"Ah! Thank you. I shall not keep you any longer. I suppose," added Eustace, with some hesitation. "I suppose it is impossible for me to see Miss Starth?"

"Certainly it is impossible. She has retired to bed. You can call tomorrow. Good evening."

Thus dismissed, there was nothing for it but for Eustace to return to his house. In spite of Mrs. Perth's calmness he saw that she was worried, and had something on her mind. He wondered if she really knew anything of Frank. But that was impossible, unless Darrel had told Mildred that Lancaster, *alias* O'Neil, was the murderer of her brother. That would account for Mrs. Perth's stiffness, as she would not be too well disposed towards Jarman for having introduced a criminal—and such a criminal!—to her and Mildred. However, nothing could be learnt until he saw Darrel on the morrow. "And if he *has* told," said Eustace, over a final pipe, "why, Mildred will be angry with me."

That night Jarman got little sleep. It annoyed him that Frank should be absent at so critical a moment. He wanted the young man to open the sealed letter, and had half a mind to open it himself. But on consideration he did not think he was justified in taking such a course. If Darrel had told Mildred, Eustace determined to explain the whole of his connection with the matter, and to assure her again of his firm belief in Frank's innocence. As soon as Lancaster revealed his new hiding-place he would take him the sealed letter, and from its contents might be gathered some clue to all these mysteries. They seemed to increase every day, and to grow darker the more he endeavoured to throw light on them.

The next morning Eustace, having had a bad night, slept well into the middle of the day. Then he had a cold bath, and having cooked his own breakfast sat down to it, somewhere about twelve o'clock. He was still worried but ate well, as he knew he had a hard day before him. But just as he was pouring out his second cup of coffee, he became aware that someone was looking at him through the window. To his surprise he saw the arch and piquant face of Fairy Fan. With a sudden start he rose and went to the door. There she was in the most dainty of costumes, looking amused at his astonishment.

"You asked me to come, so I have come," she said, stepping into the house without being asked. "I hope you don't mind my taking you by surprise in this way?"

"Oh, not at all," said Eustace, mechanically, and led the way to his sitting-room, wondering what ill wind had blown her hither. "But I wish you had given me notice of your coming."

Miss Berry—as she chose to be called—plumped into a seat, and cast an eye over the untidy table. "You didn't want to be found at breakfast so late," she said smiling. "I thought you were an early riser."

"I had a bad night," said Eustace, shortly.

Fan selected a cigarette from a box near at hand, and lighted it. "I don't wonder at that," she said through a cloud of blue smoke. "If you will shelter criminals, what can you expect?"

Jarman started uneasily. "What do you mean?" he demanded frowning.

"Why," said she, waving a daintily gloved hand, "it seems that Frank Lancaster's been with you. What a cunning fellow you are, Eustace. I guess you gave Uncle Banjo and me the outside running."

"I don't know why you want the inside."

"No. And nobody else does," she replied, smartly.

"Not even Balkis?" hinted Jarman, and could have bitten out his tongue for making a remark so calculated to place her on her guard.

As it was, she coloured and looked keenly at him. "I guess you know more about the matter than you'll give away."

"Perhaps I do," he replied, determined not to let her know the extent of his knowledge. "But if you came here to see Lancaster, he's gone."

"That's a lie," said Miss Berry, coolly.

"Search the house then," retorted Eustace, serenely, meeting her with her own weapons. "I give you full permission."

She looked at him again. "No," she said, after a close scrutiny. "I guess I believe you."

"I am flattered."

"Not a bit. You feel angry. Where is Frank?"

"I don't know."

"Oh, yes, you do," she rejoined persuasively; "and see here, there's five hundred pounds to be earned."

"So I believe," said Eustace, coolly, "and your uncle is playing the part of a philanthropist."

"You can put it that way if you like, Eustace. Come, tell me where the boy is. I wish him well."

"I doubt it, seeing that your relative offers this reward for his capture. However, I can reply with an honest heart that I don't know where he is."

Fairy Fan threw away her cigarette with an important air. "I wish you did," said she, "I want to save him from being lynched."

"Why do you wish to save him after bringing him into this state."

"I didn't," she said fiercely. "Yes, you did. For some reason best known to yourself you induced Starth and Lancaster to quarrel. Having been successful up to the point of putting a rope round Frank's neck, you come to me to ask if I will help you to adjust it."

The woman clasped and unclasped her hands nervously, and rose to pace the room. "Believe me, I come to save him," she said earnestly. "He's in great danger, and I alone can help him."

"Ah! Then you know who killed Starth."

"I don't—I don't! I swear I don't!" she cried vehemently. "So far as I know it was Frank. My uncle believes in his guilt also."

"I know. It is to his interest to believe," snapped Jarman. "How much money is involved in this business, Miss Berry?"

She turned pale, and looked down. "There is no money," she said.

"Oh, yes. We'll say about a million. Your uncle doesn't offer this reward for nothing. It's a small sprat to catch a large mackerel."

Fan threw herself down and burst into tears. "I wish I were dead!"

"Or you wish Frank were dead. Which?" asked Jarman, mercilessly.

"No, I don't. Oh! Do tell me where he is. I can save him."

"From being hanged?"

"I—I—think so. Where is he?" She stamped her foot imperiously.

Eustace smiled as he saw she was trying all her arts to make him reveal what he was determined to conceal. "I tell you I don't know," he said quietly. "Now that you have learnt that I sheltered the man, I don't mind admitting that he was here. But he has gone away, and has left no address."

"What frightened him away from this hiding-place?"

"You had better ask Darrel, who told you where to find him."

"Darrel?" Fan seemed genuinely surprised. "He never told me."

"Then who did?" asked Eustace, bluntly. Fan thought for a moment, then looked up with a winning smile. "I'll tell you that if you'll answer me a question."

"What is the question?"

"Why have you placarded London from end to end with those posters?"

CHAPTER XVI

WHAT MILDRED KNEW

Eustace looked at her much surprised. "If you don't know of those things, I don't," he said.

"Do you mean to say you didn't get them out?"

"Certainly. I saw one and was very much surprised."

"Do you know what the Scarlet Bat means?" she asked.

"Perhaps I do," he said, enigmatically.

"And the name Tamaroo?"

"Oh, it's a name, is it!" said Jarman. "Thank you for the information, Mrs. Anchor."

"Don't call me by that name," said Fan, frowning.

"Why not? You were married to the man, and the name Tamaroo was the last word he said to me."

The woman changed colour. "What did he mean?" she asked softly.

"You can explain that best," answered Eustace. "See here, Mrs. Anchor, or Miss Berry, or whatever you choose to call yourself, I want to know what your game is."

"There is no game," she insisted.

"Yes there is, else you would not have put Starth and Lancaster against one another, nor would you come down to see me and ask questions. There's some scheme in your mind, and in the mind of your so-called uncle —"

"He *is* my uncle!" she flashed out, tapping her foot.

"Bah! Do you think I believe that? Accomplice, if you like."

Fan started to her feet like a small fury. "You dare to insult me, do you?" she said. "Better take care, you low-down cad!"

"Ah!" said Eustace, calmly, "now the mask is being dropped."

With an effort she controlled herself, seeing she had gone too far.

"It's enough to make a woman angry," she said panting, "to be talked to in that way. I am perfectly honest."

"I never called your honesty into question."

108

"Yes, you did, and I'll never forgive you for having done so. I know you are my enemy now. I thought you were a fool."

"So I was in San Francisco, but I have learnt sense since. And I am your enemy, Mrs. Anchor, and the enemy of that man Berry."

"You'd better not threaten him."

"Indeed! Do you think I am afraid of him?" sneered Eustace. "I also have been in the Wild West, and I can handle my weapon as neatly as Berry did—when he shot Starth."

"It's a lie—it's a lie! He did not."

"Don't lose your temper; you'll gain nothing by it. I am on the side of Frank Lancaster, and I intend to prove his innocence."

"You can't," said Mrs. Anchor, with a pale face. "He is guilty."

"It's your scheme to make him appear so," retorted Jarman; "but I know better, and so do you. Who told you he was here?"

"That's my business," she said doggedly.

"And a very shady business it is. Do you wish to murder Frank as you murdered your husband?"

With a spasm of fury Fan snatched up a knife and flung it at him. It flew over his head. "Don't do that again," said he, "or I'll forget that you are a woman."

"The woman you loved," she said again, weeping.

Eustace grew tired of thus running in a circle.

"Don't you think you'd better try something new, Mrs. Anchor? We have had cajoling, tears, violence, temper—I'm growing weary!"

"I also," said Fan, drying her tears, and speaking in a much more business-like manner. "It's not worth while losing one's temper."

"Not with me, I assure you."

"You're a brute!" she said violently.

"Possibly. Did you come to tell me that?"

"I came to see Frank, not you. But as he is not here—and I don't think you are clever enough to deceive me—please send him my message."

"I don't know where he is, Mrs. Anchor." Jarman used the name because he could see that it annoyed her. "But the message?"

"Tell him that if he will promise to marry me I will save his neck. But I must have the promise in writing."

"I'll convey the message if I can," said Eustace, without making any comment, "on one condition."

"What is that?" asked Mrs. Anchor, turning from the mirror, before which she was adjusting her veil.

"You must write a letter to Miss Starth, deploring the death of her brother, and stating that you loved him so much that you wished to marry him."

Fan grew crimson, and her eyes sparkled. "I shall not write such a tissue of lies," she said with a stamp.

Jarman laughed, but not pleasantly. "You have become wonderfully scrupulous all of a sudden," he sneered. "But you intended to marry either Starth or Denham."

"Denham!" she said contemptuously. "I wouldn't marry him if he asked me. Why do you want me to write such a letter?"

"For your own sake," responded the big man, coolly. "Miss Starth believes that you are concerned in the death of her brother. Such a letter will convince her that you were well disposed towards him."

"Bah! She won't believe it."

"She may, or she may not. However, I want it written."

Mrs. Anchor sat down, and leaning her cheek on her hand stared musingly at the floor. After a few minutes she looked up. "You're on some game or another," she said calmly, "and for some reason you wish me to join in. Well, I don't mind. The letter shall be sent."

"Oh and don't you want to know what the game is?"

"Not at all. Whatever you are doing can't concern me. This letter will do no harm, and as I wish the message taken to Frank I am willing to buy it on those terms."

Jarman looked at her distrustfully. He wondered why she yielded so suddenly, and knowing her tricky ways, he felt sure that she had some card to play. However, for reasons of his own, he wanted the letter, and, so long as he got it, was not particular how it came into his possession. It was useless to act honourably towards a pair of sharpers like Fan and her so-called uncle. Having thus arranged matters, the little woman held out her hand.

"I have a carriage waiting to take me to Mardon," she said. "We understand one another, I hope?"

"I think we do. But I am in the dark regarding your schemes."

"I can say the same thing about this letter. I don't know why you want it written."

"Tell me who told you of Lancaster's whereabouts, and I'll explain."

"No, thanks," she rejoined, with a shrug. "Writing such a letter won't hurt me in any way, and telling you too much, might."

"As you please. Let me see you to the carriage."

She accepted his offer, and together they walked across the fields to where a fly from Mardon was waiting. Mrs. Anchor hopped into this as lightly as a bird, and again held out her hand. "Goodbye," she smiled. "You won't forget to deliver my message?"

"I will if I can, on condition—"

"Yes, I know the condition. The letter shall be sent to Miss Starth."

When the fly drove away, Eustace stood in a brown study for a few minutes. He wondered why Mrs. Anchor had so readily accepted his assurance that Frank was not in the house. Certainly he was not, but Jarman fancied that so suspicious a woman would have made sure. Yet she did not even avail herself of his offer to let her inspect the house. "I wonder what stake those two are playing for?" mused Jarman, walking down the road. "It's that million, I suppose."

But he could not be sure until he gained more explicit information. Jarman had conceived a plot, with which the letter to Mildred was concerned. By it he hoped to learn the secrets of Berry, who certainly appeared to be the head of the whole business. As to the Scarlet Bat, the opening of the sealed letter might reveal what that meant. But the letter could only be opened by Frank, and Frank was nowhere to be found. Jarman decided to tell Mildred the whole story, and then to consult her about opening the letter in Frank's absence. It seemed foolish to wait, and to leave the man in such peril. And he was in the greatest peril, now that Fan knew he had been hiding at Wargrove. Eustace felt thankful that for obvious reasons she could not take the police into her councils, else he might have got into trouble for compounding a felony.

While thus thinking a man had approached him softly, and Jarman was startled by a touch on his shoulder. He wheeled round sharply to behold Darrel. The man looked sulky as usual, and purred like a cat when he addressed Jarman.

"So your friend Lancaster has gone away?" he said quietly.

"Yes," replied Eustace, thinking it best to save time by admitting so obvious a fact; "you frightened him away."

"Ah! Then he left a letter behind him?"

"He did, Mr. Darrel, in which he stated that you knew him, and that you threatened to denounce him."

"Only if he interfered between me and Mildred," said Darrel.

Jarman flushed, and his face grew angry. "What do you mean by speaking of Miss Starth in so familiar a fashion?"

"I speak as I like, and being in love with Miss Starth—since you want me to be punctilious—I call her by the name I like best."

Jarman could have struck him to the earth, as he stood there like the Man-mountain of Gulliver. There was something insolent about Darrel which inspired the meekest of men to kick him, and Eustace was by no means a Moses. For the moment Eustace was inclined to take him up on the question of loving Mildred, but remembering that he was not officially engaged to the girl, and that should he not discover the assassin of her brother he might never be her husband, he thought it best to pass over the matter. However, he remarked on the conjunction of the girl's name with Frank's. "Lancaster was not likely to interfere between you," he said.

"Oh, yes, he was," said Darrel, in his slow, heavy voice. "Lancaster is in love with her."

Jarman felt a jealous pang. "Impossible!"

"Not a bit of it. Lancaster saw her that night in the theatre, and even then admired her more than I liked. Down here I saw them together, and he loves her. I'm in love myself, and I know. And I'm not certain," added Darrel, viciously, "that she doesn't love him."

"I tell you she can't," cried Jarman, agitated.

"Oh! Then she knows Lancaster killed her brother?"

"She knows nothing. I only speak from my knowledge of her character. She would not love a man she knew so little of as Lancaster."

"According to you, she did not know him by that name. But she is just the kind of romantic girl to fall in love with that Irish secretary of yours. He made up well for the part," sneered Darrel.

Jarman straightened his shoulders. "I don't think it is good taste to discuss Miss Starth," he said, "but I can safely assure you that she does not love the man."

"You seem very sure." Darrel scanned Eustace in his usual insolent way. "I believe you are in love yourself," he said with a short laugh. "Well, I give you the same warning as I gave Lancaster."

"I'm not disposed to take any warning," rejoined Jarman, hotly, "and if you denounce Lancaster as having been here I shall deny it."

"Oh, now that he has cut, there's no necessity for me to say a word. But don't you interfere."

"See here, Darrel," said Jarman, controlling his temper with an effort, "no man shall speak to me like this. I forbid you to mention Miss Starth's name to me again. She will choose for herself."

"I know she will. She will choose me," said Darrel, complacently.

"There's always two to a bargain," said Eustace, drily. "However, as Lancaster has gone, there was no need for you to tell Miss Berry."

Darrel looked up in genuine surprise. "I did not tell Miss Berry."

"She was down here an hour ago, and stated—"

"That I had told her? She's a liar!"

"She did not say that you had told her. But she knew that Lancaster had been here. And you were the only person who spotted him."

"What fools the others must be," said the genial Darrel. "However, that's neither here nor there. I assure you, on my honour, that I kept Lancaster's secret. He may, or he may not, have killed Starth, but so long as he leaves Miss Starth alone he is in no danger from me. I hope you will understand that."

"I understand," said Jarman, coldly. "And now we will part."

"On an understanding, however," said Darrel, striding after Eustace —"that you don't interfere with my affairs. If you do, I'll—" He stopped, and looking at Eustace with an evil face walked on. "You are warned!" he said over his shoulder.

For a moment Eustace was inclined to follow, and dash his insolent words down his throat. But such an act might have jeopardised the safety of Frank. Jarman, therefore, was compelled to swallow his anger, and greatly he disliked doing so, but under the circumstances he could do nothing else.

All that day he wondered what amount of truth there was in the assertion of Darrel that Frank was in love with Mildred. Eustace could not bring himself to believe that Frank would act basely towards him, and make love during his absence. "He knows that I adore Mildred," soliloquised Eustace as he paced his rough lawn, "and to try to get her to himself would be a base thing to do. I have helped him. He certainly would not betray me. I swear by Frank."

Nevertheless, in spite of these brave words, he caught himself frowning at the thought, and finally made up his mind to see Mildred and learn the worst. He was aware that she liked him, but that into their bargain no love had entered. If she really loved Frank, and the young man had acted honourably, why then— "But it's impossible—impossible!" groaned Jarman, clenching his hand. "He would not treat me in such a way."

Troubled in this fashion he presented himself at Rose Cottage, looking unlike his usual self. Mildred was in the garden watching the sunset and was walking towards the summerhouse when she heard him call her name. Turning with a cry of alarm, she came swiftly towards him, holding out both hands.

"Eustace, I'm so glad you have come! I was sorry that I could not see you last night. Why did you not come earlier?"

"I was busy," he said, evasively, and looked into her eyes. "Mildred, why were you alarmed when I called you?"

She faltered. "I thought it might be Darrel," she said faintly. "But he would not call you by your Christian name?"

Mildred blazed up. "I'd like to see him dare!" she said. "But he has insolence enough for anything. He persecutes me!"

"Oh, does he!" cried Jarman, angrily. "Then I'll made short work of him. You see if I don't. I'll—"

"Do nothing—do nothing!" she panted, catching his hands. "He is a dangerous man. He knows too much."

"About what I don't understand." She turned red, and her hands dropped. "Mr. O'Neil," she said, in a low voice, then covered her face.

"He has gone away. I don't know where he is," said Jarman, "but—"

"No, no! Say nothing." She dried her tears and drew him into a sheltered part of the lawn. "He is here," she whispered. "I have concealed him, and he has told me his story."

Jarman looked at her, astonished. "You know then that he is Lancaster?"

She nodded with a smile.

CHAPTER XVII

THE SEALED LETTER

Jarman was so astonished at Mildred's communication that he dropped into a garden-seat which was fortunately close at hand. It was wonderful enough to hear that Lancaster was concealed in Rose Cottage, but still more wonderful to hear that she knew who he was. Eustace would have thought it unlikely that she would have anything to do with the man suspected of being her brother's murderer. Yet she admitted the fact boldly, and actually smiled. He recalled the remarks of Darrel, and wondered if there was an understanding between her and Lancaster.

"How long have you known his real name?" he asked sternly.

"Since you went away," replied Mildred, sitting beside him. "Don't be angry, Eustace. I agree with you that he is innocent, and when he came to me for shelter, what could I do? Even if he were guilty I could not give him up." And she shuddered.

"Does Mrs. Perth know?"

"Yes. I had to tell her. But we have kept it secret from Jane."

Eustace nodded. "It's just as well. The girl might babble. How was it Lancaster dared to come here?"

"He did not know what to do, or how to escape. You see, Mr. Darrel—"

Jarman interrupted. "I know Darrel recognised him. He told me so today. And he said other things, for which I felt inclined to knock him down. And I should have done so, but that, as you say, he is too well aware of the existing state of things."

"What did he say?" asked Mildred, an angry light in her eyes.

"There is no need to repeat his insolence."

"There certainly is not, for I know quite well what he said. He is determined to make me his wife, and—"

"And he coupled your name with that of Lancaster."

"Oh, he is jealous of everyone," said Mildred, tossing her head. "You don't believe that, I hope?"

"Believe what?" asked Eustace, wishing for details.

115

But like a woman, having brought the matter to a point, she changed the subject hurriedly.

"Nothing, nothing!" she declared, hurriedly. "I am engaged to you, Eustace, if you find out who killed Walter."

"So I understand," he replied sadly. "But there is no love on your side, my dear."

"I told you plainly what I thought."

"You did, and I should not have taken advantage of your position. I think we had better—"

"Stop!" she interrupted, and in the moonlight he could see her bosom heave. "You had better not say too much. Let us leave the subject alone until we get out of these troubles."

Eustace was quite willing to do this. He could scarcely tax her with being in love with Frank on the evidence of Darrel. But he was resolved to question Lancaster at the first opportunity. Meantime, seeing that Mildred was disposed to grow angry, he thought it best to leave the matter alone.

"Where is he?" was his question.

Mildred looked round as though she thought the birds of the air might overhear.

"He is in the summerhouse," she said. "There is a small room at the back, which I fitted up as a kind of studio for painting."

"But is that safe, Mildred?"

"Quite safe. No one ever goes there but me. The summerhouse, as you can see, is quite buried amongst the trees, and I have hung some Eastern stuffs round the walls to conceal the door into the studio. Besides," she added, with a little hesitation, "no one would ever think of looking for him in my house."

"No. That is all right," assented Jarman; "but why did he come?"

"For the very reason I have stated. He was afraid lest Mr. Darrel should send a message to the police, so he gave the key of your house to old Bowles, and came in the afternoon—"

"As Desmond O'Neil?"

"Certainly. Then he told me his story. At first I was horrified, but, remembering how you believed in his innocence, I decided to help him. As the secretary, he then went for a long walk, and came back at night. I had the studio ready for him, and he has been in it ever since."

"Let me see him," said Jarman, rising.

"One moment," said Mildred, catching his hand; "you will find him different to what you expect. His disguise has been taken off."

"Were you surprised at the change?"

"No." She blushed. "The fact is, Eustace, I saw him in the theatre on that night, so I knew him again when he became himself."

116

Jarman felt a jealous pang. He began to think that Mildred loved the boy, seeing how she blushed when she spoke of him. Also her voice faltered, and she seemed embarrassed. At first Eustace almost felt inclined to speak out, and demand if she loved Lancaster; but remembering the position of the young man, and being afraid of the wrath of Mildred, he held his tongue. In silence they moved across the lawn and entered the summer-house. It was luminous with moonlight, and Eustace saw a faint sparkle of gold, the threads of the Eastern stuffs which draped the walls. Mildred gave a little cough, and repeated it twice. "The signal!" she whispered with her finger on her lips; and in spite of the gravity of the position she seemed quite to enjoy its mystery. In many ways Mildred Starth was still a school-girl.

From the other side of the wall came a cough, and this also was repeated twice. Mildred drew aside the drapery and revealed a door.

"I'll leave you now," she murmured. "You can talk to him alone. Come in and see me afterwards," and before Eustace could say a word she was gone. He saw her flit across the lawn in the moonlight, then knocked softly at the door. A key was turned, the door opened, and Frank looked out.

"Who is it?" he whispered.

"Your friend Jarman," said that gentleman, and stepped inside.

It was perfectly dark, save where a slender moonbeam stole in through the high window. Frank gave a gasp of relief, and gripped Eustace's hand in the gloom. They exchanged a hearty handshake, and then Frank pushed forward a chair. As he had been long in the darkness, he was better able to see than Jarman.

"I'm so glad you have come," said Frank, drawing another chair close to that of his friend, so that he could converse in a whisper. "I have been longing for you. You got my letter?"

"Yes. And I am much astonished to find you here."

"I thought it was the best thing I could do," said Lancaster. "After you left, Darrel—"

"I know all about it. But why did he threaten you?"

"Oh!—" Frank hesitated. He could not tell Jarman the reason, and hardly knew what to say. But Jarman brought things to a point.

"Lancaster," he said, seizing the young man's hand, "I have been a good friend to you. Have you—are you—I mean, do you treat me as a man of honour should treat another?"

"Yes. I swear I have said nothing."

"Ah! You know what I speak of?"

"I do. I can hardly make a mistake when you speak to me in such a tone. Eustace, don't think so basely of me."

"Do you love Mildred?" asked Jarman, sternly.

There was a moment's silence. "Heaven help me, I do!"

"And you have—"

"No, no!" Frank's voice broke out quickly and earnestly. "I have not said a word to her. I have not even shown that I take any interest in her. I knew she was engaged to you, and that sealed my lips. I would not have come here, but that I was driven into a corner. Darrel knew me under my disguise. I fancied he might put the police on my track. If I had gone to London, or anywhere in the country as O'Neil, the police would have caught me from the description Darrel could give. And if I took off my disguise, the description in the papers would enable them to recognise me. Eustace, I swear that if a poor hunted wretch like myself had had any corner to hide in I should not have come here. But you trust me—say you trust me?"

"Yes, I do trust you," said Jarman, a little sadly. "I know you have been driven to take up this position. But we will talk no more of the matter. When you are free from trouble then we can talk. But tell me, how did Mildred receive you?"

"She was horrified at first, but afterwards, when I confessed all, she believed me to be innocent. She told Mrs. Perth, who also thinks I am guiltless. I am safe here. Even Darrel can't find me in this place. But if you like, Eustace, I can disguise myself in another way and go abroad. I don't want to remain here longer than I can help."

"You must remain here," said Jarman, decisively. "If you try to escape you may be captured. Fan knows of your disguise."

"And Berry?" asked Frank, in alarm.

"I can't say that. Fan was down today, but she did not tell me if she had revealed anything to Berry."

"Who told her? But I needn't ask. It was Darrel."

"You are wrong. Both Darrel and Fairy Fan deny that."

"Then who could have told?"

"I can't say. But Fan came down to see you."

"To have me arrested, I suppose?" said Frank, bitterly.

"On the contrary, she wished to make you a proposal of marriage." Frank sat still for a moment, then, in spite of his troubles, laughed softly.

"You or she must be crazy, Eustace."

"Then it is she. Her message, which I promised to deliver on conditions, was that if you would marry her she would save you."

"Then if you see her again you can refuse her offer. I should not think of marrying her. I have got over my infatuation there."

"And have placed your heart elsewhere?" said Jarman, quietly.

"We agreed not to speak of that," said Lancaster, stiffly. "I am an honourable man, and in my position—oh! It's ridiculous. Don't hit a man

118

when he is down, Eustace."

"I'm not so ungenerous, I hope."

"You are the best of good fellows," said Frank, impetuously, "but my nerves are worn rather thin with all this worry. What are the conditions on which you delivered the message?"

"I'll tell you later. I have a scheme in my head to counterplot Fan and the man she calls her uncle."

"Don't you believe that he is her uncle?" asked Frank.

"No," replied Eustace, decidedly, "I don't. She met him in San Francisco, and he became her accomplice to get Anchor out of the way. I am sure that Berry—or, as he was then—Sakers, fired the shot that killed the man. But in some way the two were done out of this fortune connected with Denham and with you. They brought the boy to England to plot against you, and then intended when you were put out of the way to get the money from Natty. That poor lad doesn't know it, but I believe his life is not safe."

"You don't think they would murder him?"

"They murdered Starth. Oh, yes, I am certain on that point. If Berry didn't fire the shot himself, he got someone else to do it. But the object was to throw the blame on you, so that you might be hanged. I can't think why it should be necessary. However, we may find out from the sealed letter."

"Ah!" Frank started, and spoke in a rather agitated tone. "I forgot that in my troubles. Have you got it?"

"Yes, it's in my pocket. I'll show it to you immediately. Have you a candle here?"

"Yes. But I am afraid to use it. The light might be seen from the road."

"And if Mrs. Baker saw it she would certainly make inquiries. We'll wait for a bit. I'll show you the letter before I go, and then I must talk to Mildred and Mrs. Perth. But about Berry. I wonder if anyone knows details of his past life?"

"Darrel does," said Lancaster, promptly. "He saw him in Los Angeles."

"H'm! I wonder if he would tell me anything? He was most insolent to me today, but in your interests I don't mind putting up with that if there's anything to be learnt."

Jarman paused for a moment, and then went on: "Frank, do you think there is negro blood in Darrel?"

"It's curious you should say that, Jarman. Jenny Arrow saw that portrait of Balkis, and she thought it resembled Darrel."

"I haven't seen that portrait. Miss Cork took it away, you said."

"Yes." And Frank described how he had obtained the photograph from Mildred, and for what purpose. "I'm sure Miss Cork knows Balkis."

119

"She might—she might," mused Jarman "Well, I'll soon know her also, for I am going to look her up at the Docks."

"For what purpose?"

"Can't you guess? That woman is mixed up in this thing. Her photograph was in Starth's possession, and Berry visits her. Now you tell me that there is a resemblance between her and Darrel. I shouldn't be at all surprised to find that this negress is some relative."

"Oh, but that's absurd, Eustace. Darrel comes from Africa." Jarman laughed. "He went out there in the first instance. He talked of being in Los Angeles. That is in Mexico, and Mexico is in the same latitude as the West Indies."

"Then you think he may come from the Islands?"

"It's not improbable. Where does Balkis come from?"

"Zanzibar, according to Starth."

"Who was a born liar," said Eustace, cynically. "I shouldn't be surprised to find she came from the West Indies also. And remember, Frank, that Denham was born in Zacatecas—that's in Mexico. Your father travelled in those parts."

"Yes. But what's all this to do with me?"

"A great deal, I fancy. I am sure the money is connected with Mexico, with Balkis, with Darrel, and with Denham. Fan and Berry know about it. And the Scarlet Bat. I shouldn't be surprised to learn that it was a kind of sign connected with the affair. I can't say in what way. But we'll know soon. What I can't make out," said Jarman, nursing his chin, "is why London should be plastered with posters of the Scarlet Bat and Tamaroo."

"You don't mean to say—?"

"Yes, I do." And Eustace told Frank of the poster, and how Fan had denied having anything to do with it. "And I'm sure she spoke the truth," he said decisively, "for she asked me if I had posted the Bat. Of course, she must guess that you have it tattooed on your arm, and thought that I made use of it."

"But for what purpose? You and I are not supposed to know anything about the fortune—if there is one."

"Oh, there is one, sure enough, and the Berry lot think I know much more about it than I do. And there's another negro mixed up in the matter besides Balkis. The lawyers I called on told me that one came to ask after you." And Jarman gave details.

"Well," said Frank, more and more puzzled, "there's only one thing to be done. We must open the sealed letter."

"All right. Here you are," and in the darkness Jarman passed it along. Frank opened it, but it was impossible to see. Therefore Eustace lighted a match, which was not likely to be seen from the road, and held it while

120

Frank read the letter. The paper had a Scarlet Bat drawn in one corner with red ink, and the writing consisted of only a few words. "My son," ran the writing, "when you are twenty-five send your address to 'Tamaroo, The General Post-Office, London. To be called for.' Then wait events."

"And Tamaroo is the name on the bills!" said Eustace under his breath.

CHAPTER XVIII

A QUEER VISITOR

"Well, I guess this is a surprise," said Natty.

"And a very pleasant one," rejoined Miss Arrow.

The two were standing on number nine platform of Liverpool Street Station waiting for the Wargrove train, and the meeting was accidental. Natty did not look so well as usual, as his face was somewhat haggard. Jenny noticed this, and thought he had been sitting up all night. With considerable coolness she made the remark, which Natty contradicted.

"It isn't that," said Mr. Denham, gloomily. "I've been square enough, but I've been having trouble."

"Oh dear me!" cried Miss Arrow, sympathetically. "Not bad, I hope?"

"Sufficiently bad to make me leave for the States next week."

Jenny looked rather dismayed. She fancied herself in love with Mr. Denham, as by this time she had quite got over her romantic affection for the Irish secretary.

"I'm sorry," she said pensively. "And you will regret leaving—Mildred!" She looked at him sharply.

"I'll regret leaving all my friends. Those at Wargrove are the best I've struck in the old country. I don't know that Miss Starth's any great sorrow to me, though. She don't care a red cent for me."

"Her affections are otherwise," said Jenny, sentimentally.

"That's so, and I don't see much good my hovering round. I should like to marry a real sweet English girl."

Jenny blushed, but she was not vain enough to take the compliment to herself. Yet she could have done so, for Denham was thinking of her when he paid it. Jenny was not pretty, but she had the freshness of youth, and a sweet, frank face of her own which appealed to the man.

Denham had been so accustomed to women of the world like Miss Berry that he longed for something fresh and unsophisticated. He had been thinking a great deal about Jenny lately, and now that he saw Mildred was a star far above his reach, thought he might do worse than take the rector's daughter. The transfer of affections from Miss Starth to Jenny was a considerable effort of mental gymnastics, but Natty had achieved it.

By the time the train started he had laid in a large quantity of magazines and newspapers for the girl, and took his seat in a first-class carriage along with her. There was an old gentleman in the compartment, but they did not pay much attention to him. Nor did they read the magazines. In each other's conversation they found quite enough pleasure. After discussing Billy and the Arrow family and the departure of Natty for the States, Natty announced that he was going down to Wargrove to see Jarman.

"I want to say goodbye," said he, "and there are other things I have to do. Deliver a letter, for one thing."

"To Mr. Jarman?"

"To Miss Starth. And it's from Miss Berry. You've heard me speak of my friends, I guess?"

"Oh, yes—your most intimate friends."

"Well," drawled Natty, flushing, "they were, but they ain't now. I've had a row. Berry hasn't been acting square by me, and I don't cotton to his goings-on nohow. I'll give them a wide berth for the future."

Jenny observed a discreet silence, as she did not want to ask questions about business which did not concern her. Natty was offended.

"Guess you don't care much for me?" said he, with a shrug.

"Oh, but I—" Jenny was about to say that she did, and only changed the sentence in time. "But I like you, really."

"I'm going to stop for a few days, and we can talk of that," said Natty, looking peculiarly at her. "I suppose Jarman will put me up?"

"Oh, I'm sure he will," said Jenny. "Mr. Jarman likes you. He's rather troubled now on account of Mr. O'Neil leaving him."

"What's he gone for?"

"I don't know. I think he left without giving notice," said Jenny.

"I don't know that he ain't wise, that young man," said Natty, in a dry tone. "The billet didn't suit him."

"He seemed very comfortable!"

"What folk seem, ain't often what they feel," rejoined the American, and again fixed Jenny with his eyes. "Now, you'd never think that in your company I feel different to what I say."

"Really?" Jenny did not know where to look and was thankful that the old gentleman was in the carriage. She felt that Natty was in measurable distance of a proposal, and the timidity of maidenhood seized upon her. Consequently she became voluble, and drew Denham's attention to the scenery, to the pictures in the magazines, and to the news of the day. Natty, not accustomed to this innocence, was delighted, and thought Jenny just charming. He made up his mind to propose within the week, being used to carry through business smartly.

When the train arrived at Mardon Jenny bundled herself into a governess-cart drawn by a fat and elderly pony, and driven by one of her brothers. She offered Natty a seat, but he refused, as he caught sight of Eustace coming out of the station. "But I'll call in and see you tomorrow or this evening," said Natty. Whereat Jenny, afraid of this barefaced wooing—it was really quite improper said her heart—ordered the young Arrow to drive on. Natty watched the elderly pony toiling up the hill, then turned to greet Jarman.

"Here you are!" said Natty, shaking hands. "I've just come down to put up with you for a day or two. Can you fix me?"

Jarman was not quite prepared to extend this hospitality. He had a better opinion of Natty than of his friends. All the same, the young man was in touch with the Captain, and, being weak, was under his influence. Consequently, Berry might be employing Natty as a spy; as the report of Fairy Fan—if she made any—could not be entirely satisfactory to the little skipper. Had he been on the spot he would have made an exhaustive examination as to the whereabouts of the man he desired to hang.

Nevertheless, Jarman fancied that he could control the weak nature of Denham quite as easily as Berry had done, and since the young man had come down he saw no reason why he should not make use of him. He could trust to Mildred's cleverness to keep him away from the summer-house. Therefore, if Natty came and went at his own sweet will, Berry would be quite convinced that Lancaster had left the neighbourhood. It was a bold game, but the situation was so desperate that only boldness would allay suspicion.

"Of course, I can put you up," said Jarman. "Shall we drive?"

"No, I guess not. Let us send on the baggage and walk across. I have something important to say."

Wondering what this could be, Jarman saw that Natty's trunk was put on a fly, and, after directing the man to take it to the Shanty, walked on with his unexpected guest. Eustace had long since posted a letter written by Frank, according to the instruction of the sealed epistle, and it had been sent to Tamaroo at the General Post-Office. The man (for Tamaroo was a man according to Fan's half-confession) was directed to call at the Shanty and see Mr. Lancaster. But, needless to say, it was Jarman's intention to interview the visitor in place of Frank. Thus, if it was a plot in any way—but that was unlikely, seeing that the sealed letter came from Frank's father— the young fellow would not run the risk of being arrested.

"I suppose you know that my secretary has left me?" said Eustace, seeing that Natty did not seem inclined to begin the conversation.

"How should I know that?" asked Denham, sharply, and looking oddly at Jarman.

"You came down with Miss Arrow, and she knows. Consequently—"

"Well, she did tell me that Mr. O'Neil had made tracks," interrupted Natty, calmly, "but she did not mention that he was Lancaster." Eustace stopped and looked hard at his companion. "You recognised him, then, Denham?"

"No. I was sold—completely sold, though I knew Lancaster's looks well enough to spot him. His disguise was very clever, so I got sent up. Miss Berry told me."

"I thought as much," replied Eustace, with a shrug. "She said she would say nothing about the matter, and of course she did."

"She told Berry, and I was in the room. And then—" Denham clenched his fist and looked angry. "They wanted me to play the spy," he burst out; "but don't you think I'm down here for that purpose. I've given those two the chuck."

"Why did they wish you to play the spy?" asked Eustace, quietly.

"Well, you see, I come into money when I'm twenty-five. Not from my father. He was rich, but spent nearly all he had. He left me with enough to get along on without working, anyhow. But I was told by Berry, who is my guardian, as you know, that I might inherit a million. He would not give me particulars, saying he would engineer the job. That's what brought me over here. Now, it seems that to get this money, Lancaster has to be found, that he may give evidence. He has some papers which prove that I am entitled to the fortune. And Berry, hang, him, asked me to hunt him down."

This statement was a very ingenious one on the part of the Captain, as it simply set forth that Frank was wanted for a reasonable purpose. Jarman could not conjecture why Natty should be angered.

"I can't see that in searching for Lancaster you are playing the spy."

Denham looked surprised. "Why, you know that Lancaster was with you. Miss Berry came down, having discovered it somehow."

"Did she tell you in what way?" asked Eustace, quickly.

"No. I guess she never says more than is needful. But she saw you, and heard that Frank Lancaster had skipped. Then Berry said that he was certain you knew the whereabouts of the fellow, and asked me to come down and try to get the truth from you. That's what I call acting a spy. Well, I am here, and I came to tell you this."

"I am much obliged to you, Denham. I suppose it is in order to prove your right to this fortune that Berry offered the reward?"

"He said as much," replied the young man, "but I pointed out that if Lancaster were to come forward he might be hanged, and that no fellow could be expected to be such a fool. Upon my word!" said Denham, walking and talking very fast, "I believe for some reason that Berry wants the poor chap lynched."

"I think so too," admitted Jarman, much to Natty's surprise.

"Then you don't like Berry?"

"No, and I don't like Miss Berry. I know too much about both. It's a pity, Denham—since we are now confidential—that you are with these people."

"Well, I guess Banjo Berry was a friend of my father's, and I was handed over to him as a ward. I never liked him particularly, nor his niece either."

"Is she his niece?"

"I believe so. My father lived at Los Angeles and the Berrys were often at our house. My father seemed thick with Berry, and, to tell you the truth, rather afraid of him. He died a year or so ago, and by his will I was handed over to Berry on account of this fortune. I was shunted here to look after it, but if the getting of it includes the chance of a man being lynched—I pass. I don't need to hang on to this gang, as I've enough to marry on. Berry can go to blazes for me. I sha'n't recognise his guardianship any longer."

"I don't see that you ever needed him as a guardian," said Eustace. "You appear to be well able to look after yourself."

"So I am. Berry thinks I'm weak. So I am. And good-natured. So I am. But there's a line I don't pass, and he's skipped across it. I don't have anything more to do with him, and so I said."

"Has he any control over the money you possess?"

"I reckon not. It's all my own, and I don't let him, or anyone else, interfere. I'll just cut back to the States, I guess."

Eustace thought for a moment. "Tell me, Mr. Denham, did Berry or your father say anything about that Scarlet Bat on your arm?"

"No!" Natty stopped short and stared. "You saw that when I was bathing, I expect. I was stolen by Indians, so my father told me, and they tattooed the mark. I was a kid then, and don't remember anything about it. And the strange thing is," added Denham, "that all London is placarded with the Bat."

"And with the word Tamaroo. Do you know what that means?"

"I guess not. But you do. See here, Jarman, you're up to some game?"

Eustace nodded. "On behalf of Lancaster," he said. "And on your behalf also. You are in danger!"

Natty stared. "Danger! What do you mean?"

"I'll tell you that later. We must have a talk when we get in."

"All right," agreed the American, with a keen glance. "I'm glad I dropped across you, as I don't trust the Berrys a cent now. I always thought there was something strange about the fortune business. But before I enter your house I have to deliver a letter to Miss Starth!"

"Ah!" said Eustace, quickly, "from Miss Berry?"

"Yes. How the deuce did you know?"

"I know a great deal," replied Eustace, drily, "and I hope to know more. I'm glad you have been frank with me, Denham. I may be able to help you a lot. No, don't ask questions now. Deliver your letter, and when you come to me we can have a talk. There's the road up to the cottage. *Au revoir* for an hour."

Denham went away directly, but he looked puzzled as he flung a parting glance at Jarman. That gentleman walked on, wondering at the lucky chance which had caused Denham to change towards Berry and his fair niece. He might learn much by dexterous questions. And Denham really seemed to have good principles, when he had revolted so completely against his tyrant. Altogether, things were shaping well, and Eustace chuckled.

At the door of his house he saw a figure, and as he drew near he beheld a negro. The man was small but wiry, and of considerable age, judging from his grey wool. He was quietly dressed in a garb as black as his face, and he grinned as Eustace appeared.

"You write dis?" he asked, holding out Frank's letter, and when Jarman nodded, grinned again. "I am Tamaroo," said the black man.

127

CHAPTER XIX

A STORY OF THE PAST

"Tamaroo!" repeated the negro, showing a good set of teeth for so old a man. "I come about the letter."

Eustace looked at him, and remembered a certain negro who had been waiting for Anchor at the time the miner was shot. Evidently Anchor had been about to explain that the man was waiting, when the bullet struck him. "Tamaroo!" murmured Eustace. "I might have guessed that so peculiar a name would be connected with something barbaric. Come in!"

In a few minutes they were seated in the study. Jarman, since the departure of Miss Cork, had not sought out another housekeeper, so he had no fear of eavesdroppers. Denham was likely to be engaged with Mildred for at least an hour, so the interview between himself and Tamaroo would not be interrupted. He observed that the negro was much above the ordinary class. He had a certain dignity about him, wore none of the barbaric colours in which his race delight, and, moreover, spoke surprisingly good English. Occasionally he lisped, but on the whole his speech would not have disgraced a moderately educated white man. As soon as he sat down, Tamaroo gravely mounted a pair of spectacles, and took out a bundle of papers tied up with red tape.

"One moment!" said Eustace, loading his pipe, as he thought he could talk better while smoking. "Was it you who pasted the town with the Scarlet Bat?"

"Yes. It was me, sir." Tamaroo said. "I wanted to know where you were, and as you were hiding I could do nothing else to make you know that I wanted to see you."

"Hold on!" said Jarman, seeing the mistake. "How do you know I am Frank Lancaster?"

"You could not have written this letter if you were not, sir," said Tamaroo, decisively. "My old master gave a direction to the lady aunt who looked after you, and it was to be given to you on—"

"On the twenty-fifth of September. It's not the date yet."

128

"No, sir. But I thought you might get the letter before. The mark on your arm, sir, would draw your attention to the Scarlet Bat on the walls, and you would ask for the letter."

"But I say, Tamaroo, why do you come along before the time?"

"There is danger, sir—great danger—and I want to save you."

"Not me. You wish to save Frank Lancaster."

Tamaroo looked up quickly, and replaced the bundle of letters in his breast-pocket. "And you, sir?"

"I am the friend of Mr. Lancaster. You can show me the—"

Tamaroo was on his feet before Eustace finished, and in his right hand he held a revolver.

"Keep back!" he cried shrilly. "You have trapped me, but I fight—yes, I fight."

Jarman maintained his seat and smoked coolly. "There's no need for you to fight, man," he said soothingly. "Should I know about the Scarlet Bat and that letter if I were not Mr. Lancaster's friend?"

"Others know, and they are not friends," said the negro, doubtfully, but lowering the revolver.

"Captain Banjo Berry and his niece?"

"Huh!" Tamaroo grunted. "You know them?"

"Rather," replied Jarman, flinging himself back. "And I know much more about them than they like. They got poor Lancaster into this trouble."

Tamaroo groaned. "I know it," he said, "and if I had only come to England sooner it would not have happened. I arrived just after the trouble, and heard that my young master was accused."

"You do not believe him guilty, then, Tamaroo?"

"No, sir. Certainly I do not. Captain Berry came to England to try and get my young master hanged."

"For what reason?" asked Eustace, wondering to find his suspicions verified. "I always thought he did; but why?"

Tamaroo touched his breast-pocket. "That is told here," he said, "but I cannot speak save to my master."

"But I am his friend. I may as well tell you that after he got into trouble he came to me. He stopped for a time, then, being in danger of discovery, he fled."

"You do not know where he is?" asked the negro, disappointed.

Eustace looked at him keenly. "Well I do," he admitted, "but he is in such danger that I dare not tell. Can't I see the papers?"

Tamaroo moved towards the door. "No, sir," he said sternly; "my old master told me to read them and to give them to Mr. Lancaster alone. Oh! Tell me where he is, I beg you, sir?"

Eustace looked perplexed. He had no reason on the face of it to doubt the good faith of the man, and the sealed letter being answered in this way was a guarantee that Tamaroo was the emissary of the elder Lancaster. But it behoved him to be cautious, as he was surrounded on all sides by snares and pitfalls. Captain Berry was not the man to stop short of any crime to gain his end—witness the death of Starth and his pursuit of Frank.

"Do you know why Berry is pursuing Lancaster?" he asked, forgetting that the negro might see fit to keep his own counsel for the same reasons.

"To get him hanged to said Tamaroo, quietly."

"You said that before. But the reason?"

In his turn Tamaroo replied: "You said that before, sir. It is in the papers which I carry."

"And they will explain the whole business?"

"They will. They contain the whole story of the Scarlet Bat and of the Indian treasure—"

"Ah!" interpolated Eustace with grim satisfaction. "I knew there was a treasure. How much, Tamaroo? A million?"

"Nearly that. But you can see from the will."

"The will! Have you the will of Mr. Lancaster?"

Tamaroo nodded. "I have the will."

"And is Mr. Lancaster the elder dead?"

"Yes, sir," said the negro with emotion. "He died a year ago. And I could not see him die, alas!" he added, much moved.

"Why not, were you away?"

Tamaroo again shook his head and looked mournful. Then, sinking his voice to a whisper, he said: "My master was a leper."

Eustace jumped up with an ejaculation of disgust and pity. "For how long was he a leper?" he asked, thinking of the money.

"From the time he sent my young master to the lady aunt. It was for that reason he parted with him. I remained, but my master would not let me attend to him, lest I also should take the disease—and I had this to do." He again touched his breast-pocket.

"So it was you who sent the money from 'Frisco?"

"It was I, sir. My master told me to send it, till I could give up the fortune to my young master."

"And you have come to do that?"

"Yes, sir. But only to him will I tell the story and give the papers."

Jarman reflected. The old man was evidently most trustworthy, seeing he wished to fulfill his mission with the utmost exactitude. He could safely be told of Frank's hiding-place.

"Tonight I shall lead you to Mr. Lancaster," said Jarman, quietly.

"Thank Heaven—oh, thank Heaven!" cried Tamaroo, and the tears rolled down his black face. "It has been a care to me this trust. I wish to give it to my young master and be at rest."

"Oh, that's all right," replied Eustace, patting the old man on the back. "And we'll be able to baffle this conspiracy?"

"Yes," cried Tamaroo, wiping his eyes, "we will save my master."

"By the way," asked Jarman, suddenly, "do you know a young fellow called Natty Denham?"

Tamaroo nodded. "I do, sir. He is the son of my master's partner."

"What!" Jarman looked puzzled. "Partner in what?"

Again the negro became obstinate. "It is in the papers," he said.

"That means I'll learn nothing until Frank does," said Jarman, good-humouredly. "You are a faithful messenger, Tamaroo. Has young Denham seen you?"

"No, sir. I do not think he knows of my name, unless Captain Berry—"

"Oh, he's told him as little as he could. But, I say, does Berry know of the contents of those papers?"

"Yes, sir, He learnt them from—" Here the negro hesitated.

Eustace laughed and nodded. "You needn't worry," he said, "I know of that. Mrs. Anchor, who is now called Miss Berry, learnt about the fortune from her husband."

Tamaroo smiled grimly, and then with an ejaculation smote his hands together, looking in a startled way at Eustace. "I know you now, sir. You were said to have killed Mr. Anchor in San Francisco."

"Yes. But I suspect that Berry killed him. And you were the negro who was waiting at his house for him."

"I did not wait at the house," said Tamaroo, quietly. "Mr. Anchor was a friend of my master, and had some of the papers connected with the fortune of the Scarlet Bat. When he was going after his wife he told me to come and get them. Then he thought he would give them to you, and I waited while he visited you. But I grew weary, and followed. I saw you speaking to Mr. Anchor, and heard the shot!"

"Who fired it?"

"Captain Berry. He was then called—"

"Sakers. I know. But the knife wound?" Tamaroo looked oddly at Eustace. "I know nothing of that, sir," he said. "But we can talk again of this. I will tell you all I know in the presence of Mr. Frank. And now—"

There was a sound of laughing outside. Mildred suddenly appeared at the window and tapped on the glass to be let in. She usually did this when impatient. Tamaroo saw her face and started. Jarman went to the door and admitted her. She was with Denham.

"I have come to ask you a question," said Mildred, entering the room. "Oh!" She started back. "Who is this?"

"This," said Eustace, waving his hand, "is Tamaroo."

"What!" cried Denham, "the name on the bills?"

"Yes," put in Tamaroo, quietly; "and this—" He bowed to Mildred. "—is Miss Starth."

"How do you know me?" asked Mildred, puzzled by the recognition. "It was I who gave you the paper at the inquest," said the negro. She uttered an exclamation. "Then you know that Frank is innocent?"

"Yes," said Tamaroo, with a hanging head. "But I cannot prove it."

"Don't you think Lancaster killed Starth?" asked Natty, eagerly.

"No sir," he replied, looking strangely at the young man; "but who killed him I cannot say."

"Captain Berry," suggested Eustace.

Tamaroo shook his head. "It was not Captain Berry."

After this he refused to say any more, and sat down, seemingly quite worn out. Jarman, who wished him to be prepared for the interview with Frank, insisted that he should lie down. So the negro went to the bedroom formerly occupied by the Irish secretary. He locked the door when he entered, apparently fearful for the safety of his papers. Eustace smiled approvingly. Every action of Tamaroo's showed how devoted he was to Frank Lancaster. He returned to the room where Mildred still waited with the American.

"What is your question?" he asked.

"It doesn't matter just now," she replied, with a glance at Denham. "Later I can talk of it. This arrival of Tamaroo has driven all else out of my head."

"But do you know anything of the man?"

"I know all that Frank could tell me," she replied. "My dear Eustace, Frank has told me all of your doings since he came to you. You don't mind my calling him Frank, do you?" she said, pleadingly, as she saw him frown. "He is in such difficulties, and I am so sorry."

Jarman looked at her a little sadly, seeing that she was slipping away from him. "No," he replied, quietly, "I don't mind. Have you told Mr. Denham anything?"

Mildred uttered an exclamation. She had quite forgotten the presence of the American, and dreaded lest she had betrayed Frank. But Natty came forward with a smile.

"You need not be afraid, I guess," he said, nodding. "I'm square, and on your side."

"I thought you were friendly to—"

"To the Berrys? Not much. I've chucked them. They have been making use of me, and have been trying to get Lancaster hanged—"

"And are trying," interrupted Eustace, quickly. "It's all right, Mildred. So sure am I of Denham that I intend to trust him."

"You need have no fear," said Denham, colouring with pleasure. "I'm straight all through. Don't you trust me, Miss Starth?"

Mildred looked at him with her innocent eyes, and he met her gaze without dropping his own.

"Yes, I trust you," she said, "thoroughly."

"In that case," said Eustace, rubbing his hands, "Mr. Denham can be present when Tamaroo explains to Frank."

"Explains what?"

"The whole business of the conspiracy. It concerns Frank, and also you, Denham. Tamaroo says that your father was the partner of the late Mr. Lancaster."

"I've heard him mention Lancaster's name," said Natty, slowly; "but Tamaroo never came along."

"He lay low, as your countrymen say. But it will all be explained tonight —in this room."

Mildred uttered an exclamation. "Do you think that is wise?"

"Yes. No one is likely to come here."

"What about Captain Berry?" asked the girl, doubtfully.

"He least of all," said Denham. "He doesn't know where I am, and if by chance he does turn up, I'll keep him going till we can smuggle back Lancaster to his hole."

So it was agreed, although Mildred was still anxious. It seemed risky to her to take Frank from his safe hiding-place, and expose him to a chance of capture. However, she implicitly trusted in Jarman, and went back to tell Frank of the arrival of the negro.

"How is it you speak English so well?" Eustace asked Tamaroo.

"I was educated at a negro university," replied the man. "I am better educated than many a man of your colour, sir. But later on I will tell you my story. Tonight I must relate what I know of his father to Mr. Lancaster."

And so it came about. Leaving Natty and Tamaroo together, Eustace repaired to the summerhousetomoee about nine o'clock, and found Frank waiting for him in a state of subdued excitement. Mildred had told him everything, and he needed no explanation. The night was particularly dark, so the two men left the garden arm in arm. Mildred was walking on the lawn and watched them go, and Mrs. Perth in the house kept Jane employed lest she might learn too much.

In a few minutes Frank was in the Shanty and shaking hands with Tamaroo. The old man was much affected at the sight of his master's son.

"You are not at all like your father, sir," he said, "but like your dear mother, Heaven bless her!"

"You knew my mother?"

"She died in my arms," said Tamaroo, quietly, and then took out his bundle of papers.

Denham, Frank, and Eustace waited anxiously to hear how the old negro would begin. Tamaroo untied the bundle and selected a long, official-looking paper. "The will," he said. "By this, Mr. Frank, you inherit close on a million if you are not hanged!"

"Hanged?" uttered all three in sheer astonishment.

"Hanged," repeated Tamaroo, "before the age of twenty-five."

CHAPTER XX

A STRANGE WILL

Tamaroo smiled at the amazement expressed on the faces of his audience, although they had every excuse to look astonished.

"Do you mean to say that such a condition is in the will?" asked Frank.

Tamaroo nodded impressively. "It is set forth here," he said. "This is a copy of the will. The original is in the office of Hiram & Co., lawyers, in San Francisco."

"Are those the agents of White & Saon?" asked Eustace.

"Yes, sir. I paid the monthly money through them. I was afraid to bring the original will with me, as I thought Captain Berry might kill me to get possession of it. But he has only a copy."

"And how did he get the copy?" asked Natty, quickly.

"That is part of the story," said the negro, adjusting his spectacles. "It is all written out here. But it will be best for me to tell it in my own way, and then, Mr. Frank, you can read the papers afterwards when you have time."

Frank looked grim. "I have plenty of time," he said; "the whole twenty-four hours of the day. But tell the story in your own way."

The negro nodded, and seemed pleased that he was allowed to do what he liked. The four men were seated at the end of the room furthest from the window. Outside it was a particularly dark night, and rain was falling. At times the wind shook the house, which was old. The blinds of the big, square window at the end, where Jarman's desk stood, were pulled down, but the curtains had not been drawn. Occasionally a flare of bluish lightning would show against the blinds, and more clearly where they did not quite cover the window. What with the drench of the rain, the howling of the wind, and the rolling of distant thunder, the noise at times drowned the negro's voice. Therefore the three who listened were obliged to bend their heads in order to hear clearly. The lamp was drawn close to Tamaroo's elbow so that he could refer at his ease to the papers. But this he rarely did, as he seemed to know what they contained by heart. He began his narrative by asking questions.

"Do you remember your father, Mr. Denham?" he asked.

"Oh, I guess I do," replied Natty, nodding. "He didn't die so very long ago. We hung out in Los Angeles, and Berry was an old friend of the governor's."

"Quite so," nodded Tamaroo; "and he was the ruin of your father. He induced him to drink more than was good."

Natty, who had not quite got over the contempt of the American for the black race, would have replied in rather a fiery manner, but that Tamaroo gave him no time.

"Don't be angry, sir," he said. "All that I say is means to an end."

"Well, I believe Berry did make my father drink," admitted Denham, reluctantly. "He was always hovering round. But so was Anchor, for the matter of that. He drank also."

"And was Fairy Fan anywhere in the galley?" asked Eustace.

"Yes," said Tamaroo, who seemed to know the lady by that name. "She is the niece of Berry."

"Oh!" said Frank, "then she really is the niece?"

"Oh, certainly. The daughter of his sister, and a very wicked woman."

"You don't need to add that last," put in Eustace. "I know how she treated poor Anchor. But go on with the story."

"I must begin at the beginning, then," said Tamaroo, and cleared his throat. "I need not be very particular as to time," he said, "as the dates are all in the papers here. I'll just tell you the story as shortly as possible, and then you can read it at leisure for yourselves."

"That's all right," said Frank. "Go on. I am impatient."

"I am a very old man," continued Tamaroo. "You mightn't believe it, but I am over eighty. In my youth I was a slave on a plantation near New Orleans. I was wickedly treated by a brutal master, and Mr. Lancaster, seeing me being flogged one day, bought me out of pity. I was not very young then, but I was strong, and Mr. Lancaster found that I could work for him. I did. Heaven bless him!" said Tamaroo, with emotion. "He was a good friend to me. He set me free, and he sent me to school, where I learnt to talk as I do. Afterwards, when old, I went to a negro college and learnt still more. But when Mr. Lancaster bought me I was very ignorant. He was a handsome young man then, and fond of roving. He took me with him to the Californian diggings, and we had a wild time. It was there that we first met Captain Berry."

"What is his real name?" asked Eustace.

"I don't know; he had so many. But he was originally a sailor. I think his true name was Berry, as he used that oftener than the others, and always when he was well off. When in difficulties he called himself by other names."

"Such as Sakers, at San Francisco," murmured Eustace. "Ah! That was because he took to the sea again and lost a schooner in the South Seas. But when my master met him he was called Banjo Berry, because he played so well on that instrument. The name took his fancy, and he kept it."

"And anything else he could lay his hands on," said Denham. "I've heard him twang the banjo, and he can scrape a bit."

"Berry and my master got on very well, and were always together. I did not like him myself, and warned Mr. Lancaster against him, but my master would always have his own way. Then Mr. Denham came."

"My father?" said Natty, looking interested.

"Yes, sir. He was a gay young man then also, and he took a liking to my master. Berry was friendly with both. The three set to work to make money at the diggings, but ill-luck pursued them. At last my master grew disgusted, and thought of returning to England. But before he went he fancied he would like to travel about Mexico for a time. He took me with him, but left Berry and Mr. Denham behind at the diggings. We went into the wilds of Mexico, and had many adventures—oh very many—and were in much danger. But we came through all, and I saved my master's life twice."

"Heaven bless you!" said Frank, shaking the negro's hand.

The old man nodded with a proud look. "I loved my master. He had saved me from slavery, and what else could I do but save him? For two years we travelled in the wilds. Then we met with an Indian. He had been deserted by his tribe and was dying. My master, always kind, nursed him for a long time; but he grew weak, and at last he died."

"What sort of Indian was he?" asked Natty—"a red-skin?"

"No. We were not so far north as that. He said he was an Aztec."

"Aha!" murmured Eustace, "now we are coming to the treasure."

Tamaroo nodded. "You are clever, Mr. Jarman. Yes, this Indian told my master, when dying, that he knew of a treasure hidden under the sign of the Scarlet Bat."

"Kind of totem," said Jarman.

Tamaroo looked puzzled. "I do not know what that is," he said simply, "but the Scarlet Bat was a sign set by the great King Montezuma on a rock, under which he concealed part of his treasure. The Indian—he was a cacique—enraged by the desertion of those who should have saved his life, told the secret to my master."

"And how did the cacique know?"

"The secret had been handed down from his fathers."

Denham nodded. "I've heard of that sort of thing before," he said. "Some Indians know where the treasures of Montezuma are hidden; but the greater part of the hoard remains undiscovered. They will not reveal its whereabouts to a white man."

"True," assented Tamaroo. "They hate white men. But my master was so kind that he won the gratitude of the cacique. When the man was dying he told, and gave a chart. Then we buried him."

"And went to look for the treasure?" asked Frank.

"No, sir. It was a wild country where there were many Indians. We should have been killed had we gone alone. My master returned to the diggings and offered to share the treasure with Berry and with Mr. Denham, if they would come with him to find it."

"Did they agree?" asked Natty, eagerly.

"Of course they did, or all this trouble wouldn't have come about," put in Eustace, decisively.

"You are not altogether right, Mr. Jarman," said the negro, quietly. "Only Mr. Denham would go. Berry was making money at the diggings, and preferred the bird in the hand to the two in the bush. But he came with us for a little way. Mr. Lancaster, knowing he was a good shot and a fearless man, wanted him greatly to come, and promised him a share. But he refused and turned back. We went on without him."

"And you found the treasure?"

"Yes. We had hard work, though. It was quite a year before we came across the rock marked with the Scarlet Bat. Also we had to fight our way through a hostile country, and several of our men died. At last we reached the rock and found the treasure. With the greatest difficulty we transported it to civilisation. I need not tell you all the hardships we underwent, or how we got the treasure safely landed. But we did. I had a share, and then Mr. Denham and Mr. Lancaster divided the rest between them."

"So that's how my father made his money," muttered Natty. "He spent it on a large scale."

"He did, sir," said the negro, gravely. "He spent all he had, with the exception of that portion he saved for you."

"He didn't save much. Why didn't he leave me more?"

Tamaroo nodded impressively. "He was afraid of Berry."

Natty stared and looked angry. "My father was afraid of nothing."

"He was afraid of Berry," insisted Tamaroo. "And Mr. Lancaster was also afraid."

This time Frank protested. "I can't believe that."

"It is true enough. You see, gentlemen, both Mr. Denham and Mr. Lancaster married when they got the money. You two gentlemen"—he looked at Frank and Natty—"were born on the same day."

"That is strange," said Natty, and Frank laughed.

"It pleased both my master and Mr. Denham, for they were such good friends. So that you should both be certain of inheriting the treasure, they had you both tattooed with the Scarlet Bat."

"Oh! Was that it," said Natty, thinking of his story of the Indians. "Mine is on the left arm. And yours, Lancaster?"

"On the right. Go on, Tamaroo."

"The reason of the tattooing," continued the negro, "was that my master and Mr. Denham thought that Berry would kidnap you both."

"But what was Berry's game?" asked Natty.

"To get the money. He had bad luck at the diggings, and when he returned to San Francisco he found that the treasure had been discovered. He claimed a share, which claim was refused."

"I should jolly well think so," said Jarman, emphatically, "considering Berry did nothing towards getting it. What cheek!"

"So my master and Mr. Denham thought," said the negro, with a smile. "They refused the claim, and then Berry threatened to kidnap you two gentlemen. He thought he would then be able to force those who possessed the treasure to part with some of it. The tattooing was done so that if the kidnapping took place both of you would be recognised. But Berry never made the attempt."

"He waited for a better opportunity."

"Yes." Tamaroo nodded. "Mr. Denham went to live at Los Angeles, and spent a lot of money. His wife died after a time, and he looked after you, sir"—this to Natty—"so that you might not be kidnapped. At length Berry turned up after some years, and made friends."

"Didn't my father mistrust him?"

"At first he did, but afterwards, being shaken by drink, I think he grew afraid of Berry. He shared a portion of the money with him. That is, he gave him free house-room, and occasional sums. Berry was not satisfied, but when he found that Mr. Denham was spending the money he never attempted to kill him, knowing that what remained would not pay him to commit such a crime. He then thought of my master, who had saved his share."

"Did my father live in San Francisco?"

"Yes, Mr. Lancaster. After the death of your mother he lived like a recluse, and invested all his money. It is well invested," said Tamaroo, proudly. "I helped him. You will receive about forty thousand a year now."

"If I'm ever in a position to enjoy it," muttered Frank, startled by this good fortune. "Well, did Berry see my father?"

"He did. Mr. Lancaster was then beginning to suffer from leprosy, but the disease had not made much progress. When it began he sent you to the lady aunt, Mr. Frank."

"I was then two years of age, I remember. Go on."

"Berry came to your father, and threatened to follow you to England and kill you. Mr. Lancaster grew afraid, and made this will."

"Ah!" put in Eustace, "now we come to the interesting part. Why did he make such an extraordinary will, and place Frank in such danger?"

"It was the best he could do to save him from Berry's machinations, Mr. Jarman," said the negro, quietly. "Being a leper, he could not do much, as his disease was gaining on him, and he thought he would be sent away to some settlement by the authorities. That afterwards happened, but at the time I speak of he was still in 'Frisco."

"My poor father!" murmured Frank. "And what about Anchor?"

"Mr. Lancaster met him afterwards. But about the will. My master knew that Berry was a fascinating man with a strong influence. He thought that if he left the money to you, Berry might gain an influence over you, since you were so young, and get you to leave the money to him. Then he would murder you to become possessed of it."

"Berry would never have fascinated me," declared Frank. "I am not so weak-minded as that."

"You were young then, Mr. Frank, and Berry could have done much with you as a boy. He influenced Mr. Denham here."

"He certainly did," assented Natty, "and I'm no slouch either. But Berry, in spite of his looks and rascality, is fascinating. I was quite taken in by him. But I see through him now. Well—the will?"

"As I said," went on Tamaroo, "Mr. Lancaster did not know how to make the money safe from Berry. Therefore, he made his will leaving the money to you, Mr. Frank, and afterwards to Denham's son."

"That's to me," said Natty. "I see now, this money is the fortune I was to inherit."

"Yes. My master did not know that Berry had such an influence over your father, nor did I, or a different will would have been made. But the money was to go to you, provided that Mr. Frank was hanged before he reached the age of twenty-five. If Mr. Frank died a natural death, or was murdered, the money was to go to a charity. Anchor was made the trustee of this will."

"But I don't see where the sense of the hanging comes in."

"Well, Mr. Jarman," said the negro, turning to Eustace, who had spoken, "it's this way. My master thought that unless he put in that clause, Berry might get rid of Mr. Frank by violence."

"But if he murdered him the money would have gone to the charity."

"Quite so," assented Tamaroo, quietly. "And even if Mr. Frank died a natural death that would have happened. Mr. Lancaster knew that Berry was mixed up with people of our race who knew something of poisons."

"Aha!" said Jarman, "Balkis!"

"Yes. Balkis, sir; though I don't know how you came to hear of her."

"I'll tell you later. Go on."

140

Tamaroo paused to collect his thoughts, and continued: "So you see that the only way in which Berry could prevent the money going to the charity —in which case it would be lost to him altogether—was by getting Mr. Frank hanged. My master fancied that even if Berry did not murder Mr. Frank openly he might get some drug from Balkis which would kill Mr. Frank, without revealing that poison had been used. And that could have been done," said Tamaroo, impressively.

"Ah! I see now," cried Eustace. "Berry by means of this poison could have made Frank's death appear natural."

"Yes, sir. In which case the money would have gone to the charity. Mr. Lancaster knew that, being brought up by the lady aunt, his son would not commit a crime, so it was not likely that Berry would succeed in getting him hanged before the age of twenty-five."

"I see," said Frank, grimly; "but he has made a good shot at it. I was to be hanged for the murder of Starth, and then Natty here was to get the money."

"Yes," said Tamaroo. "And afterwards Mr. Denham was to be put out of the way, and Berry and his niece were to benefit."

"Very clever," muttered Natty. "But I'm not quite such a fool. And Mr. Lancaster is dead?"

"He is, sir. His disease got worse after he made his will, and he went to a leper settlement, where he died some time ago. As soon as I heard of his death I brought home these papers, only to learn that Mr. Frank was in danger of being hanged. To find him I plastered London with those posters. Then I—"

There was a smash of glass, and the blind of the middle window bulged out. Berry sprang into the room with a revolver. "I arrest you!" he called out to Frank, "for the murder of Starth. I arrest you!"

Jarman purposely overturned the lamp, and in the ensuing darkness confusion ensued. When it was re-lighted Tamaroo and Frank had disappeared.

CHAPTER XXI

AN UNEXPECTED MEETING

The next morning Darrel, who was still at the Rectory, paid a visit to Mildred. Had she been within doors she would have refused to see him, as she was much distressed in her mind. Frank had not returned from the Shanty, nor had Eustace appeared to explain the reason. Mildred was haunted by visions of the young man being captured, and, since she firmly believed in his innocence, felt very anxious. After a sleepless night she came out before breakfast to take the air in the garden, and so found herself face to face with Darrel in the most unexpected way. He entered the grounds with an air of possession which was intensely irritating to Mildred in her then state of mind, and she was not prepared to receive him warmly.

"You come at an awkward hour, Mr. Darrel," she said coldly, "and I am not able to see you."

"I thought you might refuse," he replied, sulkily; "but I cannot deny myself the pleasure of being the first to bring you the good news. You will be glad to hear that the murderer of your brother Walter has been caught."

Mildred nearly fainted, but saved herself by a strong effort. "Are you speaking of Mr. Lancaster?" she asked.

"Of who else?" replied Darrel, with a triumphant smile. "He is the guilty person. Last night Berry, of whom you have heard, came down and found him in Jarman's house. I believe there was a fight, but in the end the man was caught. You must be pleased."

"I am not pleased. Mr. Lancaster is innocent."

"Of course he would tell you that in his character of O'Neil," said the man, scornfully. "But it's a lie. I believe he is guilty."

"Perhaps you denounced him to Captain Berry?"

"No. I told him that if he left you alone I would hold my tongue."

The girl turned on him angrily. "And what right have you to say such a thing about me?" she demanded vehemently. "I am not engaged to you. I never shall be!"

"Oh, yes, you will," he replied, coming closer and looking into her white face with angry eyes. "You will be my wife, now that this villain is out of the way."

"Never! And Mr. Lancaster is not a villain."

"He is. He killed your brother. You cannot love the murderer of your brother."

"Who told you that I loved Mr. Lancaster?"

"My own heart. Bah! Do you think I can be deceived? Did I not see the looks which passed between you?"

Mildred looked on him with ineffable contempt. "You mean, low, pitiful coward!" she said, while he winced at the ringing scorn in her voice. "You come here to insult me, because I will not marry you. Now, hear me. I *do* love Frank."

"Ah!"—a low cry of rage escaped him—"you call him Frank."

"I do, for I love him. He has said nothing to me, and I do not even know if he returns my feeling."

"Yes, you do," said Darrel, striking his stick passionately on the ground, and glaring on her fiercely. "You two understand one another very well. I believe that you knew where he was concealed after he left Jarman. Ah!"— he read her face—"you *did* know."

"That's my business. Leave this place at once."

Darrel stood his ground doggedly. "I refuse to go. I refuse to give you up," he declared, with a growl like a wild beast disturbed at meal-time. "Your lover has been arrested. He will hang, and you will be my wife. I'll bring your pride down then."

"Never! Never! Never! Frank can prove his innocence, and I will die sooner than be your wife. You betrayed him, you pitiful coward!"

"I did not. Miss Berry learnt that he was here."

"Through you," she flashed out.

"No. On my soul!" he protested. "I said nothing. I don't know how she learnt it. But she did make the discovery, and told Berry. He came down here last night, and watched Jarman's cottage. He saw Lancaster enter, and waited outside the window. After a time he smashed the glass with his gloved hands, and sprang into the room with a revolver. Jarman overturned the lamp, and then—"

"And then," said a new voice—that of Jarman who had stolen upon the two unobserved—"then Frank escaped in the darkness with Tamaroo."

Darrel turned on the newcomer fiercely, but Mildred gave a cry of joy.

"Frank has not been taken then?" she cried, clapping her hands. "This man"—she looked scornfully at Darrel—"says he was captured."

"What do you mean by that?" demanded Eustace, who looked pale and ill, and was evidently in a sullen mood.

"Because I'm sure he has been taken by this time. I saw Berry last night —"

143

"Ah!" cried Mildred. "You came to help."

"Yes, I did. I wanted Lancaster removed from my path. Berry came to the Rectory to ask for my assistance. But he knew already where to find the man. I went with him to the cottage—"

"And you lurked outside, not being man enough to enter," said Jarman, with a sneer. "I turned Berry out pretty sharp. Being an American, he has yet to learn that an Englishman's house is his castle."

"And you have to learn, Mr. Jarman, that you have been compounding a felony in sheltering this criminal."

"Frank is not a criminal!" cried Mildred, with a stamp.

"Ah you defend your brother's murderer," sneered Darrel, savagely.

"Don't talk rubbish, Darrel," interposed Jarman. "You know well enough that Lancaster is innocent."

"He is not. He certainly escaped last night, but Berry is on his track. Lancaster may disguise himself, but Tamaroo will be spotted in a mighty short time. They can't escape."

"Why did you tell me that Frank was arrested?" asked Mildred.

"I thought you would be pleased," he said sulkily.

"No. You thought it would wound my heart, you coward! Go away!" She stamped her foot. "I hate the sight of you."

"Mildred," said Eustace, quietly, though he felt a pang at seeing how she defended Frank, "let me attend to this gentleman."

"I sha'n't move till he goes," said she, obstinately.

"You had better go," said Eustace, suggestively, to the Rhodesian.

"And leave the field to you," he answered, with a taunting laugh. "How many more lovers have you, Miss Starth?"

Mildred gave a cry of shame, and her face crimsoned. With a shout Eustace dashed forward, and before Darrel knew what he was about he swung him up in his mighty arms, and pitched him clean over the gate into the roadway, where he sprawled like a huge toad. Mildred caught Jarman by the hand, panting.

"Oh, you are a man—a man!" she said.

Darrel picked himself up, but did not show fight. His face was more like that of a negro than ever, and Eustace believed he was a half-caste, seeing how the racial type came out.

"You bully!" growled the man, fiercely, but keeping well in the roadway. "I'll be even with you. I can guess where Lancaster is hiding now, and I'll hunt him down—I'll hunt him down! He shall hang, and you, Jarman, shall go to prison for having assisted him. As for you"—he turned fiercely on the girl, who stood beside Eustace, shaking and white—"you shall be my wife. I'll break your spirit. I'll—I'll—" He could speak no more for sheer rage, and his hands trembled with excitement. Finally he gave a roar like a wounded lion, and dashed away. Mildred wrung her hands in dismay.

"He will hunt down Frank—he will hunt down Frank!"

"Nonsense!" said Eustace, roughly, helping her to a seat. "It's all bluff on his part. He can't know where Frank has fled to. So long as the boy is with Tamaroo, I am sure he will be safe."

"Did they say where they were going?" asked Mildred.

"No. There was no time. Berry, in a most wonderful way, smashed in the window. I expect he used his coat to avoid being cut by the glass. Before we knew where we were he was in the middle of the room, and covering Frank with his Derringer. The only thing that occurred to me was to overturn the lamp, which I did. Then I made for Berry, but found him already struggling with Natty. I managed to light a candle, and discovered that Tamaroo had disappeared with Frank."

"What did Berry do?"

"He accused me of sheltering a criminal. I would not let him leave the room, so that the two fugitives could get a start. Then I turned him out. I expect he joined Darrel, although I never knew that Darrel was outside, and they went away."

"But if Mr. Darrel was outside he must have seen the direction in which Frank went."

"I doubt it, the night was so dark and stormy. But, even if he did, he could do nothing. Berry, afraid of the law, as I thought he would be, did not bring a policeman with him, nor did he have a warrant. Frank can escape by half-a-dozen stations round about. They are all within walking distance. Depend upon it Tamaroo will take him to some safe place, and then we shall hear. I trust the negro."

"But about the will—the—"

"There is no time to talk about that now," said Eustace, brusquely. "There is much to be done if Berry is to be thwarted. He'll hunt Frank down with all his heart and soul, and now Darrel, out of sheer hatred, will join in. I want to save Frank—" He paused, and looked directly at Mildred. "I wish to save him for—"

She put out her hands. "No. Say nothing now. Afterwards we will talk— we can—oh! Believe me— I—I—shall keep my bargain."

"Your bargain was not that I should save Frank, but discover the assassin of your brother," said Eustace, gloomily. "But to do the one I must do the other. Frank shall be saved, and the man who killed Walter shall be caught. And then"—he paused again with a shiver—"and then—we will talk, as you say."

"But I want to say—"

145

"Say nothing, Mildred. Child," he said, as she rose, "all I wish is to see you happy. I have made one mistake. Do not let me make another. No, don't speak. I'm only a man after all, and I am not equal to—to—" He passed his hand across his forehead, then started briskly. "But this is not business," he broke off, and held out his hand. "Give me the letter."

Amazed by his sudden transition from sentiment to business, Mildred did not quite comprehend. "The letter?" she stammered.

"Yes, the letter written by Miss Berry to you, saying that she loved your brother, and wished to marry him. Denham gave it to you."

"Yes, yes. But how did you—"

"I got her to write it," said Jarman, quickly. "She wanted me to deliver a message to Frank for her, and I agreed to do it on conditions. They were that she should write such a letter."

"I wondered that she should," said Mildred, searching in the pocket of her dress. "I came to talk to you about it last night."

"That was the question you wished to ask?"

"Yes. But the arrival of Tamaroo put it out of my head. Did she love my brother?"

"No. Nor did she intend to marry him."

"Then why did she write a lie?"

"Because she would write anything to secure her own ends," said Jarman, taking the letter. "This will not hurt her in any way, and as I asked her to write it she did. I am only beating her with her own weapons."

"What do you intend to do with the letter?" asked the girl.

Eustace put it away, and smiled faintly. "I am going to show it to a black lady called Balkis."

"I heard something about her from Frank. But why—"

"Don't ask me questions, my dear," said Eustace, impatiently, for he felt that he could not talk about the negress without exposing the opium smoking of the dead brother; "there is no time. I go to London in an hour. First I look in at that house in Sand Lane—"

"Where Walter lived?"

"Yes. Frank told me that when he called to see your brother on the day of the murder one of the windows was open. Tilly, the servant, in her evidence said that the windows were all bolted and barred. I am going to ask why she told the lie. I suspect that she knows that someone got into the house, else she would not have given false evidence. And that someone is the murderer."

"Oh, I hope you will be successful!" cried Mildred, clasping her hands. "And afterwards?"

"I go to the Docks to see Balkis. I'll tell you all about it when I return. Keep up your spirits, Mildred," said Jarman, holding out his hand. "I'll

146

save Frank yet."

She bent down, and, before he could stop her, kissed his hand. "Oh, how noble you are—how noble!" Then she ran into the house to prevent further betrayal of emotion.

Jarman turned away sadly. "No hope for me," he thought. "She loves the boy, and he her. The two young things have been loyal to me, and have not come to an understanding. Shall I be less noble? Well, well, well!" He passed his hand across his face with a sigh. "We shall see."

At the Mardon railway station Jarman saw Darrel getting into the train. He gave a scowl as his eyes fell on his enemy, but made no remark. Thinking that the Rhodesian was losing no time, and wondering if he really knew where the hunted man was to be found, Eustace slipped into a third-class smoker. He dismissed the big man from his thoughts, as the only chance of saving Frank lay in getting evidence to prove his innocence. And Jarman hoped to get a portion of such evidence from the servant, Tilly Samuels.

On arriving at Liverpool Street he took the underground train to South Kensington, and soon found himself in Sand Lane. At the door of the house formerly occupied by Starth he saw two women. One was Tilly, who was weeping, and the other—Miss Cork.

CHAPTER XXII

MISS CORK EXPLAINS

The housekeeper looked lean and shadowy as usual. She was still dressed in grey, and wore her hair screwed into the same door-knob that Jarman knew so well. But her face wore a smile, and she was staring at Tilly with passionate affection. When she heard Jarman's foot on the pavement, she turned round with the look of a tigress ready to defend her cubs. But at the sight of her old master she changed colour, and made as if to run away. But Eustace caught her by the elbow, and prevented her departure. Tilly, who wore the blue dress and the picture-hat, looked amazed and indignant.

"'Ere, sir," she said shrilly, "jes leave my mother be, d'ye see!"

"Your mother?" said Eustace, recalling Miss Cork's mention of a stolen child.

"Jus' so," snapped Tilly, making warlike demonstration with the yellow umbrella. "I'll call the policeman round the corner, an' he's a friend o' mine. It's bad enough for that old Betts to keep m' box, without m' mother being hit," and she again began to weep.

"Hush, child," said Miss Cork, sharply, and removing her arm from the grasp of Eustace. "I must speak with this gentleman. I had hoped never to see you again, Mr. Jarman"—with a curtsey—"as I have behaved ungrateful. But if you will put temptation in poor folks' way, you must take the consequence."

"But what temptation are you speaking of?"

"That's a long story," said Miss Cork. "We can't talk here, and Mrs. Betts, who employed my child, has turned her out of the house."

"Without m' box," snivelled Tilly, wiping her eyes with a pair of cotton lavender gloves. "Alt's presents is in it, too."

At that moment, looking very small and very fierce, and very like that celebrated Mrs. Raddle who persecuted Bob Sawyer, the mistress of the discharged servant appeared at the door. "Don't stop the road up before my house," she cried, shaking a mittened fist. "Not a box or a character will you get till you give up your wages for giving me only three days' notice."

"That's the way she goes on, sir," sobbed Tilly, "as if m' mother didn't want to take me away and make a real lady of me."

"Wait a moment," said Jarman, who knew the landlady, having once or twice visited Starth at these rooms. "I can arrange this. Now, Mrs. Betts," he said, striding to the door, "what is the matter?"

"Oh Mr. Jarman, I'm that ashamed, really, so unpleasant, what must you think?" simpered Mrs. Betts, becoming suave.

"I think that I want to have a talk with this young lady and her mother," said Eustace, grimly. "And I'll be glad if you'll let us have a room for half-an-hour."

"Lady! Mother!" gurgled Mrs. Betts. "Well, I'm sure, and what's the world coming to I'd like to know, when gentlemen—"

"Oh, allow me to know my own business best," interrupted Jarman, impatiently. "Tilly's mother was my housekeeper."

"That alters the case," said Mrs. Betts, blandly. "A room is at your service, sir, but I don't give box or character until—"

"I'll pay you Tilly's wages, and you can give both."

Tilly set up a shrill cry of triumph over Mrs. Betts, and would have darted into the house, but that she was withheld by Miss Cork. "We must speak to Mr. Jarman first," said the ex-housekeeper.

"And I must have the money—fifteen shillings—before the box—"

Eustace nodded. "I am in a hurry, Mrs. Betts," he said, walking into the passage. "Let me have a room and half-an-hour with these two."

Quite satisfied, though rather perplexed, the landlady showed her visitor into a small room on the ground floor. It was badly furnished and worse lighted. But at least it was a place where Eustace felt he could talk privately to Miss Cork. Tilly and her mother entered, and Jarman closed the door.

"I shouldn't tork loud," said the small servant, pointing to the key-hole; "her ear's allays there."

A shrill voice through the key-hole replied that this was untrue, and bestowed several unflattering epithets on Tilly. Afterwards the retreating footsteps of Mrs. Betts were heard, and Tilly giggled over her success in detecting the old lady. But Eustace was too worried to take any interest in this comedy. He stationed Tilly near the door that she might give notice if Mrs. Betts returned, and then addressed himself to his old housekeeper.

"Well, Miss Cork, and what have you to say?"

"I beg your pardon, I am not Miss Cork. As I have found my child, I can take my real name, which is Selina Burl—Mrs. Burl. I now go out charing, and never will I be parted from my child again!"

"You need not be, so far as I am concerned. But now explain. Why did you leave me without notice?"

"I saw a picture of the black woman who stole my child."

"You mean Balkis?"

"Yes. I mean the woman who keeps an opium shop at the Docks."

"Did she steal your child?" asked Eustace, wondering.

"Years ago," sighed Mrs. Burl, while Tilly looked on intelligently.

"Why should she steal your child?"

"Ah, that's a long story. I'll tell it to you if you like, sir."

"I'm ready to hear it," answered Eustace, wondering at the coincidence which had brought his former housekeeper into contact with Balkis.

"Burl drank," began the lady, abruptly. "He was a house-painter, and earned wages of the highest when not at the bottle. He turned me out into the street one night with Tilly." Mrs. Burl pointed to her newly-found off-spring, who giggled. "We lived near the Docks, by reason of the cheap rents. I had nowhere to go and was found by that black woman, who called herself Balkis."

"How long ago did this happen?"

"Never you mind," replied Mrs. Burl, drawing her shawl closely round her. "I'll tell what I can, and that which I don't tell don't matter. Balkis (as she called herself) said she wanted a servant, and took me in. She gave no wages, but a comfortable home. We—Tilly and me—stopped with her for some time. Then I left."

"Why did you leave a comfortable place?" asked Jarman.

Mrs. Burl pursed up her lips, and shook her head. "It weren't respect-able," she said, nodding. "No; though in one way it were. I haven't a word to say against Balkis, who always kept herself like a lady, though she was the colour of the tea-kettle. But you see, Mr. Jarman, she kept an opium shop, and a gambling den."

"Ah, did she. What did the police say?"

"Now you come to the reason of my leaving, sir. The police knew noth-ing about the gambling. I don't think they minded the opium smoking. Such people came there!" Mrs. Burl shuddered. "Chinamen and Lascars, and low sailors, and sometimes gentlemen who were fond of the pipe. But all that was almost public, as you might say. The gambling"—here Mrs. Burl lowered her voice—"it took place in the secret rooms."

"What do you mean by the secret rooms?"

"What I do say, Mr. Jarman," replied Mrs. Burl, with several nods, and an air of mystery. "The opium shop was near the river, and respectable to look at outside, being painted and kept clean. But the rooms—which I cleaned—were almost under the river, and furnished like Buckingham Palace. Balkis used to boast that if the police ever found out her rooms they would never leave them alive."

"Did she mean to murder them?"

"Ah, that's just what I don't know. She's a terrible woman, and has all kinds of ideas—very wicked ideas, though I must say that she is respectable for the most part. All she wanted was to make money, and she made it quicker out of the gambling rooms than in any other way. The piles of gold and notes I've seen there, sir, you wouldn't believe. And the Chinamen played an evil game called Fan-tan—"

"I know it," said Eustace, who had been in Canton.

"Then you know a wicked thing, Mr. Jarman, begging your pardon. But I had a quarrel with Balkis, as she would not give me money to dress Tilly, and I threatened to leave. Balkis said that I could go, and then like a fool, knowing the terrible woman she was, I said I'd tell the police about the secret rooms, and the gambling."

"That was indeed foolish, Mrs. Burl."

"Ah, it was, sir, and soon I found it. Balkis, when I was asleep, took Tilly—who was then a child—from my side, and hid her away."

"In effect, she kidnapped her?"

"Yes, Mr. Jarman, she did; and when I woke fair distracted, she said I would never see my child again until she made her money out of the gambling. When she shut them up and returned to America—"

"Ah!" said Eustace, "she came from America."

"She did, Mr. Jarman, from a West Indian island. But when she went I was to have Tilly again. I implored her to give me my child, but she only laughed. She declared if I said a word about the gambling rooms that I would never see Tilly again. Then she turned me out, and I went searching for Tilly, for many a long month, till I was taken up for vagrancy, and you found me."

"Why didn't you tell me this before?" asked Eustace. "I could have told the police and have recovered your child."

"That's just why I held my tongue," said Mrs. Burl, quickly. "If the police had been informed, I would never have got Tilly again. When I was with you I several times went to ask Balkis about Tilly, and she assured me that she was well."

"I was brought up in a wurk-hus," put in Tilly, "and then Mrs. Betts took me, so I've bin 'ere since, though the situation ain't worth much."

"I see," said Eustace. "Well, Mrs. Burl, and how did you recover Tilly?"

Mrs. Burl moved uneasily. "Now I'm coming to my ingratitude, sir. I was afraid when I saw the picture of Balkis which Mr. Lancaster left."

"Hullao!" cried Eustace, with sudden suspicion. "How did you know my secretary was Lancaster? And what do you know of him?"

"I know all that I read in the papers," said Mrs. Burl, with hanging head, "and when I went sometimes to see Balkis I heard Captain Berry talk of how he wished to get Mr. Lancaster."

"Captain Berry? You know the whole gang?"

"Ah, that I do, sir, and will give you any information I can, now that I have my Tilly safe. Balkis wanted to catch Mr. Lancaster also, because he had killed Mr. Starth, of whom she thought much."

"She was in love with him?"

"Well, sir, you might go so far as that. She loved him, and thought Mr. Lancaster guilty. So when I found out that you were hiding Mr.—"

"Wait," said Eustace. "How did you learn that?"

"I listened and then I knew," murmured Mrs. Burl.

"I see," said Eustace, sternly, "and you betrayed the poor wretch."

Mrs. Burl began to weep. "I am ashamed of myself—"

"You may well be," said Jarman, bitterly. "I can guess what you did. Having told Balkis that you could inform her and Berry where the man they wanted was to be found, you promised to denounce him if Balkis gave you Tilly."

"Yes," faltered Mrs. Burl. "I told her, and she said that Tilly was with Mrs. Betts. So I came here, and Tilly gave notice, and now we are going away. But I am ashamed."

"I don't want any apologies," said Jarman, coldly. "It is worse than useless to hear them from so ungrateful a woman as you are. Come to the facts. Balkis told Berry."

"Yes, sir," whimpered the woman. "And she told Miss Berry, who also came to the opium shop—but not to smoke. I will say—"

"That's enough," said Jarman, cutting her short in disgust. "I know now how Berry and his niece came to find Lancaster. You have got your child as the price of your treachery, so there is no more to be said. But the least you can do is to give me the address of Balkis."

"Oh, I'll do that," said Mrs. Burl, sobbing. "I ain't afraid of her now I have my Tilly. But don't go into them secret rooms, sir, for you'll never leave them alive. I should be sorry to see any trouble come upon you, Mr. Jarman."

"That comes well from you!" retorted Eustace, ironically. "However, here is a piece of paper and a pencil. Write down the address of Balkis while I talk to your daughter."

Mrs. Burl obeyed with sighs and sobs, but seemed glad to be let off so easily. Tilly looked up alertly.

"Wotever 'ave you to say to me?" she asked, with wonder expressed on her wizened face.

"This," said Eustace, sharply. "At the inquest you said that all the windows and doors were bolted. You know that one of the front windows was open."

Tilly began to whimper in her turn. "I was afraid of Mrs. Betts," she cried. "She's such a 'ard woman, and would 'ave given me beans, if she'd found as I'd gone out leaving the winder ajar."

"Then the window was open?"

"Yes, sir. The right-'and winder, but the blind was down."

"That wouldn't keep out anyone. Have you any idea who got in and murdered Mr. Starth?"

"Why, sir"—Tilly's eyes opened widely—"didn't that yeller-'aired—"

"No, he didn't, and you know he didn't."

"S'elp me, sir, I never—"

"You know more than you said at the inquest," said Eustace. "Tilly," interpolated her mother in severe tones, having written the address, "tell all. It's the least we can do to this kind gentleman after the way we've treated him."

"You needn't blame Tilly," said Eustace, drily. "You are in fault, not she. Come now"—to Tilly—"do you suspect anyone?"

"No," said Tilly, defiantly. "I don't!"

Eustace thought for a moment. Then he took out a sovereign, and tossed it to Mrs. Burl, "Go and get the box," he said, "and call a cab. I'll speak with Tilly alone."

Mrs. Burl, accustomed to obey Eustace, went out at once, with a final recommendation to Tilly to tell all.

"Now then," said Jarman, when alone with the small servant. "Did you pick up anything?"

"Yes," said Tilly, in a frightened voice, and fished in the pocket of her blue dress. "This and this. One was in the kitchen, the ribbon, and t'other was on the sitting-room floor."

The object found on the sitting-room floor was the invitation sent by Starth to Lancaster asking him to call. Probably Starth, for the furtherance of the plot, had taken it out of Frank's pocket when he lay insensible, intending to destroy it, but had forgotten to do so. It must have lain unnoticed on the floor till picked up by Tilly. "And you found this before the police came?"

"Yes, sir. I should have told 'em, but I was that scared as I didn't."

"You did very wrong," said Eustace, severely. "The coroner insisted that the deceased did not ask Lancaster to see him, and this is the proof that he did. What about the ribbon?"

"I found it in the kitchen," said Tilly, in a subdued voice. "It is a tarting ribbon, and I thought it pretty."

"Have you worn it?"

"No, sir, and I ain't told anyone of it."

153

"I'll take charge of these," said Eustace, putting the articles into his pocket. "Say nothing about them. Now, did you find the window as you left it when you returned?"

"No," whimpered Tilly. "When I went in to lock it for the night it wos close shut and locked."

"Did Mrs. Betts do that?"

"No. She weren't in the room."

"Observe," said Eustace, "how foolish you have been not to state this. The person who killed Starth must have entered by the window, and have locked it when within. He afterwards left by the door."

"She couldn't have got in through the winder."

"What do you mean?"

"Well, sir," said Tilly, with hesitation, "that tarting ribbon wos worn by a woman, as it ain't a necktie."

Eustace was also of this opinion after some reflection, and wondered if Starth could have been killed by a woman. He asked Tilly several other questions, but could learn nothing new from her. Then, having taken possession of the address—that written by his former housekeeper—he left the house. The last he saw of Mrs. Burl, she and Tilly were struggling with Mrs. Betts for the possession of a very small green trunk, and the waiting cabman was applauding the fight. Evidently some new trouble in connection with the three days' notice was taking place.

However, Eustace had more serious things to think of, and washed his hands completely of Mrs. Burl, after her ungrateful behaviour. He lost no time in taking the Underground to the City, and thence departed for the Docks. After a dull journey he repaired to the address mentioned in the paper. It was a certain number in a narrow lane which led down to the water's edge. On the right-hand side of this Eustace found a respectable-looking house, painted a spotless white, and with green shutters. It would not have disgraced a new suburb. The doorstep was also white, and the brass knocker polished to a painful brilliancy. Amidst all the other frowsy houses that of Balkis looked fresh and clean and genteel.

The door was opened by a lean Chinaman dressed in blue. He made no remark, but conducted Eustace into a room furnished in the Chinese manner. Jarman was left alone for a few minutes, then a huge negress entered the room, and he recognised her as Balkis from the picture. It was not her looks that made him start but her garb. She was dressed in a brilliant tartan gown, and the ribbon picked up in the Sand Lane house by Tilly was of the same pattern.

CHAPTER XXIII

BALKIS

For a moment or two Eustace and the negress eyed one another. He was admiring her shapely form and stately bearing. Although black, she was comely, and in spite of the character given to her by Miss Cork, *alias* Mrs. Burl, looked a good-natured creature in the main, although Jarman granted that she could be furious when aroused. On the evidence of the tartan ribbon, he wondered if she had been lurking in Mrs. Betts's kitchen on that fatal day, and whether she had killed the man she professed to love.

On her side Balkis was—as the Americans put it—sizing up her visitor. Her customers were for the most part Lascars, Malays, Chinamen, and sailors. But occasionally a gentleman from the West End would come to her respectable house to smoke a sly pipe of opium. Some even came to gamble, and Balkis was wondering if this well-looking man was a smoker or a gambler. She waited for him to speak, being shrewd and not caring to venture an opinion until she knew precisely what his business was.

"Do you know an old man called Tamaroo?" asked Eustace, suddenly.

Balkis looked at him serenely. "I never heard of him," she said.

Jarman noticed that she spoke almost as well as Tamaroo himself, and wondered that, within so short a space of time, he should come into contact with two educated members of the African race.

Evidently she was on her guard, so Eustace tried another shot.

"I was directed to this house by Mrs. Burl," he said.

This time Balkis showed emotion, and, to speak truly, became rather ferocious.

"She's a bad woman. An ungrateful woman! I saved her and her child from starving, and she—"

"She threatened to betray you," finished Jarman, serenely.

Balkis stared, and looked still more unpleasant. "There is nothing wrong that she could say. If you belong to the police you've wasted your time. I am quite respectable."

"Even to keeping those secret gambling-rooms?"

"What!" She glared at him like a tigress. "Burl told you that, did she, and after my telling her where to find Tilly?"

"After taking away Tilly from her for years," said Jarman, calmly.

"You know a great deal of what does not concern you," said Balkis, placing her hands on her hips, "and if you've come to threaten, I am quite able to defend myself. There's no gambling here, and no secret rooms. If you want a clean mat and a pipe you can have it. I have never been in trouble with the law yet."

Eustace produced the piece of ribbon. "Do you know where I found this?" he asked, dangling it between finger and thumb.

"You bought it, I suppose," she said quietly.

Eustace shook his head. "Observe, it is of the same pattern as your dress —as the ribbon you wear round your neck."

"What's that to do with me?"

"Simply this. It belongs to you and was lost in a house in Sand Lane, Kensington, where a—"

Balkis made a step towards him, and her big eyes rolled savagely. "Why are you talking like this?" she asked hoarsely.

"If you know Tamaroo he will tell you."

"Tell me yourself, mister."

"There's no reason why I should not. I have come here for certain information, and I don't go away till I get it."

"Information about what?" she demanded unpleasantly.

"About certain people whom you know. Captain Berry, his niece, Tamaroo, and Lancaster."

"Lancaster—the wretch who murdered my Walter!" cried Balkis, with a tragic air. "See here, mister, I have men below—foreign men, who carry knives. At a word from me they'd cut your tongue out."

"At the risk of having a hole drilled through them," said Eustace.

Balkis seemed disconcerted, as she apparently did not expect that he would be armed. "Who are you—your name?"

"Eustace Jarman."

To his surprise Balkis made a clutch at his hand, and shook it warmly. "Why didn't you say so before? Where do you live?"

"In Essex—at Wargrove."

"Who had you for housekeeper?"

"Miss Cork, who now is Mrs. Burl."

Balkis clapped her huge hands. "You're the right man. I expected you would come and see me."

"You expected me?"

"Yes. Tamaroo told me you would come, sooner or later. And then I heard of you in 'Frisco. Mrs. Anchor! Eh?" said Balkis, archly.

"Oh, so you don't come from Zanzibar?"

"Who said I did?"

"Walter Starth told Lancaster."

The face of the negress grew sad. "Yes, I told Walter that, for—for reasons with which you have nothing to do. Well, what do you come to me for, Mr. Jarman?"

"To see if you are the friend or the enemy of Berry?"

"I am neither the one nor the other," she said frankly. "I knew him in San Francisco, and in Jamaica. He is a sailor, and found me out through following my Walter."

"Why did he follow him?"

"I can't tell you that yet," she said suspiciously. "Walter came here to smoke. He was fond of a pipe. He met Captain Berry up West, and Berry followed him here. Then we recognised one another, and good old Banjo often came here to smoke a pipe. But why do you ask these questions?"

Eustace reflected. She appeared to be frank, and certainly did not side with Berry to any great extent. He thought it best to trust her, for even if she made use of the information he gave her it would not benefit her in any way.

"You loved Walter Starth?" asked Eustace.

The big negress, who had been standing, dropped into a chair.

"With all my soul!" she said vehemently. "Ah, you think because I am black that I have no feelings. But I did love him. He was going to marry me—yes. I am rich, and I could have bought him."

"You certainly gave him your photograph," said Jarman; "but if you come from America, how did you write those Arabic words?"

"I did not. It was a Malay who wrote them for me. I wanted Walter to think that I came from Zanzibar. I did not want him to know anything about San Francisco."

"Why not?"

"I sha'n't tell you. I have my own secrets. Again I ask why you question me in this way?"

"Because I am a friend of Lancaster's, and I want to prove his innocence."

"He is not innocent!" cried Balkis, with a lowering brow. "He killed my Walter. Tamaroo says he did not, and I have not made up my mind to harm him yet."

"Harm who—Tamaroo?"

"No; the man Lancaster. I can get rid of him in my own way."

"I see. You have something to do with Obi."

Balkis shuddered, and her face turned grey. "Hush! Say not that dread name," she said, looking round fearfully. "Why do you, a white man, talk of Obi? You are not of us—you know nothing of the fetish."

"No; but I have travelled in the West Indies. You know how to prepare the poisons that are used in connection with Obi"—again the negress shuddered—"so you propose to get rid of Lancaster by giving him poison. Well, that is better than being hanged. But how are you going to get Lancaster here? He has disappeared."

"I know how to get him when I want," said Balkis, sulkily. "Tamaroo is his friend, and Tamaroo also loves the fetish."

"Not to such an extent as to make Lancaster over to you for you to practise your devilish arts on him," said Eustace, indignantly. "Or do you intend to put him into your secret rooms, and get rid of him as you would rid yourself of the police did they raid the place?"

"Burl again!" said the woman, with a snarl, and showing a magnificent set of white teeth. "She told you a lot. If I get her here again she will have the chance of seeing how I can rid myself of those I do not like." She paused, then said abruptly: "There are no rooms."

"That means you don't trust me yet," said Jarman, feeling in his pocket. He determined as a last resource to make use of the letter written by Fairy Fan. For this moment had he procured it. "Did Starth love you?" he asked, looking at her.

"Yes. He was going to marry me. But he was killed, and I shall avenge his death. If Lancaster killed him Lancaster shall die."

Jarman spoke plainly. "Do you know Miss Berry? Well, she also loved Starth, and he promised to marry her."

Balkis gave a yell like that of an enraged lioness. "It is not true—not true," she said, in guttural tones. "A lie! A lie! A lie!" She danced and stamped as she reiterated the word. "He loved me, and me only! He said so! He was to marry me."

"He was to marry Miss Berry. Here is the proof," and Eustace handed her the letter, which she snatched from him eagerly.

To arouse the jealousy of Balkis had he got this letter written, and had put it to a use which Fairy Fan never expected, or she certainly would not have written it. Eustace guessed that a semi-civilised creature like Balkis would be insanely jealous, and that if she found the man she loved adored another woman would make short work of that woman. Had Balkis been on the side of the Berrys, Jarman hoped to detach her from their interests by means of this letter. But Balkis apparently cared neither one way nor the other. Still, to make her talk more freely, it was worth while trying the experiment. The ruse was successful, for the great black creature after reading the letter went fairly mad.

"She shall die—she shall die!" was her cry, and again she stamped, crushing up the letter in her strong fingers. If Fairy Fan now came within reach of those fingers Eustace thought she would have short shrift. But he was not sorry. The crimes of Mrs. Anchor needed some such punishment.

Suddenly Balkis thrust the letter into her pocket, and seizing Jarman's hand kissed it savagely. "You are my friend. I swear by you! I will do what you want," she said hoarsely.

"Then tell me who killed Starth."

"I cannot—unless it was Lancaster. Tamaroo says no; but, then, he is the friend of Lancaster."

"How did you meet Tamaroo?"

"I knew him in San Francisco. He also is Obi-worshipper. He knew I was here in London, and when he came he visited me. I told him all I knew about Captain Berry."

"Did Tamaroo come after Starth died?"

"No. A week before he died."

Eustace thought. Tamaroo said that he arrived after the death, and in that way explained his inability to find Frank. But it seemed that he was really in town beforehand. "Did Tamaroo know Starth?"

"No," said Balkis. She paused and looked questioningly. "You heard of the Scarlet Bat?" she asked.

"Yes. Tamaroo told me all about it."

"Ah!" Balkis drew a long breath. "Me also he told, and how Berry wished for the money. He learnt that Berry came here, and asked questions. I told him all. When he heard that Berry knew my Walter he said he would go to Walter to hear more of him. I told him the house, and sent that ribbon with Tamaroo so that Walter might know he came from me."

"Oh, then Tamaroo was in the house when the murder was committed?"

Balkis looked strangely at him. "Tamaroo did not kill my Walter," she said. "If he had, I should have killed him." And, although Jarman urged her to say more, she declined to do so.

Then he thought of the likeness remarked upon by Jenny between Mr. Darrel and Balkis. "Do you know a man called Darrel?"

"I do. He comes from Jamaica. Why should I tell you a lie. He is a cousin of mine."

"I thought so," said Jarman, drawing a deep breath.

"Yes. He has our blood in him. He comes here at times, but he never calls me cousin. He thinks himself white, but he has our blood."

"Well, Balkis, you know now how Miss Berry has treated you."

"I shall kill her!" said Balkis, gnashing her splendid teeth; "and I know how to kill her painfully."

Jarman shuddered, so ferociously did she make this speech. He thought he would not like to offend this creature. "And you will help me to save Lancaster," he said eagerly—"to save him and baffle the Berrys?"

"I do not know," she said sullenly, and heaved herself up from the chair. "If he is innocent he shall not die. If not, he shall die. Come!"

"Where will you take me?" asked Eustace, following her to the door, but feeling in his hip pocket that his revolver was loose.

"To my secret rooms," said Balkis, looking back with a grin.

"Ah, then Mrs. Burl is right. You have secret rooms."

Balkis nodded, and led him down a long passage.

"And I can kill in them," she said in a matter-of-fact tone. "But not you. You are my friend." She grinned again. "I shall let you see that woman die if you like."

Jarman shuddered again at the venomous tone, and in spite of his courage felt a trifle nervous. However, he had his revolver, and, if it came to the worst, resolved to fight. Now that he had launched himself into the adventure he was resolved to carry it through. He had promised Mildred to save Frank, and this was the only way to do it. Balkis could tell the truth, and he wished her to do so.

The negress led him to a trap door, and they descended to find themselves in a long stone passage. At the end of it was an iron door, which she opened. Eustace was conscious of a blaze of light, and in the glare saw—of all people—Tamaroo and Frank Lancaster!

160

CHAPTER XXIV

TAMAROO SPEAKS

"You did not expect to find me here?" said Frank, after he had shaken hands warmly with his friend.

"The very last place in which I should have looked for you. How did you come?" He glanced inquiringly at Tamaroo.

"I brought him," replied the old negro. "When you overturned the lamp I drew Mr. Frank away in the darkness. We went to the nearest railway station and came to town. Then did we seek this shelter. The Captain will never think to find us here. What of him?"

"He is furious, and quite at a loss to find you. But—" Eustace glanced at Balkis, where she stood with folded arms staring at Frank with no very pleasant expression.

"There is nothing to fear," she said, guessing Jarman's meaning. "As yet I am not sure if this man killed my Walter."

"I did not," interposed Frank. "I told you so before."

"And I also assured you of his innocence," said Tamaroo, uneasily.

Balkis still continued to glare. "As I say, I am not sure," she declared obstinately. "If you did not kill my Walter you will come to no harm. Here you can stay until I send you out of the place to foreign parts. But if you killed him"—she looked savage—"there will be no escape for you. Now you know!" And with this not very reassuring speech she passed through the door again, shutting it with a clang.

Eustace heard a key turn in the lock and recalled the warning of Mrs. Burl.

"Are we safe here?" he asked Tamaroo, who appeared quite easy in his mind. "I was told that these rooms were dangerous."

"Dangerous?" echoed the negro, looking round. "Why should they be dangerous?"

Jarman repeated the warning of Mrs. Burl and the boast of Balkis. But Tamaroo merely laughed. "There is no danger," he said decisively. "I am quite sure that. Balkis will do nothing to harm us."

"She does not seem to be very well disposed towards Frank."

161

"Because she will insist that I killed Starth," said Frank. "No doubt Berry has been poisoning her mind. However, Berry will not look for me here."

"Darrel might," hinted Eustace, uneasily.

"Nonsense! How can he find this place?"

"Oh, he knows it! My belief that he had the negro blood in his veins is true. He is a relative of Balkis, and sometimes comes here; but he is not proud of the relationship."

"But even if he does know this place he'll never think that I am here."

Eustace looked doubtful. "I had to pitch him out of the garden of Rose Cottage," he said. "He was impertinent to Mildred."

"To Mildred?" repeated Frank, with an angry flush.

"Yes," responded Jarman, keeping his eyes away from Frank's face. "He said—well, never mind what he said. I punished him for his insolence, and he went away, vowing that he would hunt you down."

Tamaroo laughed. "He will never come here," he said. "He must know that Balkis is on the side of the Berrys, and will believe that this is the last place I would bring my master to. The very danger of the refuge makes its safety."

"I am not sure that Balkis *is* on the side of Captain Berry now," was the reply of Eustace. "She certainly will not help him, if only because she hates Fairy Fan," and Eustace related how he had made use of the letter Miss Berry had written.

Tamaroo nodded approvingly. "That is a good plan," he said. "If she thinks the white woman loved Starth, she will not help her plots. Balkis was madly in love with Mr. Starth."

"She says he would have married her," said Jarman.

Frank laughed. "I don't believe that. Starth was nice in his ideas of female beauty, and would not marry a black woman. Moreover, he was desperately in love with Fan."

"Balkis knows that, and hates Fan accordingly," said Eustace, grimly. "But Starth might have married Balkis for her money."

"She is certainly rich," put in Tamaroo, meditatively. "Already she has made up her mind to return to America. She goes next week."

"And what will you do with Frank then?"

"Take him abroad. I have arranged it all with Balkis. She knows many sailors, and can get some captain to give Mr. Frank and myself a passage— say to Spain. There we will wait till there is a chance of learning who killed Starth."

Jarman looked attentively at the negro. "You do not know who is the guilty person?" he asked meaningly.

"No." Tamaroo looked surprised. "Why should I?"

"Well," said Eustace, quietly, "I went to Sand Lane to examine Tilly, the servant. She said that the right-hand window of the house was open—"

"I remember that. I told you so," said Frank.

"Yes, and on your report I questioned Tilly. She admitted that she told a lie at the inquest. The window was open when she left the house. On her return"—here Eustace looked again at Tamaroo—"it was locked, which proves that the assassin entered by the window, and, after committing the murder, locked it so that no one should get into the house, and discover the crime. Then he left by the door."

"Why do you look at Tamaroo when you say that?" asked Frank.

"Because Tilly found a scrap of tartan ribbon on the kitchen floor similar to that worn by Balkis. I brought it with me, and Balkis acknowledged that it was a piece she gave to Tamaroo, when he decided to see Starth."

Frank wheeled round and looked anxiously at the negro. "Did you see Starth?" he demanded. "I thought you did not arrive in London till after the murder, and for that reason you could not find me."

Tamaroo considered for a few minutes. "I did say that," he admitted; "because I thought it wise for the moment to conceal that I had been in Starth's house. I thought you might mistrust me."

"I should never do that," replied Lancaster, patting the old man on the back. "But why did you visit Starth?"

"I should like to know that also," said Eustace, who was not so easily convinced of the negro's innocence.

The man gave him a reproachful glance. "I acted for the best, Mr. Jarman. You can trust me."

"I think I can," answered Eustace, cautiously. "And yet—why did you visit Starth?"

"To explain that, I must remind you of the murder of Anchor in San Francisco. It was Sakers who shot him. I was glad of it."

Eustace looked as surprised as Frank. "I thought Anchor was the executor of my father?" said the latter.

"He was, and he intended to betray his trust. He was so madly in love with his wife that he could not give her up. She threatened to leave him and go with her uncle if he did not let her share in the money of Mr. Lancaster. Anchor had the papers—some of them. But I had others which he wanted, so that he could dispose of the money. He intended to join his wife in Chicago, and, with Sakers, to arrange for the robbery. I do not know how he intended to manage it. But I do know," added Tamaroo, emphatically, "that it was his intention to return to his house, where I was waiting for him, to get the papers from me, and to leave me dead behind him."

Eustace could scarcely believe this, "If you heard how the man spoke to me—"

"I know. It was to throw dust in your eyes. You would report that Anchor was at enmity with Sakers and Mrs. Anchor, and thus no one would suspect him of the robbery. When he spoke to you, Mr. Jarman, he had the papers on him. Sakers—or rather Berry—knew this. He intended to kill Anchor, and to rob the body of the papers. However, he chose the wrong moment, as you were talking to the man. You chased Sakers, and he could not search the body. I did so."

"Ah! You were on the spot. You said something about it."

"I learnt—in a way that it is not necessary to explain—that the man intended to betray his trust. Mrs. Anchor gave the information."

"Was she at the house?"

"Yes, and I was waiting there for the return of Anchor. I left the house and went to your rooms, Mr. Jarman, where Mrs. Anchor said her husband had gone. I saw the shot fired, and saw also that Sakers fled, pursued by you. When the street was quiet I came to see the body, and got the papers from the breast-pocket."

"But what about the Chinaman, Lo Keong, who stabbed him?"

"It was not a Chinaman," said Tamaroo, quietly. "I stabbed him."

"You?" Jarman was beginning to see the connection between the San Francisco crime and the Sand Lane murder.

"Yes, I," said Tamaroo, perfectly calm and collected, while Frank shivered. "Anchor was a traitor. He was betraying a sacred trust. When I took the papers he opened his eyes. I saw that he was still alive, so I stabbed him."

Jarman jumped up, and even Frank recoiled from the negro. "You had no right to kill the man," said Eustace, hoarsely.

"I did not. The shot was a fatal one. I simply stabbed him to make sure. You need not rebuke me, Mr. Jarman. I did it then and I would do it again."

"Did you do it again?" asked Frank, remembering the death of Starth.

"You are thinking of Sand Lane. Yes, sir, it was I who stabbed Starth."

Eustace shuddered. "Was he alive?"

"No. He was quite dead. But I stabbed him in order to frighten Mr. Berry. When he saw that the man had died from wounds similar to those Anchor had died from, I fancied he would be afraid, and abandon his scheme to get the money."

"Did Berry know that you stabbed Anchor?"

"No. Nor does he know that I stabbed Starth. But, seeing that there was a shot wound and a knife wound in the two cases, he must have gathered that someone else was mixed up in the matter. Such a knowledge would make him careful."

"It didn't, however," said Frank.

The young man did not like the way in which Tamaroo had behaved, for, although he had not murdered either Anchor or Starth, still he had mutilated them. But then, in spite of his veneer of education, Tamaroo was a negro pure and simple, with the savage instincts of the African race. To rebuke him would be as futile as punishing a dog for barking. Tamaroo had only obeyed his nature. And Eustace, on his side, shrewdly suspected that Balkis—also an African—would act in the like barbaric fashion did she think it necessary. The race instinct held good, in spite of the fact that both these black people were educated.

"Tell me exactly what occurred in the house," said Eustace, "and also explain why you went to see Starth?"

"When I came to England I stopped here for a time," said Tamaroo, "as I knew Balkis in San Francisco, and knew that she would not betray me to Berry."

"Why not, considering—"

"That is a secret of Obi," said the old man, with a savage look. "I was here in these rooms, which are not generally known to the outside world. Starth and Berry came here, and I knew them, but when they were here I always kept out of their way. From listening I became aware that there was a plot against you, Mr. Frank, to have you hanged. Starth and Berry were the movers, also Miss Berry. Starth was to receive his share on condition that he inveigled you to his house, and there you were to be saddled with the guilt of murder."

"But Starth did not expect to be killed himself?"

"Oh no! But Berry intended that he should be the victim. That was why Miss Berry made trouble and created rows between Starth and you, Mr. Frank. Berry, at the theatre on the previous night, brought about that quarrel so that you might be accused. Then the next day Starth wrote the letter asking you to visit him. How Starth fancied that the crime was to be brought about I don't know. He drugged you, and then waited for the arrival of Berry to carry on the rest of the plot."

"How did you come to know all this?"

"I gathered it at various times, and thought out the rest," said Tamaroo, nodding. "Of course, some of it is my own fancy."

"Theory," grunted Eustace, admitting, however, that the negro had pieced things together very cleverly. "Well, you went to Sand Lane?"

"Yes. As I thought that this trouble was coming, I pretended to Balkis that I wished to see Starth, and she gave me the tartan ribbon she wore as a sign that I could be trusted."

"In what way?" asked Frank.

Tamaroo shook his head. "I can't tell you that. There was something in Starth's life which Balkis knew, and which gave her a hold over him. He

165

was always afraid of people of my colour. Unless I had taken the tartan ribbon he would not have spoken."

"Did he speak?"

"I never saw him," replied the negro, simply. "I did not get to the house till nearly seven. The window was open, and as I saw no one about, and could get no answer when I rang, I climbed in. I then locked the window, so that no one should enter in that way to interrupt between Starth and myself."

"There was no chance of that."

"I don't know, Mr. Jarman. I had entered that way, and, seeing what a plot was in progress, others might have come in. I then went down the stairs to see the servant, as Balkis had mentioned her."

"Balkis knew Tilly," murmured Eustace. "And then?"

"There was no one there. I went up the stairs, and found Starth dead. He lay in the middle of the room, and you, Mr. Frank, were unconscious on the sofa—drugged as I saw."

"Why did you not give the alarm?" asked Lancaster, angrily. "I could not, sir. I was a stranger and a man of colour. Also I had entered by the window. Had I given the alarm I should have been arrested and perhaps hanged. You can see my difficulty."

"Yes," admitted Frank. "I see it was an awkward position."

"I thought it best to go away and say nothing. I knew that Starth had been shot so as to inculpate you, and that you would be arrested. Had that happened I should have come forward. As you escaped I waited, hoping to trap Berry in the dark. I wished to find you, and to tell you what I knew. That was why I posted the Scarlet Bat over London. I knew that it was tattooed on your arm, and that if you became aware of the posters you would, out of curiosity, inquire for the sealed letter."

"That's exactly what happened," said Eustace. "But you say that Starth was waiting for Berry after he drugged Frank. Perhaps Berry came and shot Starth with Frank's pistol, and then departed."

"No," said Tamaroo, decisively, "I can't think that. Berry wanted to enjoy the money, and wouldn't have risked the murder."

"Then I can't say who shot the man if not Berry," said Jarman. "However, on what you say, we'll try and bluff Berry. And before you Berry," said Jarman. "However, on what you say, we'll try and bluff Berry. And before you left, you stabbed the body?"

"Yes, I did," rejoined Tamaroo, defiantly. "The man was dead and I thought to frighten Berry. There was much at stake. I then left the house, but I don't think anyone saw me going, as it was growing dark. That is all I know. What else is to be found out must be discovered by you, Mr. Jarman."

"I'll do my best," said Eustace. "But who am I to follow?"

Providence answered that question. There was the sound of the door opening. Balkis entered, and after her came Captain Berry, his niece, and Darrel. The Rhodesian, fulfilling his threat, had hunted Frank down, and was face to face with his prey.

CHAPTER XXV

NEMESIS

Fairy Fan cast a scornful glance round the room. It did not deserve such disdain, as it was magnificently furnished, although the display of colour was rather barbaric. The walls were lined with tall narrow mirrors framed in gold, and with painted panels let in between. The hangings were of crimson plush embroidered with gold, and the blue carpet was profusely sprinkled with yellow flowers. There were red velvet divans against the walls, many gilt chairs with spindle-legs, and numerous card-tables with green-cloth tops. At the further end of the room a door—likewise sheathed in iron—led into an inner and smaller apartment, similarly furnished. And everywhere glittered electric lights in opaque globes. Apparently Balkis had spared no cost to make her subterranean gambling-rooms as gorgeous as possible. When she saw Miss Berry sneer at the—in her opinion—matchless magnificence of the place, her black eyes sparkled with fury.

But the men had more important things to think about than the furnishing of the room, with which they were well acquainted. Berry surveyed Frank with glee, and rubbed his hands. He looked harder and more evil than ever, and openly gloated over his victim.

"I guess you're fixed this trip, young man," said he, cheerfully.

Frank turned a disdainful back on the little scoundrel, and addressed himself to Darrel, who glared at him with sulky triumph.

"You betrayed me, I suppose?" he said, with contempt.

"I knew that Tamaroo would bring you here," replied Darrel, coolly, "and I have brought Berry to have you arrested."

"That is out of the question," put in Jarman, decidedly.

"Why so?" demanded Berry, with a snarl.

"Because I know too much about you and your niece here. If this case comes into court, I'll have Captain Banjo Berry, *alias* Sakers, arrested for the murder of Anchor in San Francisco."

"I did not murder him."

"I can testify to that," said Fan, who was listening eagerly. "He was with me in Chicago at the time."

"You were not in Chicago," cried Tamaroo. "You came back to your own house, and told me that your husband had gone to see Mr. Jarman. I followed him, and I saw Captain Berry kill Anchor."

The little skipper clenched his hands. "It's a lie! Who'll believe the words of a black man?"

168

"I am not black," said Eustace, coolly, "and I can swear that you fired the shot. Your niece made out that her husband was killed by an old miner whom he had cheated. That is untrue. You shot him, as you hoped to get the papers dealing with the Scarlet Bat treasure from him."

"He intended to give them in any case," said Mrs. Anchor.

"I know that," said Tamaroo; "and he asked me to come to the house, so that he might get the rest of the documents from me. But I guessed his trick, and I followed him. I took the papers from his body and I knifed him."

"You?" cried Fan and Berry together.

"Yes. He was a traitor, and he died. You killed him, Berry, but I put the finishing stroke. And I also stabbed Starth."

"Ah!" cried Berry in triumph. "You murdered him."

Frank darted forward and placed himself before the little man. "If that is so," he said, "I must be innocent."

"You are not," snarled Berry. "You shot Starth, and this black fellow finished him off."

"Starth was dead when I put the knife into his heart," said Tamaroo. "You were afraid when you found that he was killed as Anchor had been killed in San Francisco."

"You gave me a bad quarter of an hour, I admit," said Berry; "but I guess Lancaster will swing, and you'll get gaol, Tamaroo."

"Nothing of the sort," said Jarman, coolly. "You can't do what you like, Berry. I'll see to that."

"See to yourself," said Berry, wrathfully. "See to your own life. If I give the word, neither you nor Lancaster will leave this place alive. I can depend upon Balkis."

"Yes," said Balkis, "you can depend upon me."

Her eyes were fixed on Fairy Fan with a vindictive expression, and her words bore a different meaning to what Berry gave them. He quite believed that Balkis was on his side, and went on in triumph.

"There are men in the pay of Balkis who would knife you as soon as I chose. Take care, Jarman, I am not to be trifled with. I mean to get that money."

"Forty thousand a-year," put Tamaroo; and Fan's eyes sparkled.

"So much as that?" she said, clasping her hands.

"Yes," said Frank. "I don't suppose I'll spend half of it."

"You!" cried the Captain, with a howl of derision. "You won't spend it. You hang and the money goes to Denham."

"Supposing it does," said Eustace, suddenly—"suppose your clever plot comes to a successful conclusion, how are you going to get the money from Denham?"

"He'll do anything I wish him to do."

"Oh no, he won't. You disgusted him by asking that he should play the spy on Lancaster. He came down to me, and, in conjunction with Tamaroo, I have opened his eyes to your rascality. Denham is on the side of Lancaster, and your plot to coerce him has failed."

Fan laughed derisively. "I can twist him round my finger."

"Oh no. He is in love with Miss Arrow, the daughter of the rector of Wargrove. He will have nothing further to do with you, Mrs. Anchor."

Berry's face was changing colour. He recognised that he had made a mistake in letting Natty get beyond his influence, and did not know what to do for the moment. If he had Lancaster hanged, Natty would get the money —that was always intended—but now Natty was on the side of the enemy, he and Fan would never enjoy the forty thousand a-year. Perhaps it would be better to make some bargain with Lancaster. Darrel guessed that the little skipper thought of hedging, and hastily interposed.

"Let's get this over," he said. "Here is Lancaster, whom we know is guilty of murder. Balkis had better conduct us to the upper part of the house, since she does not wish the police to come here. Then Lancaster can be arrested."

"If the police came here," said Balkis, before anyone could speak, "not one of them would leave again. These rooms are known to none but those who have gambled here, and when I go to America next week no trace of them will remain."

"How do you intend to destroy them?" asked Berry, derisively.

The black woman looked at Fan with an evil eye, and smiled slowly. "You may learn that before we part," she said.

Frank was growing weary of all this hesitation and of these vague threats. He resolved upon a bold stroke in order to bring Berry to his knees.

"I'm sick of this hole-and-corner business," he cried. "Let us do what Darrel suggests. I shall submit to arrest."

"Frank!" said Jarman, hurriedly; and Tamaroo also protested.

"I intend to give myself up," said Lancaster, determinedly. "Had I not been a moral coward I should have done so in the first instance. I am perfectly innocent of this crime, and I shall stand my trial."

But this proposition, as Frank anticipated, was not at all to the taste of Berry. He was about to object when his niece stopped him. With an engaging smile she came forward and took Frank's hand. "Listen to me, my dear," she said sweetly. "You were always my favourite, and I have loved you always. Promise to marry me, and you shall go free to enjoy the money."

"Along with you, I suppose?"

"Along with me," she answered, still smiling. "It is not hard."

"No, but it's impossible, I guess," said Berry, grimly. "I ain't going to let you and Fan skip with the dollars after all my trouble."

"And I'm not going to let Lancaster escape," chimed in Darrel. "I want to see him hanged."

"He shall never be hanged!" said Tamaroo, much agitated.

Eustace, who had his eye on the savage face of Balkis, suddenly addressed Miss Berry. "You say you love Lancaster?"

"I do. I have always loved him."

"That is untrue. You only want to marry him because you can't get the money in any other way. There is a chance, I see, of you three thieves falling out." He looked scornfully on Berry, Fan, and Darrel. "In that case an honest man, such as Lancaster is, may come by his own."

"You talk nonsense," said Fan, doggedly. "I love Frank—"

"Pardon me, you loved Starth."

Fan objected loudly, while the eyes of Balkis flashed. "I never did, Eustace, I hated him."

"You loved Starth," repeated Jarman, mercilessly. "I have it in your own handwriting."

Without a word Balkis darted forward, and held out the letter. The other woman laughed. "That is a trick of Mr. Jarman's," she said.

"It is not a trick," hissed the negress. "Look you, I loved Walter with all my heart and soul. He would have married me. Yes, you may laugh"—she glared like a brave lioness on Berry and Darrel—"but he would have married me. I loved him, and this white woman stole his love."

Fairy Fan changed colour at the sight of this rage on the part of Balkis, and even the Captain looked uneasy. He was well aware that Balkis had it in her power to make things unpleasant for him, and was quite willing to save his own skin by deserting his niece. Fan still kept her courage, and denied the letter.

"I wrote that with a purpose. It is not true. I swear it!"

"Though you swore a hundred oaths I should not believe you," said Balkis, stamping. "You loved my Walter, you took him from me. I will punish you. I will—I will!" She shook her fist in a paroxysm of rage and dashed into the inner room.

Fan stared at Eustace. "This is your work," she said, looking pale.

Jarman nodded. "I got the letter for this purpose. You will not pacify that savage jealousy easily."

Miss Berry slipped her arm within that of her uncle. "I am quite safe," she said coolly. "No harm can come to me."

"Wait a moment," said Berry, removing his arm. "You left me in the lurch, Fan, when you married Anchor. I'm going to make my own bed this time, and lie on it."

"What do you mean?" she asked quickly.

"This," said the little scoundrel, coolly. "Natty's given us the go-by, so there ain't much chance of getting the money through him."

"There's less chance of getting it through me," said Frank, quickly, "if that's your meaning, Berry. I intend to give myself up."

"Don't be a fool," said Darrel, quickly, and looking uneasy.

"I've been a fool long enough. I'll give myself up."

Eustace nodded. "That's the best thing to do," he declared, for he had been observant of the Berry face. "Stand your trial, Frank. I have got evidence that will stand you in good stead."

"But see here," cried Berry, looking more and more dismayed. "If you can be proved innocent—"

"Ah! You admit that I am innocent," said Frank, quickly.

"To all here. But it depends upon yourself if I prove it in open court. What will you give me?"

"Wait a moment, Frank," interposed Jarman, preventing the young man from replying. "Do you mean to say, Berry, that you can prove the innocence of Lancaster?"

"No, he can't," said Darrel. "It's impossible."

"Not if I get five thousand a-year for life," said Berry, coolly.

"Then I must have half of it," put in Fairy Fan.

At this moment Balkis called them into the inner room in an imperious voice. At first they were unwilling to go; then they decided to obey, seeing that the negress might prove dangerous. She was seated at the head of a table under a kind of canopy.

"You say that Lancaster is innocent?" she asked Berry.

"I do," he replied, "if I get five thousand a-year; and a mighty small sum that is, considering the cards I hold."

"But what about me?" said Fan, looking disagreeable.

"Oh, you shall be rewarded," said Balkis, blandly. "I don't believe you loved Walter after all."

"No. I love Frank here, but since he will not marry me, let him give me the same sum as he gives my uncle."

"That means I have to pay ten thousand a-year," said Frank.

"Out of forty thousand. It's cheap at the price."

"I refuse to allow this," said Darrel, loudly. "Balkis, you are my relation. Stand by me."

"Ah! You remember I am of your blood when you want me," said the negress, bitterly. "Well, I shall do what you wish."

"Then I wish this," said Darrel, strong in this support. "Do not let any of these people leave this place alive till I get what I want. Lancaster must be hanged, I must marry Mildred Starth, and I must have twenty thousand a-year given to me."

"Very modest you are!" murmured Jarman; while Tamaroo, glancing at Balkis, smiled slightly.

"What about us?" asked Berry and Fan.

"I will see that you have money also," said Darrel. "I am master of the situation now."

"And you intend to hang me?" cried Frank, his blood up. "Then not one of you will get a penny. Denham shall have the money if I die."

"Or the charity," put in Eustace. "Frank has only to commit suicide, which is better than being hanged, and the money goes to the charity. I think you'd better make terms, Berry."

"I intend to. Leave me alone, Darrel. Lancaster, will you give me and Fan ten thousand a-year between us if I prove your innocence?"

"Yes, I will do that. I'll make an agreement if you like."

"Oh, I can trust you. You can do nothing till you have the proof. I have the confession of the person who killed Starth. It is locked up in my strong-box at my rooms. The key is on my watch-chain. When we leave here you will come to my lawyers, and we can arrange with Tamaroo here about getting a document drawn up. When all is tight and right, you will get the paper that proves your innocence."

"And whose guilt?" asked Frank.

"I can tell you," said Eustace, quickly. "I have suspected the man for some time. Darrel, *you* shot Starth."

"I did not," said the big man, hoarsely.

"Yes, you did," said Berry, relentlessly. "I can chuck you now, since I am right myself. I found you in the room with the dead body. I let myself in with my latch-key. I could have denounced you, but having my own game to play I let you off on your signing a confession. You did so in the room at Sand Lane."

"It's a lie—it's a lie!" said Darrel, turning grey.

"It is true, I believe," said Eustace, quickly. "Tamaroo says that Berry was coming to the house."

"I was," said Berry. "You may as well know all. I wanted Lancaster hanged to let Natty have the money—"

"We know all that," said Frank. "Go on. Tell us something new."

"I will tell you—" began the Captain, when Darrel, dashing forward, caught him by the throat. The two rolled over on the floor, while Fan shrieked, and jumped on a divan to be out of the way.

Balkis rose to her feet and waved the other three men out of the room. "Go! Go!"

Jarman and Frank, however, did not move, but Tamaroo, who seemed to understand Balkis, caught their hands, and dragged them out. The negress came after them rapidly, and slammed the door to. As she did so there was a shriek from Miss Berry. Tamaroo still dragged the men towards the outer door. "Come up! Come up!" he cried. "There is danger—danger!"

Eustace was brave enough, but he felt a qualm at this mysterious danger, of which he knew nothing. "Come, Frank, let us get the police quick!" and he darted along the passage and up through the trap-door. Tamaroo followed, and Lancaster. And still they could hear the men fighting within and the shrieks of Fairy Fan.

Balkis, at the door of the inner room, taunted the three. "You white woman loved my Walter and took his love. You shall die! You, my cousin, killed my Walter. You shall die! You Captain Berry, brought about the death of my Walter. You shall die!"

From within rose a wail, and then came the curses of Darrel and Berry, who felt that they had been trapped. Balkis heard them beating at the door, and, laughing loudly, mocked them. Then she pulled a lever which was hidden behind the hangings. There was a roar, a long wail, and then came sobbing, With a delighted smile the negress listened, then she glided from the apartment.

When the police arrived they found the respectable house empty. The negress had vanished. The trap-door was open, and down here Jarman led them, hoping to save the wretched three. But it was too late. As the police and Frank and Eustace darted towards the inner door to open it Tamaroo rushed between and spread out his hands.

"It is too late!" he said, pointing to the lever. "She has let in the water. The river fills that room, and those three are drowned!"

It was so terrible to think of this doom befalling the wicked trio that Frank sat down and fairly sobbed.

"Nemesis!" said Jarman.

CHAPTER XXVI

A WEDDING PRESENT

In the summerhouse where Frank Lancaster, when an outlaw, had sought refuge, sat Mildred and Eustace. Frank had stood his trial, but the proceedings were merely formal, as the confession of Darrel, which Captain Berry had obtained, proved his innocence beyond doubt. The girl should have looked much more delighted than she did, now that the man she loved was cleared of suspicion. But she seemed nervous and apprehensive, and her face was pale. Eustace had come down from London to tell her that Frank was free, and to intimate that he would be down in the afternoon after an interview with White & Saon relative to the will.

"Are you not pleased, Mildred?" asked Eustace, looking at her gravely.

"Very pleased," she replied, with an effort. "It is the best of news to think that Frank is free, and will be recompensed for all he has undergone."

"He has youth, health, strength, and forty thousand a-year," said Jarman, looking away, "so he ought to be happy."

"I hope so—I hope so," said Mildred, casting down her eyes. "And it is owing to you that he has been cleared of this terrible charge."

"I am glad to have been the agent. I always believed in his innocence. But circumstances had more to do with the affair than I. I simply took advantage of my luck."

Mildred shook her head. "You have had more to do with the matter than you will admit, Eustace. But tell me exactly what has taken place. You have been too busy to explain clearly."

"There was so much to do in connection with the trial," said Jarman; "and I think you know the greater part of the facts."

"Never mind. I wish to hear them again."

Eustace nodded gravely, and began without preamble. "As you know, Berry and his niece came to England, knowing the will of the late Mr. Lancaster, which they procured through Anchor. He intended to play traitor, and in some way arranged to get the money by ridding himself of Tamaroo. But Berry wanted Anchor out of the way, so that he might get the papers

175

and fortune to himself. He shot Anchor, as I told you. Then I chased him, and it was Tamaroo who got the papers."

"And who stabbed the man," said Mildred, shuddering—"you told me."

"That was a savage thing to do," admitted Eustace. "But, in spite of his education, Tamaroo is a savage at heart. And in any case, Anchor could not have lived after Berry's shot. Well, when Natty's father died, Berry contrived to be appointed his guardian. He exercised a great influence over him, and it was his intention to give Natty the fortune by having Frank hanged."

"And was Natty to marry Miss Berry?"

"Mrs. Anchor, you mean. I don't know. Perhaps; but I don't think she cared for the lad. He, when in possession of his fortune, would no doubt have been induced to sign a will in favour of Fan and her uncle, and then he would have been got rid of. It was with some such plan that the two came to England. They made the acquaintance of Frank by Fan writing and asking him to compose her some songs."

"Was it a trap?" asked Mildred.

"A decided trap. I don't know how they intended at first to bring about his being accused of a crime, but chance threw Starth in Berry's way, and then they saw what to do. Your brother hated Lancaster and was always quarrelling with him. It was not Frank's fault. Berry made as much trouble as he could, and Fan by flirting with your brother and then with Frank made matters worse. The affair culminated in the quarrel in the Piccadilly Theatre, in which Frank used rash words. Then the next day Walter wrote, asking Frank to call."

Mildred clasped her hands, and looked up nervously. "Was that a trap also, do you think?"

"Yes," said Eustace, decidedly. "Your brother was in the scheme to get the money. He knew that Lancaster would have to be hanged, so that it might come into Denham's possession and then into Berry's. I expect they promised him a share."

"But did they intend to give it to him?"

"No, they did not. Your brother was their dupe. Berry arranged that Starth should get Frank down to his place and drug him. Then when he was insensible a crime was to be committed and Frank was to bear the blame."

"Horrible! Horrible!" said Mildred, hiding her face. "And to think Walter should behave so. But who was to be killed?"

"Your brother," said Eustace. "Walter did not know who the victim was to be, and, after drugging Frank, waited for Berry. The rest of the scheme was to be carried on, as I believe, by Berry killing your brother, and then by Frank being accused. But Walter never thought that he would be the victim."

"Walter really drugged Frank?"

"Certainly. He put opium in his tea. When Frank was insensible he searched him for the letter asking him to call, as he wanted that evidence out of the way."

"But for what reason?"

"Why, to make it clear that Frank had called on him voluntarily. Had the letter been shown, it might have pointed to the trap. Well, in searching for the letter—which was thrown on the floor, and found by Tilly—Walter discovered Frank's revolver, which he placed on the table. It was the merest chance that Frank carried it, and, of course, it was a card quite in the hands of the plotters. Walter waited for Berry, but Berry was late. Now I will tell you of Darrel's confession."

"Where was it found?"

"In Berry's strong-box. The police took the key from his dead body, and searched his lodgings. They found the confession, which exonerated Frank entirely."

"Tell me the exact words."

"I can't give them very exact. But the meaning was something like this. Darrel loved you, and wanted to marry you. Walter at first approved of the match, but afterwards he intended to marry you to Natty, and so brought him down."

"I should never have married him," said Mildred, in a low voice.

"Walter, no doubt, thought he could force you. But Darrel got wind of this through Balkis, who was his cousin. He came to remonstrate with Walter. Darrel was half a savage also, with his African blood, and your brother and he came to high words. Then Darrel confessed that Walter insulted him so that he snatched up Frank's revolver from the table and shot Walter through the head. He says in his confession that he didn't intend to kill him."

"Do you think that is true?" asked Mildred.

"I can't say. Darrel was a most violent man, and his love for you amounted to a frenzy. However, he shot Walter, but before he could get out of the house Berry entered."

"How could he enter if the door was closed?"

"He had a latch-key, which he had procured from Walter. I daresay he intended to kill Walter—either shoot him or stab him—and then go away, leaving Frank to bear the blame. He went to Frank's chambers to prove an *alibi*. But when he found Darrel in the room he saw that the deed was done. To make himself safe he made Darrel sign a confession, and kept it in his strong-box. Then the two agreed that Frank should bear the blame. Now you can see, Mildred, why Darrel was unwilling to denounce Frank when he recognised him here. He feared to be implicated in the case. But his rage

177

got the better of him, and he took Berry and Fan to the secret rooms of Balkis."

"What has become of Balkis?"

"She has disappeared; no one knows where. I expect she had made all arrangements and has departed for the States. It's just as well, as she is wanted for the murder of those three."

"Why did she murder them? I thought she was friendly with them."

"She was in a way. But she was madly in love with your brother and was under the impression that he would marry her. He might have done so, for Balkis is rich. However, if he got Lancaster's money he intended to marry Fairy Fan. When, by means of that letter, I proved that Fan had been making love to Starth, Balkis was furious. Then, when she found that Darrel had killed her lover, she determined on his death."

"Had Frank killed Walter, would Balkis have—"

"I am sure she would," interrupted Eustace, quickly. "She was a most furious woman, and would have stuck at nothing. And she didn't. She resolved also on the death of Berry, because he had caused all the trouble, and had really brought about the death of your brother by his machinations. So she closed them in the room and let the river in. The three poor wretches were drowned like rats in a trap before I could get back with the police."

Mildred shuddered with horror. "Had she designed all this?"

"No. To do her justice I don't think she did. The trap was arranged for the police should they have made a raid on the gambling-rooms. It seems that the inner room was only divided from the river by a thick wall. There was a tunnel through this, closed at the lower end by an iron slide, which was worked by a lever from the outer room. Balkis shut the three in, and Darrel was fighting with the Captain. Then when she got rid of us—I went to fetch the police, remember, as I suspected foul play—she must have worked the lever and admitted the water. Great Heavens!" said Eustace, covering his face. "I can imagine the feelings of those poor wretches when they saw the water pouring into the room. Bad as they were their punishment has been terrible."

"Were they all three dead?"

"Yes. The police shut the slide again by means of the lever and the water was drained. The bodies were found, and by this time they have been buried."

"Balkis disappeared?"

"Yes. She must have made preparations for flight. In any case she intended to leave for America a week after the crime was committed. Her money was all invested abroad, and she no doubt got on board some boat that sailed immediately for Spain or the Continent. She had many friends

178

amongst the sailors who patronised her opium shop and gambling-rooms, and had no difficulty in getting away."

"Then Frank was arrested?"

"I wrote to you. He gave himself up by my advice. I related everything to Inspector Herny. He searched for the key of the strong-box and found it on Berry's watch-chain. Then we found the box in the Bloomsbury lodgings, and obtained the confession. Frank made his statement in court, and then the confession was read. He has been discharged without a stain on his character. And now he is with Tamaroo seeing White & Saon about the will."

"I don't like Tamaroo after his stabbing my brother and that poor Anchor," said Mildred, looking pale.

Eustace shrugged his shoulders. "Tamaroo is half a savage. But you will not see much of him. Frank has arranged to pay him an income, and he is going back to America next week. He has discharged his mission, and nothing more remains to be done."

"And Frank?" said Mildred, in a low tone. "What of him?"

Eustace looked at her from under his eyes, and winced. He knew well what was in her mind. "Frank," he said, in a hard tone, "is going down to see Miss Drake at Kingsbridge. There he will make arrangements for her comfort, now that he is in possession of the money. After that I can't say. But, Mildred"—he took her hands—"I have done what you asked. Your brother's murderer has been discovered, Frank is free. What of my reward?"

"I will marry you," said Mildred, faintly. "I promised to do so, and I shall keep my word."

Eustace smiled, but there was a look of pain in his eyes. "What of Frank Lancaster?" he asked.

"Say nothing about him," she answered, pressing her hand on her heart. "If you have any love for me—"

"Ah, my dear, I have so much love that—well we will see. I am going to town again today. Frank is coming down. I want him to see you, as he will give you a message from me."

"Can't you tell me what it is? I don't want to see Frank."

"I can only write the message," said Eustace, rising. "You will know what I mean by five this evening." He looked at his watch. "I have just time to catch the train. And now, as we have arranged to marry, will you not kiss me?"

Mildred put her arms round his neck and kissed him. "God bless you for all you have done," she murmured.

"Oh, He will. Does He not give you to me? Goodbye, and"—he kissed her twice—"don't forget me."

Mildred sank into a chair as Eustace hurried away. At the gate he looked back and waved his hand, but she never looked up. With a sigh, Jarman went to his own house. There he packed a few things and departed, leaving old Bowles in charge of the Shanty.

Mildred buried her face in her hands and wept. She loved Frank. Never till this moment did she realise how much she loved him. And she knew that he loved her as devotedly. But she must keep her promise to Eustace. He had borne the heat and burden of the day. He had worked nobly, and she could not break his heart by refusing to give him his reward. But she knew not how she would be able to bear being his wife when she so dearly loved Frank.

"I should have spoken out," she moaned. "I should have told the truth. He would not have insisted on my fulfilling a rash promise. Yet—he is so good, so noble. No. I must keep my word. Frank himself would insist on that. And Frank, I shall see him again to say farewell. Oh, Frank—Frank—my darling!" and she wept afresh.

From these sad thoughts she was aroused by the coming of Mrs. Perth full of news. "My dear," said the old lady, "I have just come from the Rectory. Would you believe it? Mr. Denham is to marry Jenny Arrow. It's all settled. They marry in a month, and go to the States."

"I am very glad," said Mildred, drying her eyes.

"Well, I am too—but such indecent haste. However, it's none of our business. My dear"—the old lady sat down and patted Mildred's hand —"why are you crying? Are you not glad that this poor young man has been proved innocent?"

"I am more than glad, because I love him."

"Ah!" said Mrs. Perth, again patting the hand, "I thought so. And I must tell you one thing, my dear. He loves you. He told me so."

"Don't—oh don't!" cried the girl, tortured beyond endurance. "I am to be married to Eustace Jarman!"

"Mildred—no!"

"I promised to marry him if he—oh, don't talk of it," and Mildred ran into the house.

Mrs. Perth shook her head sadly, and slowly followed. She thought Mildred was wrong. "It will not be a happy marriage," said Mrs. Perth.

That afternoon Frank arrived at the Shanty. He looked sad, and not at all like a man whose character had been cleared, and who had come into a fortune of forty thousand a-year. He was alone, as he intended only to stop the night and to return the next day to London on his way to Kingsbridge. Only at Jarman's urgent request had he come down to see Mildred, as he felt that he could not trust himself in her presence. At first he thought he would send the letter with which he had been entrusted by Eustace. Then he decided not to be a coward, but to deliver it himself. He therefore braced his nerves for a final interview, and walked over to Rose Cottage.

Mildred was in the drawing-room and saw him at once. The lovers looked at one another, and each strove to be calm. There was no need of explanation, as they understood. Without a word Frank gave Mildred the letter. She laid it aside. "Will you not read it?" asked Frank.

"After you are gone," said Mildred, in as steady a tone as she could command.

"No. You must read it now. Eustace wants a reply, he told me."

"Why is he so cruel?" muttered Mildred, opening the letter languidly.

Frank watched her as she read, and sighed to think that she would be the wife of another. However, he wished to be true to the friend who had done so much for him, and in his heart resolved to give Jarman half his money when the wedding took place.

Mildred flushed as she read the letter, and her eyes sparkled. On finishing she handed it to Frank without a word, striving to repress her agitation. Rather astonished at this emotion, Frank read it also. Then he too flushed, and well he might.

The letter was from Eustace and stated that he saw how Mildred and Frank loved one another. He wished them both to be happy and released Mildred from her promise.

Marry Frank, my dear, for I see I was wrong to ask for such a promise. I am old and you are young. Marry Frank. I send him to you as a wedding present, and I am sure you will not want a better. Bless you both. I am going to America for a time, but when I return. perhaps there will be a corner near the fire for your sincere friend

EUSTACE.

The letter read, Frank and Mildred looked at one another. They could find no words to speak of this wonderful self-sacrifice on the part of Eustace. Mildred burst out crying, but the next moment she was in the arms of Frank, and he kissed away her tears.

"He gave me liberty, he gave me life, he gave me fortune, and now," said Frank, softly, "he gives me you."

"God bless him!" sobbed Mildred.

"Amen to that," echoed Frank, and they kissed again.

www.ingramcontent.com/pod-product-compliance
Lightning Source LLC
Chambersburg PA
CBHW011445170626
46816CB00008B/2529